Tony Peake was born in Sc[...]
from Rhodes University, he [...]
worked under Charles Marov[...]
the Open Space Theatre. A s[...]
History and Drama, was foll[...]
and jobs in modelling, acting [...]
now a literary agent. As a short story writer, he has con-
tributed to *Winter's Tales*, the *Penguin Book of Contemporary
South African Short Stories* and *Seduction*, a themed anthology
which he also edited. His first novel, *A Summer Tide*, was
published in 1993.

Also by Tony Peake

A SUMMER TIDE

as editor

SEDUCTION

SON

to the

FATHER

Tony Peake

An *Abacus* Book

First published in Great Britain in 1995
by Little, Brown and Company
This edition published in 1996 by Abacus

A CIP catalogue record for this book
is available from the British Library.

ISBN 0 349 10807 2

Typeset by M Rules
Printed and bound in Great Britain by Clays Ltd, St Ives plc

Abacus
A Division of
Little, Brown and Company (UK)
Brettenham House
Lancaster Place
London WC2E 7EN

For Peter

One

The night Carlos Tarifa entered our lives was the night I finished reading Jed *The Chronicles of Narnia*. He'd not been well that week – some bug at school – so I made an early supper, and after our obligatory skirmish over whether he needed a bath, insisted he hop straight into bed.

'But it's *Tomorrow's World*!' Disappointment vied with outrage in voice and face.

'No world tomorrow,' I replied crisply, 'without sleep tonight.'

He was, on the whole, an obedient child; even our arguments about bathing were conducted, or so I sensed, less out of perversity than because he imagined that as a ten-year-old it was expected of him. His television viewing, however, one interrupted at one's peril. There weren't many programmes to which he was addicted – *Match of the Day*, an hour of magic on Saturday, *Tomorrow's World* – but they were the rubrics of his week.

'Tell you what, though,' I added as reparation. 'I'll finish *The Last Battle*.'

There was a moment's hesitation; then, effecting a raucous transformation into his preferred mode of transport, the motorbike, he yelped the word 'Deal' and roared off down the corridor. He knew we were still on Chapter Twelve. *Tomorrow's World* against five times his usual quotient of reading: little wonder he'd acquiesced.

'Teeth!' I called after his vanishing form. 'And don't leave your clothes on the floor!'

When, minutes later and armed with a glass of wine, I made my own more sedate advance on his bastion of untidiness, he was already in bed.

'Smell!'

I leant forward to be met by a burst of peppermint.

'Page one-four-six,' he instructed. '"Through the Stable Door".'

I read for almost an hour, until long after I'd finished my wine and my voice was so hoarse I had to whisper the final paragraph:

> And as He spoke He no longer looked to them like a lion; but the things that began to happen after that were so great and beautiful that I cannot write them. And for us this is the end of all the stories, and we can most truly say that they all lived happily ever after. But for them it was only the beginning of the real story. All their life in this world and all their adventures in Narnia had only been the cover and the title page: now at last they were beginning Chapter One of the Great Story which no one on earth has read: which goes on forever: in which every chapter is better than the one before.

I closed the book and, not for the first time, probed my glass for any last drops it might contain.

'Are they really dead?' Jed was staring at me with troubled eyes. 'Can't they ever come back?'

'Not to Narnia.'

'He comes to me, you know. In my dreams.'

'Who?'

'Aslan. He comes through the wall and he stands where you're standing now and . . .' He stopped, as if fearful that by voicing the visitation, he might cause the wonder of it to be diminished.

'And what?'

'Nothing.'

He gave the word such finality that I was left with no alternative but to busy myself with tucking him in.

'Sweet dreams.'

'And you.'

I gave his coverlet a final, unnecessary tweak; then, switching off his light, returned to the washing up, another glass of wine, my evening's marking.

'I don't understand,' my father had said the last time I'd visited him, 'why you make yourself responsible for the child. It's not as if he's yours.' We were at the scullery window watching Jed, plastic sword in hand, hack an explorative path through the tangled grass. 'Unless, of course,' my father had continued, 'there's something you're not telling me about this Jacqui creature?'

'I happen to like him,' I'd said. 'He's a nice kid. Also lonely. Or is it bourgeois to show a child affection?'

Which hadn't been the truth at all; or rather, not all of it. But I wasn't in the habit of confronting the truth. Not with my father, not with myself.

I rinsed the last of the pots, poured the last of the wine into my glass, went to put the bottle in the bin, then – because the bin was overflowing – tipped its contents into a refuse bag, added the pile of newspapers from the living room, the contents of all the ashtrays, and, tying the bag shut, took it downstairs to deposit in the bin by the front door.

The flat, which, *pace* Jed and her consequent single-parent status, Jacqui had acquired from a housing association, was on the middle floor of a terraced house in West Kilburn, sandwiched between an elderly widow who, apparently as a result of poor hearing, played her television so loudly that if she listened to *Coronation Street*, we did too; and, on the floor above, a Scottish couple who never disturbed anyone except in the middle of the night, when they would frequently wake the entire street with the sound of their shouting followed, for our benefit alone, by the sound of their bed-springs: domestic violence as conjugal foreplay.

When I'd moved into the flat three months previously, Jacqui had filled me in on the details of these immediate neighbours. Mrs Sargeson was eighty-five and had been a widow for thirty years. Upstairs Keith had, in his youth, served a sentence for armed robbery. Jean, his wife, worked at the checkout of a nearby Iceland. Mrs Sargeson was shopped for on a weekly basis by a niece who lived in Hackney. Jean was so houseproud she hoovered once a day.

Now, as I paused by the bin to look the length of Victoria Villas, I imagined that just as all the other houses had been sliced, like ours, into flats, so if one sliced them further – sliced them open, that is – one would find a million echoes of the muted soap opera at number 10: the predictably young and the predictably old, the predictably married and the predictably single, the predictably desperate.

Five doors up, a woman in a candlewick dressing gown was also stuffing a refuse bag into the bin that stood by her door. A black youth in dazzling trainers jived down the road in time to his Walkman, whilst from the opposite direction, complete with briefcase and newspaper, came a regulation yuppie who, on seeing the youth, cut sharply across the road to continue his journey on the other side.

The woman, having disposed of her rubbish, paused a moment on her front step and, as the yuppie hurried past, lifted hand to hair in a gesture of furtive vanity.

I replaced the lid on the bin – taking care, because of cats, to see it fitted properly – and when I looked up again, found that the street was empty. My snatch of urban ballet was over, we were between scenes, Victoria Villas oddly forbidding in its regimented drabness now that it had returned to being a set. The orange street lights which had, a moment earlier, lent the scene a certain seedy glamour, were, *sans* performers, as stark and uncompromising as rehearsal lights. No Aslan here, nor even the potential for such.

I went upstairs to my marking.

'Paperwork away!'

I was halfway through a grammatically erratic hymn to the glories of the Reeperbahn when Jacqui, a bottle of champagne in each hand, appeared with a flourish in the doorway. 'This calls for celebration.' Marching imperiously into the kitchen, she dumped the bottles on top of my marking.

'Careful!' I set about rescuing my essays.

She came in close. 'Now, now! Don't be a sourpuss.' She grasped my face firmly in both hands and kissed me wetly on the lips. 'Right!' She shrugged off her cape. 'You do the honours.' She collapsed onto a chair. 'God, what an evening!'

On anyone else, her body-hugging dress, jet-black like her stockings, hair and eyes, would have looked severe. Particularly since she'd scraped her hair away from her ears and piled it high on her head. But with Jacqui, although the effect was elegant, it was also haphazard, almost child-like – the result, perhaps, of the single bloom with which, in defiance of formality, she'd spiked her coiffure.

Obedient to the last, I reached for one of the bottles.

'From Suzy?'

Suzy ran a company called Parties Unlimited, and when beleaguered by the demands of organised frivolity, would summon Jacqui to the rescue. Tonight it had been a do to celebrate the pairing of Bruce Willis with Julia Roberts in the season's latest thriller.

Jacqui giggled. 'Not Suzy. Tristar, or Paramount, or whatever they're called.'

'You stole it?'

She shrugged. 'There were whole cases of it in the cloakroom, just going to waste. Waste not, want not. Surely your mother taught you that?' She opened her little black bag and took out a packet of cigarettes. 'Want one?'

'You forget. My mother's dead.'

The cork shot free of the bottle, and I handed her her glass.

'Mmm!' She licked her lips. 'Good, huh?'

The expression on my face as I sampled the champagne must have been more telling than I thought, for she said triumphantly: 'You see. You want it too. Don't pretend you don't. I mean, why drink plonk when there's this stuff?'

I raised my hands in mock surrender. 'All right. I give up. Bruce Willis proposed to you?'

She wrinkled her nose. 'Too uncouth.'

'You mean he was there?'

'Of course he was there. And Julia Roberts. Jeremy Irons. Roger Moore. Carlos Tarifa.'

It was the particular emphasis she afforded his name that gave the game away. Unlikely though it seemed, the person responsible for Jacqui's excitement was a Spanish opera director.

'You'd better start at the beginning,' I said. 'You know, as in once upon a time . . .'

She gave a self-satisfied smile: 'Once upon a time there

was an opera director called Carlos Tarifa. He was excessively famous. Even people like me, who know fuck about opera, knew about Carlos Tarifa. Mainly because of the money. And the arguments he had with his stars. And his villa, of course, which was always being photographed.' She paused to draw breath. 'He was also excessively, and I mean excessively, charming.'

'You spoke to him?'

'Of course I spoke to him.'

'About what?'

She put down her glass, and, fumbling through her bag, produced a passport-sized photo of Jed. 'It might have escaped your notice,' she said sternly, laying the evidence between us, 'but my son is quite a looker.'

Once again I raised my hands. 'Slow down. You're way too fast for me.'

She leant across me for the bottle. 'We got talking. Carlos and I. He thought I was Spanish.' She pulled the bloom out of her hair and tossed it onto the table. 'This, I suppose. Anyway, it turns out he's making a film. About Murillo.'

'The painter?'

'You know his work?'

I shrugged. 'Lots of beggar boys. Right?'

She allowed herself a gulp of champagne. 'He had nine children, apparently, but they almost all died. Wifey too. The film will be a real tear-jerker, all about the relationship between this lonely old painter and one of the beggars. One of his models.' She tapped Jed's face with a scarlet fingernail.

'Jed?' My champagne went down the wrong way, and it was some minutes before I could rephrase the question: 'You mean you suggested Jed for the part?'

Once again she fished in her bag, this time to produce a

card. 'Carlos Tarifa,' it read, followed by an exotic-looking address: the address, no doubt, of the fabled villa. At the bottom, scrawled in pen, was a London phone number.

'All I did,' said Jacqui, 'was show him the photo.'

At this point her excitement got the better of her, and she began to pace the room.

'Can you believe it? Carlos Tarifa actually wants to meet Jed!'

'And you're going to take him?'

'Take him?' Disbelief caused her voice to spiral. 'Of course I'm going to take him. I mean, imagine if he got the part! Imagine what it would mean!'

'A massive disruption?'

She stopped pacing and regarded me in silence. 'My God!' she said eventually. 'Teachers! So he misses some school? You think it won't be a learning experience, two months in Spain? Working on a film?'

Stung, I hit back: 'And the money. Don't forget the money.'

'What's wrong with money? You think money isn't important? Shit, you socialists make me sick.'

'I'm not a socialist!'

'You could have fooled me.' She grabbed the champagne bottle and emptied it into her glass.

'I'm sorry.' I reached for her hand. 'I don't mean to be a killjoy. I just think it's something to consider.'

'The future,' she snapped. 'That's what I'm considering.'

Then, with a sudden smile, she relinquished her glass and struck a flamenco pose. 'The food, the sun, the fucks!'

She beat a tattoo on the floor with her feet, and, moving into an impromptu dance, stamped a circle round the table, arms sawing the air – at which point Mrs Sargeson, whose hearing was defective only when it suited her, hammered on her ceiling, bringing Jacqui's dance to an abrupt conclusion. Scowling, she collapsed into her chair.

'You see? How can I go on living here?'

I knew what she meant. Delighted though I was with my room in the flat, it was true that, viewed objectively, 10b Victoria Villas left a lot to be desired. A box-like hall-way carpeted in stained, brown cord gave onto a bedroom not much bigger than the double mattress on its floor (Jacqui's), an even smaller bedroom for myself, and – at the end of a narrow corridor, opposite the bathroom – a third cage for Jed. The largest room in the flat, to the left of the hall, was the living room, which, in a misguided attempt to disguise its ordinariness, Jacqui had painted in contrasting swathes of black and blue, furnishing it with black leather furniture, lacquered tables and sheepskin rugs. The only other room, adjacent to the living room, was the kitchen, where the decorative input had been provided by Jed in the form of innumerable drawings of his imaginary cities, their buildings odd, angular and thrusting, their modes of trans-port suitably futuristic.

I tapped a truce on my watch. 'I don't know about you, but yours truly has a dawn patrol.'

'Not so fast!' She was out of her chair in a flash. 'You have to help me with this.' She flourished the remaining bottle of champagne.

Laughing, I shook my head. 'If I drink any more, I'll be good for nothing in the morning.'

'So? I'm good for nothing now, or so you keep telling me. We'll be company. Equals. Isn't that what you socialists want?'

'For the umpteenth time, I'm not a socialist! Just because my father . . .'

But she'd lost interest in our sparring match. Flopping into my lap, she put her head on my shoulder and threaded a finger through my hair. 'Perhaps I am irresponsible,' she whispered. 'But if she wants to get on in this shit-hole of a world, if she wants a little fun, how else is a girl to behave?'

I leant into her neck and nuzzled against the soft and scented hollow behind her ear.

'Put out or be put out?'

She giggled. 'Something like that.'

'Just be careful,' I countered, 'that's all. He's only ten — and as you say, it's a shit-hole of a world.'

She ran a delicate, teasing finger down my cheek. 'Ah! But we have you. You'll look after us. Fight the dragons. Guard the lair.' She removed her hand from my cheek and, with a chuckle, slipped it between my thighs. 'God knows, you have the weapon!'

I shifted uncomfortably in my chair.

'All right,' she said. 'I haven't forgotten.'

She stood up, and, reaching briskly for the remaining bottle of champagne, stowed it in the fridge.

'Though I do sometimes wonder,' she added quietly, 'if what happened in Devon can really have been that terrible.'

Two

*I*f life is cause and effect, the effects are not always as might be wished or predicted. For his only son, my father had foreseen university, followed by a career of some political or social import; an educated enhancement of his own untutored, latterly despairing, involvement with the Communist Party. I'd also envisaged university, though more as an escape from the tedium of South London than as the start of a career; and after that – well nothing very specific, really, except to be rid of the obligations and trauma of childhood. To be my own person.

The reality was three years of indifferent sociology at the then North London Poly, no resulting skills to speak of, and then the commune, a childish reaction to what had preceded it, and the very reverse, it turned out, of what it was supposed to be: obligation and trauma of another kind. Hence my flight, on the eve of my twenty-fourth birthday, to the sudden safety of my childhood home.

My father suffered my dismayed, dismaying presence for almost a year; until, losing patience with my inexplicable passivity, he demanded I fend for myself. I found a room in Clapham and, with a view to putting my country, and therefore my past, behind me, took a course in teaching

English as a foreign language. A month later I landed myself
a job at the Camden Centre, which was where I'd been for
a term and a half (eye on an eventual placement in Italy, say,
or Spain) when I happened on Jacqui.

Run on a shoestring out of a shabby industrial unit in a
mews off the Camden Road, the Camden Centre believed
in maximising the value of its teachers. Free periods were a
rarity, and my classes ran the gamut from introductory
(hopeless but keen) through intermediate (moderately
accomplished and bolshy) to advanced (accomplished and
therefore keen again). On the Friday I met Jacqui, I'd
decided the moment had come to demand of Gloria and
Ernesto a richly deserved, also much-needed, increase in
salary.

They were an unlikely couple, Gloria and Ernesto, to be
running anything as demanding as a school, however fly-
by-night. Their real talent, to which the school often
seemed little more than an adjunct, was for running each
other down.

The daughter of a Sussex vicar and an ex-dancer, Gloria
had started life as a dancer herself, graduating from local talent competitions to the crowning glory of a touring
production of *The Sound of Music*. She had stayed with *The
Sound of Music* for three years, maturing each December
into an ever older von Trapp – until, presumably, she would
have had to play Maria herself, at which point, sadly, her
contract was terminated and her career went into abrupt
decline. It was while dancing in a Soho club that Ernesto,
fresh from Mexico City, had spotted his nemesis, whisked
her off to the register office, introduced her to Catholic
motherhood and persuaded her to put her savings at the
disposal of his dream: the Camden Centre.

Gloria had not adapted well to Ernesto's demands, and in
defiance still behaved like an actress, showering everyone –

even the students – with the epithet 'darling', plastering the walls of her office with posters of past triumphs, and conducting her frequent arguments with Ernesto so histrionically – and so publicly – that one could seldom visit their office without being audience to a scene out of Osborne.

That Friday was no different.

'Peasant!' I heard her shrill as I came down the corridor. 'I don't give a shit about your grandmother. We English do not pay our bills on time. If we did, this country would really go under.'

I didn't catch Ernesto's reply, but whatever it was, it inflamed her still further, because as I opened the door, she was off again.

'Raising cattle on the Rio Grande,' she spat, 'is *not* the same as running a school. Despite' – this for my benefit; she'd noticed my arrival – 'the bovine qualities of our intake.'

Although motherhood had had a less than flattering effect on Gloria's figure, she was still an imposing woman, and it came as no surprise that diminutive Ernesto should be lurking against the wall whilst his wife, from behind the desk, described vivid circles in the air with her arms.

'Darling!' She switched her attention to me. 'Tell this oaf how it works. Do you pay your bills on time?'

'Well, actually,' I said, racing for this unexpected opening, 'funny you should ask. No, I don't.'

'See!'

'But that's only because I never have enough in the bank.'

'Who does?' Gloria still had Ernesto pinned to the wall with her gaze.

'In fact, it's why I wanted to see you.' I approached the desk. 'You said when I started . . .'

'Sit down, darling.' Alert to my implied request, Gloria

switched seamlessly to a quieter, more wheedling tone. 'Ernesto sweet, any coffee in the pot?'

I held up a hand. 'Not for me. Really.'

She got up and crossed to the filing cabinet, on which stood a tray of coffee things.

'Gloria, *por favor*!' Ernesto was gesturing urgently at Gloria's stomach. 'Coffee is not good for him.'

I hadn't realised number four was on its way.

'It's my body,' snapped Gloria. 'I'll decide what to put into it.' She stabbed Ernesto with another of her looks. '*And*, in future, at what time of the month.' She emptied a cup of its dregs. 'Leave motherhood to me and do your job.' She waved her cup in my direction.

Ernesto cleared his throat.

'Peter,' he began, 'believe me, we'd give you a rise if we could, *seguro*, but what you must realise . . .'

'What Ernesto is trying to say' – re-caffeinated, Gloria had returned from the filing cabinet – 'is there have been complaints.'

'Complaints?'

'Darling, don't get me wrong! You're one of our most valued teachers. But some of your students . . .' She ran a skittering hand through her hair. 'Put it this way, they don't find you *simpatico*.'

Ernesto shrugged uncomfortably. 'Funny, no? How Spanish words—'

Gloria didn't let him finish. 'Peter knows what it means.'

'I'm not sure that I do,' I said stiffly. 'Are you trying to tell me I'm fired?'

'Heavens, no!' This time the gesture was with the eyes, which flashed ceilingwards in pretended horror. 'But if we lose any students, then the fees are down, and the margins are hellishly tight as it is.' She came round the desk and rested a hand on my shoulder. 'Darling, I'd love nothing more than to give you a rise, we both would, but just at the moment . . .' She squeezed my shoulder. 'All I can promise is that at the end of term, as long as no one leaves, we'll think again. Now!' She returned to her desk. 'Did I tell you that next weekend we're planning a little party? For the students? We thought it'd be fun if they each bought a bottle of wine from their country of origin, I'll lay on some snacks, and Harriet' – Harriet was the eldest of their off-spring – 'Harriet's going to dance. Did you know she'd started lessons?'

I stood up. 'What a pity,' I said firmly. 'I'll be away.' I had no intention of paying to see Harriet's dancing debut with a bottle of English wine.

Gloria frowned. 'I think it would help your case with the students.'

I met her gaze head-on. 'Is that a threat?'

'Darling, really!' She attempted, rather clumsily, to look shocked.

Ernesto took my arm and led me to the door. 'You come if you can,' he said soothingly. 'No big deal if not.'

Alone in the corridor, I leant against the wall and closed my eyes. Escape to Europe seemed more of a dream than ever.

'Peter! You okay?' The voice belonged to Jean-Luís, disturbingly attractive addition to my beginners class, who was hovering by the common-room door, sombre features knitted in a frown. 'You look – how you say? – sad?'

I managed a smile. 'Just preoccupied.'

His frown deepened. 'Pre-occ-u-pied.' He repeated the word slowly, savouring each syllable of its seductive strangeness.

'Busy,' I proffered.

He smiled. 'Ah, busy! Busy, of course. Busy. Business. Businessman. Yes?'

I nodded. 'Exactly.'

'So!' He rubbed the palm of his hand down the side of his skin-tight jeans (a gesture I followed with surreptitious skill). 'Maybe you like some fun?'

I raised an eyebrow.

'I had a friend. A – how you say? – maker of books. Brazilian also. He have a new book, and tonight, at the Embassy, he drop a party. For book. You can come?'

'Have,' I corrected. 'An author. He has a new book, and he's throwing a party.'

Jean-Luís looked at me blankly.

'I have a friend,' I repeated. 'He's an author. He has a new book. You throw a party.'

Jean-Luís smiled. 'So,' he said, 'is good when you come. You make my English more smooth.'

His eyes were fixed on me expectantly – and because, like anything else, when you practise the avoidance of personal truth you become adept at it, I was able to tell myself that it would indeed be a help to Jean-Luís's English were I to accompany him; and anyway, after my brush with Gloria and Ernesto, didn't I merit a treat?

'Okay,' I said casually. 'That would be nice. What time?'

His features broadened in a smile. 'Eighteen hundred?'

'Six o'clock?'

He shrugged. 'You English. Very behind, no, with time?'

Now it was my turn to smile. 'Old-fashioned, you mean, or simply late?'

'In Brazil,' he continued, 'eighteen hundred, nineteen hundred, twenty hundred.'

'We English,' I said, 'like to be different. In fact we insist on it. Where shall we meet?'

'Here? By a quarter after . . .' He paused, then grinned disarmingly: 'five.'

'Right!' I said. 'Here at a quarter-past five.'

My final class of the afternoon overran, and it was five-thirty when I got to the common room.

'You English. Late. Like you say.'

He had donned a black cotton jacket and slicked back his hair.

'I'm sorry. Difficult class. You look smart.'

He flicked a deprecating finger at the jacket. 'The Embassy, no?'

I glanced worriedly at my own rather threadbare jacket and rumpled corduroys, over which – the patina of my position – there lay a film of chalk dust. 'Will I do?'

'Do?' He looked puzzled.

'Am I smart enough?'

Again that smile, part comprehension, part seduction. 'A-one okay! Come, we go.'

I let him lead me from the building. As we passed Gloria's office, we caught a snatch of her hectoring voice, and, in the background, Ernesto's placatory mumble. Jean-Luís chuckled.

'Marriage!' he whispered, and once we'd gained the relative quiet of the mews: 'Your parents? They make fight?'

'My mother died,' I explained, 'when I was very young.'

'I'm sorry.' He put out an instinctive hand and squeezed my arm.

'It was a long time ago,' I said hastily. 'I don't even remember her.'

'My parents,' he continued, 'too much fight. All the time. My father, he have many women. Very sexy. My mother, she get – how you say? – mad. Break plates. Not good.'

We emerged from the mews into the rush-hour madness of Camden Road, a Calcutta-like cacophony of buses, bicycles, cars, and a pavement clogged with hurrying, harassed pedestrians.

'Where is the Embassy?'

'Marble Arch. We take the tube?'

'I'm in your hands.'

Though as I stood behind him in the queue for the ticket machine at Camden Town, I had my doubts. The curl of hair on the nape of his neck became secondary to another, more pressing consideration: could I cope with an entire evening of halting conversation? Suddenly I hated myself.

He turned to whisper in my ear. 'Rio.'

'I beg your pardon?'

He gestured towards the handful of tramps policing the queue for charity.

'In Rio also,' he explained. 'Much poor people. Too much. *Em todo o mundo.*'

On the platform, and shouting to make myself heard above the tannoy, I prepared an escape route: 'Will it be long, this do? I don't want to be late.'

Did he hear or understand me? I can't be sure. He simply smiled a response, whereupon speech was rendered impossible by the arrival of a train.

At Marble Arch we were carried to the exit by a tidal wave of commuters and disgorged, hot and bothered, on the north side of Oxford Street. Jean-Luís took my sleeve and pulled me into the road.

'Crazy!' he shouted over his shoulder. 'This rushing hour.'

'Worse than Rio?'

He deftly avoided a cyclist. '*Igual.* Come! Is only two blocks.'

Judged on its facade, the Embassy was less government outpost than post office. Only after we had passed through the security door set in a dingy little foyer did anything approaching ambassadorial splendour become apparent: a wide sweep of staircase dominated by a gargantuan palm. I followed Jean-Luís up the stairs and into an oblong room which, like the building itself, was a mix of the formal and the haphazard. A ceiling punctuated at regular intervals by wooden chandeliers, each painted gold. Walls hung with the photographic likenesses of generals, accreting chronologically from turn-of-the-century quaintness to their more recent brethren, clad in sixties-sinister sunglasses and suits. A smattering of leather-backed chairs. Two huge wooden cabinets, ornately carved. And, in the centre of the room, a table covered in tatty green baize on which were scattered books, papers and the occasional bowl of snacks; in the far corner, a humble desk, two metal filing cabinets and a portable radiator.

The room was filled with chattering people: middle-aged men whose tailored suits and consorts betokened prosperity, younger men displaying their worth physiognomically, a myriad women in the ubiquitous costume of the style-conscious: black leggings, black dress, untrammelled hair. A waiter stood at the door, tray of drinks at the ready. We helped ourselves to some wine.

'Come,' said Jean-Luís, 'we find my friend.'

We muscled into the room. On my right two businessmen, one clutching an outsized cigar, were conversing quietly. Behind them two women (their wives, presumably) were staring in mute fascination at a point to my left. I followed the direction of their gaze and saw a darkly exotic woman in a sheath of turquoise slip her hand into the pocket of the man she was addressing – I thought, at first, to take out a packet of cigarettes; though when her hand remained in the pocket, and the man began to squirm, I realised with a shock that it was another kind of tube altogether the woman was seeking.

I was prevented from seeing what happened next by

Jean-Luís, who grabbed my arm and frogmarched me
across the room. 'There he is!'

He (the novelist) turned out to be a small, squat man
with bottle-thick glasses, a shock of untidy hair and unfortunate skin. Not that his looks deterred admiration. He
was surrounded by a positive harem of excited beauty.

'He writes much sex,' Jean-Luís whispered. 'So women
want him.'

I found myself pumping the novelist's hand and, because
of his glasses, being subjected to a scrutiny of such intense
magnification that I was reduced to the order of a labora-
tory specimen.

'So!' he smiled. 'It's you we have to thank for the manner in which our friend is learning to murder the language
of Shakespeare and Agatha Christie.'

Not sure how to take this back-handed compliment,
and somewhat thrown by his eccentric pairing of writers, I
was about to mumble some inane reply – and pretend, too,
that I had read his books – when he pre-empted me by
continuing smoothly: 'What you lack, though, at this
school of yours, is an efficient dating system. Which is why,
I think, Jean-Luís is such a fan.'

He gestured with an amused shrug to his left, where, I
now saw, Jean-Luís was in earnest conversation with one of
the harem.

'We novelists,' said the writer, tapping the side of his
acned nose, 'have our uses.'

A look of surprise (and perhaps disappointment) must
have passed across my face, for I was suddenly aware of
being under the microscope again.

'But then nothing,' he chuckled, eyes swimming up to
engulf me, 'is ever as it seems.'

There's a good deal I could have replied to this, but at that
moment a mountainous man in a loose linen suit waddled

up, and, grasping the writer firmly by the arm, began, with the briefest of nods in my direction, to steer him away.

I shot a furtive look at Jean-Luís. The writer had been correct. Nothing was as it had seemed, neither Jean-Luís's interest in me, nor – which was more disturbing – my supposed disinterest in him. As I watched the effortless way in which he made the girl laugh at some joke, I was stabbed not with relief, but by loss. And again by self-hatred.

My thoughts (more coherent in retrospect than they were at the time, certainly more specific) were interrupted by a voice at my elbow.

'You don't happen to have a cigarette?'

It was the woman in turquoise. Up close, there was a coarseness about her features which, at the age she was (late twenties, I guessed) made her look considerably more interesting, more varied and challenging, than the anodyne beauties dotted elsewhere about the room. Her eyes, as deep-set as they were coal-black, regarded me provocatively.

I presented my packet.

She frowned. 'Only three left. No good at all.' She extended a hand to snare a passing businessman. '*Por favor!*' She vamped him quite shamelessly with a Mary Pickford-like fluttering of the eyelashes. '*Voce tem um cigarro?*'

The businessman made a courtly bow and drew a packet of cigarettes from his pocket. He was about to open it for her when she reached across and, eyelashes still fluttering, took it out of his hand and opened it herself.

I shot the businessman an apologetic look, but he was apparently used to being accosted in this manner, for with an infinitesimal shrug of the shoulders, he was already melting into the crowd.

'These should keep us going.'

'I really think . . .'

She wasn't, however, to be rebuked.

'Matches?'

Surrendering myself to the inevitable, I reached into my pocket and, cupping my hands round the flame, lit our respective cigarettes. She exhaled her smoke in a sensuous plume.

'You seem to have lost your friend.'

'My friend?'

'The matinee idol.' She took another pull on her cigarette, and without changing conversational gear, asked sweetly: 'How long have you been together?'

'Together?'

'Lovers, then.'

'Lovers? We're not lovers!'

'Then you'd like to be. I saw the way you looked at him. And I can quite see why. Bruised but fierce. The perfect combination.'

Drawing myself up to my full height, I said stiffly: 'Jean-Luís is a student. At the school where I teach.'

Seeing that she had perhaps gone too far, she leant forward and fixed me with a winning smile. 'I'm sorry. Just jealous, I suppose. A handsome Anglo-Saxon in a room full of Latins. You shouldn't blame me. You have interesting eyes. Sad. I'm a sucker for eyes. What's your name?'

Among his many criticisms of me, my father's chief complaint has always been that I am too impressionable; and in that moment, I was forced to accept that he might be right. Despite myself, I felt my outrage evaporate.

'Peter. Peter Smallwood. And yours?'

'Jacqui.'

With what seemed like utter seriousness, except that in the very formality of the gesture lay the joke, she extended a hand. '*So* nice to meet you.'

'And now,' she continued briskly, 'another glass of wine, don't you think, before we eat?'

'Eat?'

'We can't stay here.' She flagged down a passing waiter. 'Embassies always run out of wine just when the party gets interesting. And anyway, we've both been jilted. We deserve some reward.'

I remembered the man in whose pocket she'd been rooting, and grabbed the opportunity, or so I thought, to embarrass her as she had embarrassed me.

'And how long have *you* been together?'

'Oh,' she said airily 'on and off for about two months. He's the Minister for Overseas Development. Very me. But now I find there's some señorita with a basket of fruit on her head back in São Paulo to whom he was engaged when they were both in their cots. *And* his money's all tied up in trusts.'

I smiled into my wine. 'Forget me, then. I'm penniless.'

'I know. You told me, remember? That you teach?' She laid an unsettling hand on my arm. 'But you, I'd guess, know about foreplay. Brazilian diplomats do everything, and I mean everything, by the book. In Jorge's case, in a rather poor translation.'

I was suddenly very uncomfortable, and in order to defuse the situation, attempted a joke in return.

'I'm afraid I go by the book as well. In fact, I'm governed by books. Whole piles of them. Waiting to be marked. Waiting now, if I don't want to lose my job.'

'You can't ditch a girl when she's starving. Besides, I want to know everything about you, not just the boring bits like your job.'

The evening that followed I can only remember in snatches; a series of *tableaux vivants* viewed through an alcoholic haze. We went first to a wine bar behind Oxford Circus where Jacqui knew one of the waitresses, a glacial blonde with a passion for horses who, when she wasn't waiting table, was galloping point to point in the country. Jacqui, it transpired, knew the man with whom the waitress lived, and as she served us our rather indifferent quiche, the two of them giggled over the ease with which he could be made to subsidise his lover's equestrian pursuits. Then, over our second bottle of wine, Jacqui grilled me about my past – my father, my mother, what I was prepared to reveal about the commune, the school. About her I learnt only that although she enjoyed such Latin looks, and although I detected a hint of Australian in her accent, she was in fact English, had a son called Jed, didn't live with Jed's father, whoever he was, and apart from occasional jobs for Parties Unlimited and a stint as an actress, didn't seem to have any visible means of support.

When we'd finished the wine, and after a whispered consultation between Jacqui and her waitress friend, the upshot of which was that we only owed a tenner for the meal, I found myself settling the bill for both of us and agreeing with Jacqui that it would be 'a gas' if we went into Soho. A friend of hers (she seemed to collect friends the way some women collect jewellery; a piece for each occasion) was singing in a club.

We went first to a pub in Old Compton Street that was bristling with men.

'I hope you don't mind,' she whispered in my ear as she pulled me towards the bar, 'but you don't get hassled in places like this. As a woman, that is.'

Then, thankfully, we were in a much quieter establishment in a street off Shaftesbury Avenue, reached down a long flight of steps. We sat in a velvet booth, in the company of an elderly man with a pigtail, and railed against the licensing laws.

How we got from that basement to the club where Jacqui's friend was singing I can't remember, though I can see Jacqui arguing with a Schwarzenegger clone outside a vast panelled door, and myself standing on the pavement for what felt like eternity under the clone's disinterested gaze while Jacqui went off to find a phone – after which, as if by magic, the clone ushered us through the door and we found ourselves in a huge vaulted room pulsating with light, music and people.

The singer turned out to be a dreadlocked Jamaican who, in between sets, insisted we join him at a table near the stage for a bottle of champagne. At some point I lost Jacqui entirely, and found myself in earnest conversation with a Scot who was in London to sell a film script. I also have a vague recollection of jiving with the singer.

Then we were in a welcome taxi and Jacqui was helping herself to the last of my money in order to pay the driver. Next, in a tangle of sheet and limb, we were on a mattress on the floor of a small, box-like room, attempting to make love. Then there was light coming through the curtains and a rather hesitant, serious-looking boy was asking me if I took sugar in my tea.

Not surprisingly, I had a monumental hangover, and it was all I could do, after I'd swallowed some Panadol and phoned the school to tell them I had 'flu, to drag myself onto the sofa in the living room and lie there groaning. Jacqui, by contrast, seemed entirely unaffected by the excesses of the night. A model of briskness, she dressed and breakfasted Jed, packed him off to school, then made us both coffee, and, coming to join me on the sofa, asked quietly: 'What else happened in this commune?'

'What do you mean?'

'Last night,' she said, 'when we got back here and things . . .' She paused. 'You said that since the commune you hadn't been able to. You know, fuck.'

I stared into my coffee.

'I thought communes,' she went on, 'were havens for that sort of thing. Free love.'

Still I didn't reply, and after a further moment, she leant forward to run a finger down the side of my face. 'Poor Peter. Frightened, lonely and depressed.'

'I beg your pardon?'

'A phrase of Suzy's. For having a hangover. Frightened, lonely and depressed. Rather neat, don't you think?'

I nodded in rueful, relieved agreement; able, thanks to her change of tack, to attempt an explanation.

'It's not because I don't want to.'

She put her hand to my lips. 'Go back to bed. That's what you need. Not interrogation.'

I fell instantly asleep, waking only when Jacqui came to tell me it was one o'clock. Surprisingly, I felt fine: weak still, but purged and cleansed, as if the night hadn't happened.

'Feeling better?'

I grinned. 'Neither frightened, lonely nor depressed.'

'Good,' she said. 'Then lunch.'

We ate in an Italian restaurant on the High Road, just a couple of streets from the flat, and this time, to my surprise, Jacqui picked up the bill.

'About last night,' she said over coffee. 'You mustn't worry. Masculine men have their uses, but God, they can be boring. And anyway, I'm not looking for marriage. I'm not that sort of girl.' She giggled. 'Or rather, when I do marry, it's going to be for reasons of which you wouldn't approve.'

'I remember. Money, right?'

She nodded emphatically. 'Mountains of the stuff.'

Back at the flat, after Jed had returned from school, she made us both tea, then allowed Jed to turn on the television.

'So,' she said, eyeing me over her mug. 'Would you like to stay for supper?'

It occurred to me then that for all her friends and all the parties, she was actually quite lonely. Added to which was the oddly liberating fact that although she had inadvertently discovered something about me that no one else knew, she wasn't insisting on explanations.

'Yes,' I said. 'Thank you. I would.'

We had a surprisingly cosy and relaxed evening. Jacqui bathed Jed, then while she cooked I read to him in the living room, two whole chapters of his current book, and let him explain to me the intricacies of a spacecraft he'd built out of Lego.

After Jed had gone to bed, Jacqui said: 'He likes you.'

'He hardly knows me.'

'Children are quick.'

I didn't stay the night, nor did she suggest it – another liberation. But the next day I phoned her, and the day after that, and although we didn't see each other again until the following week, it came as no surprise when, three weeks later, she said: 'Wouldn't it be easier for you, with the school, I mean, if you lived on this side of town?'

'I suppose.'

'Because I've been thinking. Why not move in here? Jed's as easy as pie, but it's still a strain, looking after him on my own, and the two of you get on so well together.'

'Goodness,' I said. 'Is this a proposal?'

She laughed. 'A business proposition. Pure and simple.'

'Pure and simple?'

'If we keep it that way.'

Three

Usually I was the one to make the morning tea – even at weekends when, though technically the duty fell to Jed, the tepid brew that he concocted and delivered, sloshing, to our bedsides was so lacklustre that after he'd returned to his television, I would creep into the kitchen and remake it. Unusually, then, on the morning after Jacqui's meeting with Tarifa, I woke not to the alarm but to the subtler clink of cup against saucer.

Heaving myself upright, I saw to my surprise that the tea-bearing, kimono-clad Jacqui had already bathed and washed her hair.

'Goodness!' I said. 'You shouldn't. Now I'm in shock.'

'Goodness, honey, has nothing to do with it.' She handed me my tea. 'He said to ring at eleven, and I have to take Jed shopping first. Do you have any cash?'

I nodded towards my trousers. She got out my wallet and opened it.

'Thirty.' Without consultation, she returned a fiver to the wallet and pocketed the rest. 'I'll pay you back tomorrow.'

Jed, a miniature Caesar in the toga-like drape of his towel, put his dripping head round the door.

'What do I wear?'

'I've already told you,' snapped Jacqui. 'It doesn't matter. We're going shopping.'

'Well, hello,' I said. 'Mr Hollywood.'

He shot me a look of conspiratorial delight. 'No school!'

I pretended commiseration. 'Fame has its price.'

'Wait till Wesley hears.'

Wesley was Jed's best friend, and in the best tradition of male friendship, their rivalry was as intense as it was ongoing.

'All Wesley will hear,' interrupted Jacqui, 'if you don't get a move on, is the sound of my hand connecting with your backside.'

Jed risked a final look on me – this one designed to indicate, via an inexpert rolling of the eyes, the impossibility of mothers – then vanished.

'That child!' sighed Jacqui, vanishing with him.

A moment later she was back, a swirl of pink in one hand, in the other a more subtle beige.

'What do you think?'

'For what it's worth, I see Mrs Worthington in black. With a rope of pearls.'

'The pink,' said Jacqui. 'It's less executive.'

She tossed the rejected beige onto the chair. I threw back the covers and got to my feet.

'My, my!' Jacqui's chuckle was brief but suggestive.

I reached for my underpants. 'Never seen one before?'

'Not often on you.'

'Morning glory. It doesn't mean a thing.'

This time her chuckle contained a tinge of malice. 'Methinks the lady doth protest too much.'

She shrugged off her kimono and wriggled into the tube of pink.

'Well? Was I right?'

She did a pirouette for my approval.

'No knickers?'

She stuck out her tongue. 'Those come later. Well?'

'Sensational.'

Jed appeared at the door.

'I'm dressed!'

'Get yourself some cereal.'

She put a hand on his head and swivelled it to face the kitchen. At the same moment I reached across to pluck a strand of hair from the back of Jacqui's dress. Momentarily the three of us were linked, then Jed darted off in the direction of the kitchen and Jacqui knelt to retrieve her kimono.

'You don't know what you're missing,' she said lightly.

'I forgot to tell you,' was my reply. 'It's my half-day. I promised my father I'd do his hedges.'

'Do?' She gave the word the lilt of a joke.

'Cut,' I said. 'I do it every May. All I'm saying is that maybe I'll be late.'

'Well,' she smiled. 'We'll be here. Unless we're on the town. Celebrating.'

It was the combination of untrammelled hedge and Gothic eccentricity that gave my father's house its character. The other dwellings in Winterbourne Road dated from the seemly thirties, their gardens mere asphalt squares to facilitate off-street parking; their only extravagance, architecturally speaking, the occasional bay window or the addition of pebble-dash. Number 15, by contrast, was ebulliently Victorian, a gaudy configuration of turrets and steepled windows, actual gargoyles and a chapel-like porch, all hedged about by an excess of green.

Elevation to the propertied classes had coincided for my father with marriage. The year was 1965. My father was forty-seven; Cecily, my mother, twelve years his junior. Both long-term members of the Communist Party, they had known each other since the early fifties, though it was only as his half-century loomed that my father had felt impelled (why, I don't know) to upgrade their relationship from comrades to partners. My mother's dowry of an inherited house can hardly have been a factor. Not in my father's eyes.

Or so I surmised. About the nuances of his political and personal odyssey I knew very little. Simply that when, at the age of twenty, he had enlisted with the International Brigade and taken up arms against Franco, he had been a firebrand, and that by the eighties, when I was old enough to observe him for myself, the flame had virtually died. Whether this was the result of Spain, where, for all the glory, the fight had actually gone against him, or whether it was due to later events (his growing realisation that England could never be converted to the cause of communism, the ethical problems posed by Stalinism, the death of my mother, the compromises forced on him by the need to earn a living), I could only guess at. If the mood took me. Which, as a child, I can't say it did.

My childhood revolved around lodgers not parents. Not remembering my mother – she died when I was two – I had little cause to miss her; and though I noticed, of course, that other boys had mothers, I can't recall envying them. Mothers meant having to wash behind your ears, being home before dark, keeping your room tidy. Besides which, as I say, the party members to whom my father rented rooms were a constant source of companionship and haphazard treats. Admittedly some of the women, funny-smelling creatures in steel-rimmed spectacles, were cold and unapproachable, others too ready to lecture me on the exploitation of the female; but almost all were at some point compromised by maternal instincts, and would lavish me with stories, take me on outings, arrive home with ice-cream or the promise of a film. Likewise the men, anarchists all, and determined to treat me as an equal.

It was only when I reached my teens that I began to resent
these lodgers. Although content to discuss and re-discuss
with them the fate of British coal, my father seldom had the
time to talk to me. My concerns (parties, acne, shyness) were
unimportant; bourgeois and frivolous. It was then that I gave
the house its sobriquet of Hotel Gumm; then that I launched
my campaign to turn my father against his lodgers by drawing his attention to the fact that most of them were in arrears
with their rent, and that, as for championing the dignity of
labour, where housework or the garden were concerned,
theory invariably triumphed over practice.

My father gave short shrift to my observations. Dust on
the mantelpiece, he told me, was neither here nor there;
besides, no community was without its give and take.

This skirmish over his lodgers became, in time, our principal means of communication, and the afternoon I went to
cut the hedges was no exception. I had a key, and, letting
myself in, squeezed along the bike-cluttered hall to find my
father in the kitchen, fussing over a plate of sandwiches.

'Ah,' he said, peering over his horn-rimmed spectacles.
'There you are. I was beginning to wonder.'

'It's only two. I don't get off until one.'

When young (I have a picture of him in Spain, standing
to moral attention beside a truck) my father's features were
starkly ascetic: sharp nose and chin, hair a brilliantined
carapace. Age had unravelled him. Now his hair was unruly,
his chin a confluence of wrinkles, the forehead less certain.
All that hadn't changed were the eyes. 'Sad,' Jacqui had
said when she'd met him. 'Like yours, but even sadder.' And
it was the eyes that held me presently, appraising me with
their particular brand of tired scepticism. He gestured to the
sandwiches.

'Ham all right?'

'Just fine.'

'Jim had some people round last night. You might be lucky enough to find a beer in the fridge.'

And indeed, on the bottom shelf, alongside a rotting lettuce and a plate of congealing spaghetti, were two surviving cans of Carlsberg.

'Want one?'

He shook his head.

'So,' I said, commandeering a chair at the table, 'what was it this time? The resuscitation of the USSR?'

'His birthday, actually.'

'Stalin's?'

There was a pause.

'Twenty-five.'

'Same age as me.'

'Since you mention it.'

My father's jibe was deadlier than mine. At twenty-five, lodger Jim had two degrees to his name, lectured at the London School of Economics and had recently published his first book: *Beyond the Barricades: Sexism in the Printing Industry*. I decided to change the subject.

'And you? Are you well?'

'As you see.'

Disinterring two plates from the stack on the draining board, he sat opposite me and pushed a plate in my direction. We bit into our sandwiches. For a while there was silence.

'And school?' he asked eventually. 'How's school?'

'Much the same.'

'Still having problems with Gloria?'

'I haven't got the rise, if that's what you mean.'

He took up a second sandwich. 'You should speak to Roger. He's been doing research into the working conditions of teachers, I'm sure he'd—'

I didn't let him finish. 'You forget. The Camden Centre isn't unionised.'

He shot me a look of barely concealed satisfaction. 'Precisely.'

I was taken back in time, to when I was ten again, Jed again, tucking into the tea my father had prepared on my return from school. Now, as then, he sat in judgement with his jury of unwashed plates, whilst I fought a panicked path through the cross-examination. I stood up and brushed the crumbs from my lap.

'Hedges.'

The electric cutters and extension cable were on a shelf in the pantry, wedged above a pile of paint tins, cobwebbed evidence of the house's innumerable lodgers. At the bottom of the pile was the Midnight Blue with which Claire, circa 1975, had, without calling a house meeting, painted the bathroom, thereby bringing her tenancy to a sudden end; and immediately under the cutters a tin of Apricot White, current colour of Jim's tenancy in the room at the top of the house.

I plugged the cable into the socket by the stove, and, opening the window, dropped it over the sill. Outside, I unreeled enough to allow me to reach the bottom of the garden; then, cutters at the ready, allowed myself to be swallowed up by the undergrowth.

'Some tea?'

It was an hour later and I had worked my way back to the house, where my father stood framed in the kitchen door, a pile of newspapers in his arms.

I switched off the cutters. 'Please.'

He gestured to the papers.

'These are going in the shed. I'll get some bags. For the cuttings. Then I'll make tea.'

He returned a moment later with an armful of black plastic bags.

'If there aren't enough, just leave what's left.'

'You mean someone else will do it?'

I hadn't meant it as a taunt particularly, but it came out that way, and he chose to acknowledge the charge.

'You offered to do the hedges. No one forced you.'

I compounded my error by adding: 'You mean you'll call a house meeting?'

This time I'd gone too far, and, dropping the bags in a pile at my feet, my father turned away, muttering darkly: 'Your tea will be in the kitchen.'

The weekly house meeting was to 15 Winterbourne Road what family Eucharist was to your average English village: sacred and indispensable. It was where the household worshipped at the shrine of its own importance. Levity was sacrilegious, and, watching the set of my father's departing back, I couldn't believe I'd been foolish enough to flaunt my political atheism. Snatching up a bag, I began to fill it furiously: secular atonement.

By the time I'd finished my penance, there were ten bags of clippings stashed under the kitchen window, and, wiping the sweat from my brow, I felt sufficiently shriven to venture inside. My father had not only made my tea, he'd even poured it. I lifted the mug to my lips, and ignoring the fact that the tea was already cold, drank it before the table which was also the altar around which the house would congregate to decide on its weekly rota of shopping, cooking, washing up and television viewing – and on which, I now noticed, my father had left an inadvertent, ironical and coded reminder of the limits of our relationship: a well-thumbed copy of *Great Expectations*, open at Chapter Seven.

I broke out crying, and begging pardon, and hugged Joe round the neck: who dropped the poker to hug me, and to say, 'Ever the best of friends; an't us, Pip? Don't cry, old chap!'

I didn't read any further. I couldn't. Dickens' prose had swum out of focus. This was the only book my father had read me as a child. Pip's story mine; his legacy, his loneliness, his uncertainty – all mine. Mine then, mine now. No change. Which was why I understood Jed. We shared a mutual need: for greater security, greater love. Aslan.

I wiped my cheek with my sleeve, and, collecting the cutters, trailed the cable round the side of the house so that I could attack the hedges at the front.

'Hello, Peter!'

It had gone six, and I was stuffing the last of the cuttings into their bags. I looked up, and at the gate, hand poised by the latch, was the angular form of Barbara, her aubergine-tinted tresses an unlikely halo for a face whose severity demanded to be framed by something less voluptuous than hair.

'You look hot.'

I gestured at the bags. 'Hot work.'

'I wondered who was responsible for the hedges.'

Barbara was a recent addition to the house, and though she didn't for an instant allow this to undermine her natural bossiness, was still familiarising herself with protocol.

'If I had my way,' she continued, opening the gate, 'I'd get rid of them. Unnecessary, don't you think?' She stepped smartly round the bags of clippings. 'But I've got a meeting. Excuse me if I rush.'

A short while later I re-entered the kitchen to find my father decanting wine into a jug.

'Want some?' he queried. 'Roger made it.'

I walked across and laid a hand on his shoulder.

'I'm sorry. I didn't mean to upset you earlier.'

He stiffened. 'Did you? When?'

'About the house meetings.'

'Oh, that!' He tugged at his cardigan, thereby disengaging himself from my touch. 'I'd forgotten. Not bad.' Glass at his lips, he gave vent to an unexpected giggle. 'A good nose.'

I decided to let the matter drop. 'You'll never guess what's happened to Jed. Or what might be happening. Jacqui was at this party, and guess who she met? Carlos Tarifa. You know, the opera director. He's making a film. About Murillo. The painter. And he's told Jacqui there might be a part in it for Jed. They met this morning. Tarifa and Jed.'

'Dulwich,' said my father.

'I beg your pardon?'

'There are Murillos in the Dulwich gallery. Beggar boys. Hideously sentimental. Just up Tarifa's street.'

'You know him?'

'Of course not. But I've heard him being interviewed. Does Jacqui know how he started?'

'How do you mean, started?'

'He was a protégé of Picasso's. They designed the sets together, in the fifties this would have been, for a production in France of *The House of Bernada Alba*. The Lorca play. You know about Lorca?'

'Sort of.'

'Butchered,' said my father. 'Outside Granada. For his politics and his poetry and being . . .' He searched for the correct expression. 'A lover of men.'

There was an awkward pause which neither of us, it seemed, knew how to break. Then he reached for the jug and held it questioningly aloft.

'I wish,' I said quietly, extending my glass, 'that we talked like this more often.'

'Like what?'

'About Spain, for example. You've never really told me what happened to you there.'

'Are you interested?'

I took a sip of my wine. 'I don't mean the politics, I mean . . .'

My father let out a short, harsh laugh. 'Until you realise,' he said, 'that the politics *are* what happened, that politics aren't decoration, some sort of afterthought, but life itself, then I don't see the point.'

We were back in our usual positions, he on his team, I on mine, aiming the conversational ball at our respective goals.

'No,' I said woodenly, 'of course.'

We were rescued by Barbara, who put her head round the door to ask my father whether he was coming to the meeting.

He shook his head.

'I don't think,' he said slowly, 'that we have much in common these days, your group and me.'

I got to my feet.

'If you'll excuse me,' I said, 'I'd better get back.'

My father didn't miss a beat. 'Of course. You'll be wanting to hear how Catholicism feels about Jed.'

'Catholicism? What's Catholicism got to do with it?'

'In Spain?' His chuckle had a decided edge to it. 'Everything, of course.'

Four

N ot surprisingly, Tarifa – and what Tarifa was promising – was again the topic of conversation that evening.

'I'll admit,' said Jacqui as she ladled a mess of scrambled eggs onto a plate for Jed, 'that I've only seen one side of him, and obviously he was out to please – but the charm of the man! You could drown in it. Supper's ready!'

'And Macauley Culkin?' Our incipient film star had slipped into the kitchen to take his place at the table. 'How did you find Señor Tarifa?'

Jed prodded his food with a suspicious fork. 'What's in these eggs?'

'Bacon,' said Jacqui briskly, 'and tomato.'

'What's this?'

With the tip of his fork, Jed held aloft what looked like a strip of overcooked skin.

'Onion.' Jacqui was inspecting the wine rack. 'Is this all we've got?'

'But I don't like onion! You know I don't like onion!'

'Yes,' I said to Jacqui, and to Jed: 'Put it on one side.' Then I reiterated my question: 'Did you like him?'

'He spoke funny.' Jed's principal concern was disinterring onion from egg.

'Bulgarian Merlot.' Jacqui sounded less than delighted. 'You open it.' She passed the bottle across Jed's head. 'Jed, for heaven's sake, just eat. Onion can't harm you.' She sank onto a chair. 'Now, where was I?'

'Drowning in charm.'

'It's his energy, I suppose. Why is it so seductive? Energy?'

She lit a cigarette. Jed forgot the onion and went through an elaborate pantomime of blowing away the smoke.

'Overact like that,' snapped Jacqui, 'and your career will be over before it's begun.'

I'd opened the bottle, and now I filled a glass for her.

'His energy,' I prompted.

'Well,' she said, taking a sip of her wine, 'one can see he's got an enormous ego – too much self-confidence – and I'm sure he can be monstrous. I mean, he hasn't got where he is by being nice. But somehow he just sweeps you along. And God, is he knowledgeable!'

'*Tomorrow's World*,' said Jed. 'He hadn't heard of *Tomorrow's World*.'

'Ah,' said Jacqui, 'but what about Spurs?'

Jed showed enthusiasm for the first time. 'He knows Gary Lineker!'

'So,' I said, looking from mother to son. 'He made an impression.'

'Laugh if you like,' said Jacqui, 'but wouldn't you be thrilled if it happened to you? In fact . . .' She stopped in mid-sentence.

'Yes?'

She shook her head. 'Nothing. For God's sake, Jed, just eat!'

'What?' I persisted.

But she wasn't to be drawn. 'The only thing I'm not sure about is this producer person. You know, the one we're supposed to meet. Al something or other.'

'Bacardy,' said Jed. 'Like the drink.'

'Who told you that?'

'What?' He shot me a look of puzzled innocence.

'That Bacardy's a drink.'

'Haven't you seen the ad?' He enacted amazement at what he supposed to be my ignorance. 'The one where they pretend that by pressing the arm of your seat . . .'

Jacqui was also looking at me askance. 'Why the outrage? It's only a drink. I mean, it isn't smack we're discussing here.'

Jed pounced on this new word. 'What's smack?'

'What little boys get when they don't finish their supper.' Jacqui stubbed out her cigarette and immediately lit another.

'So what else has he done?' I asked. 'This rum producer?'

'Very funny!'

'Well?'

'That's what I wish I knew.' She reached for the bottle. '*Gun Law*? Does that ring a bell?'

'*Gun Law*?'

'Gun something.'

'Guns to Murillo. I can see why you're worried.'

'I'm not worried. I just wish I knew a little more about him.' She stood up. 'Right! Bath and bed, young man.'

After Jed had had his bath, and I had read to him, we settled in the living room to finish our wine. Jacqui leant forward on the sofa, her finger tracing a ring round the top of her glass.

'I've done something rather naughty, though.'

'Naughty?'

'Promise you won't be angry?'

'What?'

'Promise first.'

Curiosity unmanned me. 'All right. I promise.'

'Besides,' she continued casually, 'when we were talking about his villa the other night, I got the distinct impression . . .'

'Jacqui, no!'

I knew, without her having to say another word, exactly what was coming.

'Actually,' she said, reaching for a cigarette, 'it wasn't me at all. It was really Jed. He was the one who kept mentioning you, so naturally Carlos made me promise you would come too. I mean, see it from his angle. Jed has to fly to Spain to meet this producer. Carlos has to make sure he doesn't feel out of his depth.'

'The answer, Jacqui, is no. Emphatically no! This is between you and Jed. I don't want any part of it.'

She put down her glass and took a deep breath. 'I won't point out how important this is to me, or how I could do with some support, or how it won't cost you a thing, or how it's for three days max, and over a weekend, too, so that wretched school of yours won't even notice your absence . . .' She paused. 'I'll only say that when I agreed we would go to Spain for a further meeting, the first thing Jed said, the very first thing, was: "Is Peter really coming with us?"'

She'd won, of course, hands down. Or rather, Jed had. All I could do now was hope that by acquiescing I wasn't letting myself in for something that would spiral out of control.

'And if he gets the part?' I asked quietly.

'It's an audition,' she said. 'That's all. We're talking one weekend. What comes after . . .' She drained the last of her wine. 'Another bottle?'

Great Expectations, I was thinking. *Great Expectations indeed.*

★

The next morning – having opened and drunk not only that other bottle, but half of a third – I woke with a throbbing head to the shrill insistence of the phone. At first I just lay there, waiting for Jacqui to answer it. Then, when she didn't, I got up and blundered into the living room.

"Allo!' The voice was female, heavily accented, and fragmented by crackle. 'Is that Jacqui?'

'Jacqui's asleep,' I muttered, 'but if you just hang on . . .'

'You must be Peter.' By rolling the 'r', the voice gave the second syllable of my name more weight than the first. 'The handsome and mysterious Peter.'

'Who is this?'

The voice wasn't in the least put out by my acerbity.

'A distant admirer.'

'Look, if this is some kind of joke . . .'

The voice fragmented further, but into a laugh this time. 'Always I joke, and always it gets me trouble. My name is Zeynep. I am ringing for Carlos. To make arrangements for your visit.'

I found myself apologising. 'I'm sorry. It's just that you woke me up. Look, you'd better speak to Jacqui. Just a minute.'

'You are booked on Iberia flight five-four-seven.' The voice didn't intend to let me go. 'Friday the eleventh at thirteen-thirty. Your tickets will be at the desk. Iberia, Heathrow. There will be a car at Barcelona. If you have any problems, you phone me. Zeynep. My number is—'

'Hang on! I need a pen.'

I scrabbled on the coffee table for pen and paper.

'Right. Iberia flight five-four-seven. Friday, one-thirty. Zeynep. And your number?'

She gave me the number. 'You sound nice. Very English. I like the English. So charming.'

There was a click and the line went dead. Dazed, I went

into the kitchen to make some much-needed tea. Jacqui was just surfacing when I entered her room.

'Who was that?' she asked sleepily.

I told her.

'Already? God, they don't waste time, do they?'

'Who is she?'

'Zeynep? Carlos's assistant. Turkish, I think.' She sat up. 'She had some tragedy with her parents, something to do with the government, the Turkish government. Fraud or politics. He wasn't precise. Anyway, they ended up in jail, and she ended up in Spain, where Carlos took her in.'

'He told you all this yesterday?'

'The Spanish are like that.'

'Indiscreet?'

'Friendly. He told me lots about himself.'

'I think,' I said, settling on the chair, 'you'd better fill me in. So I know what I'm facing. Like, for example, how a weekend which won't interfere with my job can start on Friday at lunchtime. Just before a class.'

'God!' Jacqui took a sip of her tea. 'And I'm the one who's supposed to want everything her own way!'

'You said . . .'

She held up a hand. 'I said Jed wanted you to come with us. That's all. If you can't handle the school, then you're a damn sight more feeble than I thought.'

'Of course I can handle the school.'

'So what's the problem?'

And in the event, there wasn't a problem. The plan I concocted in response to Jacqui's challenge succeeded beyond my wildest dreams. Armed with three of my most diligent pupils, I bearded Gloria in her office the following afternoon.

'Heavens!' she exclaimed as I led my posse into the room. 'A deputation.'

I could see she was thinking we had come to complain, and in order to maximise the psychological advantage this gave us, I didn't start speaking immediately, but waited until we had encircled her desk.

'Trouble?' she demanded querulously, in passable imitation of Edith Evans.

'On the contrary. I just wanted to let you know about next weekend. With Hannah here as a leader, and Klaus and Suzanne, I've asked my classes to spend the Friday out and about in London, and to write up what they see.'

Suspicion mingled with alarm in Gloria's eyes. A consummate bullshitter herself, she was extraordinarily sensitive to the ability in others.

'I got the idea from an article I read in the *TES*. The International School in Paris did it last year, and it was so successful, they're thinking of making it part of their syllabus. What I've done is choose three parts of London, which each class has to visit in the course of the day. They write about what they see, and how it compares to similar parts of their own city. The week after I'll be organising a series of seminars in which we'll discuss their findings.'

It was nonsense, of course. There had been no such article in the *TES*, no such experiment at the International School, but, as I'd hoped, the combination of our presence in the office, plus the magic words *TES* and International School – as potent in TEFL circles as the Nicene Creed – won Gloria over completely.

And having cleared that hurdle, I found myself in the grip of an excitement every bit as potent as Jacqui's. For the first time ever I was leaving England, and not only that, but at the behest of Jed, and to visit Spain, fabled part of my father's past. I was doing something unexpected, daring, the outcome of which I couldn't guess at. I was surrendering myself to the inevitable.

F i v e

'*A*re you still with us?'
It was 11.30, and for some reason known only to London Underground, our tube had been standing at Acton Town for at least ten minutes, during which time I'd been staring blankly at the deserted platform.

I snapped out of my reverie and grinned apologetically at the enquiring Jacqui.

'Wesley's been to Heathrow three times,' said Jed suddenly. He, I'd discovered earlier, had been only the once, and it irked him. 'He goes to Florida.'

'So now you're going to Spain.'

'Florida's further. Isn't it?'

'Sure. But Spain's older.'

'Oh, my God!' Jacqui was scrabbling in her bag. 'The passports!'

I laid a reassuring hand on her arm. 'I've got them.'

'Fucking train. Why won't it go?'

Whereupon, as mysteriously as it had stopped, it started again.

Passing through passport control was like stepping, albeit innocuously, from one realm into another; and in Jed I had the perfect companion with whom to share my sudden excitement.

'Come!' I said, taking his hand. 'Over here!'

I led him to the duty-free shop, where – in tacit acknowledgement of our passage into the unfamiliar – a sort of tawdry magic was on sale. He made a bee-line for the electronic games.

'Would you like one?'

He stared at me in disbelief.

'You mean it?'

I found Jacqui at the bar, nursing a cognac.

'Bit early?' I queried mildly.

She shrugged. 'When in Spain. Or on the way. You really shouldn't have.' She nodded at Jed, hunched over his game at a nearby table.

'Keeps him occupied.'

She smiled. 'You're very good with him, you know. The best of all my men.'

Now it was my turn to smile. 'But I'm not one of your men.'

She considered me over the rim of her glass. 'Don't I know it.' She threw back the remains of her cognac. 'Sure you won't join me?'

'Quite sure.'

On the plane, though, I changed my mind, and whilst not exactly keeping pace with her, still drank enough to turn my excitement at going abroad into a benignity as limpid as the sky itself. At thirty thousand feet, where the sun made perpetual summer, the world, when glimpsed, was as manageable as the game over which Jed was still hunched. A touch of the button, and this mountain, or that country, could be removed from the screen. Then we were banking steeply and being told to fasten our seat-belts. Jed lost interest in his game and became caught up in the business of landing.

'Where's the runway?' he asked nervously. 'It's all sea.'

I looked over his shoulder and saw only the placid stillness of the Mediterranean, pierced here and there by a
fishing boat.

'In a minute,' said Jacqui. 'Watch.'

The sea continued to unfold beneath us. Then, true to
Jacqui's word, the land put in its appearance: a stretch of
coastline, a proud hill, the cluttered harbour, suburbs,
motorways.

We were met by a smiling spheroid of a man, as orbicu-
lar as he was cheerful, who hovered by the exit from the
baggage hall with a scrap of cardboard on which, misspelt,
was Jacqui's name.

'That's not right,' said Jed immediately. 'They've added
an "e".'

'Just as long as the car's air-conditioned,' groaned Jacqui.
'I had no idea it would be this warm. Imagine August.'

Our driver relieved me of our trolley and herded us outside to a gleaming limousine.

Jacqui and I sank into the back. Jed opted for the seat
that opened down behind the driver.

'It's like a taxi,' he said, clearly relieved after the novelty of
the bus which had driven us from the plane to the con-
course, the echoing marble floors and unfamiliar posters of
the arrivals hall, to encounter something which felt familiar.

Jacqui lit a cigarette. 'If this is a taxi,' she said, 'I'm a vestal
virgin.'

Pausing only to insert a cassette into the player (a cassette,
it turned out, of Spanish love songs sung by a woman
whose voice was so tremulous, so vivid, that it approached
absurdity), the driver swung the car out of its parking place.

'What's a vestal?' asked Jed.

'I thought you'd want to know what a virgin was?'

He didn't acknowledge my little joke.

'Well?' he demanded.

'I'm tired,' said Jacqui, 'and if I have to listen to any more of your wretched questions, I shall have a break-down. Right here in this car. Where neither of you can avoid it.'

The tinted windows of the car framed cooled vignettes of urban sprawl: the motorway on which we sped into Barcelona; a grid of elegant boulevards; the clotted centre; then a long, straight road that unravelled northwards along the coast, beach to our right, the railway and a line of hotels to our left.

'It could be Durban,' said Jacqui at one point.

'How do you know Durban?'

'A guy I knew once.' She was staring at Jed.

'South African?'

'When I was an actress. We did a tour.' There was a far-away, almost regretful look in her eyes. 'Another life.'

'Good life?'

She snapped back into the present and began to stroke the leather seat. 'This is the good life.'

The coast was no longer flat. We were climbing steeply, away from the hotels; and the sea, when we glimpsed it, was far below us.

'Soon Tarifa,' said the driver, turning over the cassette.

Jacqui rolled down her window, allowing the sun-released smell of the Mediterranean into the car: pine needles, rosemary, thyme.

'Did he talk about his past at all?' I asked. 'When you met him?'

Jacqui looked at me blankly.

'Tarifa.'

She shrugged. 'His work. A little.'

'How did he get started?'

'He didn't give me a copy of his CV, if that's what you mean.' She returned her attention to the view.

'Only wondering.'

We rounded a headland. The coastline fell away in a series of jagged coves, whilst out to sea, on the calm, flat surface of it, the wake of a solitary speedboat made an enormous arrow in the water.

'Tarifa!' said the driver, gesturing ahead.

Before I could follow the direction of his arm, we'd turned another corner and begun to drop into one of the coves. The road twisted tortuously round the cliffs, all the while keeping pace with the speedboat.

Then, without warning, the driver was pulling off the road through an iron gate that seemed to open into thin air: until, that is, one was through it and realised it gave onto a small, circular parking place.

We were on the edge of a cliff, some three or four hundred feet above the sea, and in the lee of a scrubby mountain that continued to climb sheerly behind us. We helped the driver remove our cases from the boot, then followed him to a gate at the far end of the parking space that led via a steep flight of steps to a green wooden door set into a rough stone wall. The driver buzzed the intercom, and when it buzzed a reply, leant towards it and broke into a stream of unintelligible Spanish. There was a moment's pause, a click, and the door swung magically open. The driver stood back to let us pass.

We stepped into another world. The sea was a constant – still there below us, still flat, still calm – but where the mountainside had been bare and forbidding, all scrub and pine trees and angry red earth, the courtyard we entered was cool and creeper-clad, overhung with palm trees and circled by brilliant flowers. The driver motioned us to drop our cases by the fountain which played in its centre.

'Look!' said Jed. 'Goldfish.'

And indeed, the fountain was teeming with them, some gold, others a sleek, buttery white.

'*Muy bueno, no?*' said the driver.

I nodded. '*Muy bueno.*'

There was a clatter of heels from the stairs that led up to the courtyard on the other side, and a diminutive woman in a blue cotton dress, her hair a halo of tight, blonde curls, flew into view. I guessed her to be in her fifties – her sun-bronzed face was attractively wrinkled, her shoulders stooped – but there was something ageless about her too: a certain insouciance in the way she wore her years.

'Those stairs!' She was grimacing. 'Terrible! But how was the trip? Did you have a good flight?' Taking Jed's hand in hers, she continued without pause. 'I'm Zeynep. Such a silly name. Jed! Now that's a proper name. You have a kind mother. Not like me.'

She turned to Jacqui: 'I can see where he gets his looks.' And to me: 'So this is the man with the velvet voice.'

She had the knack of the truly charming: she made you take her flagrant flattery utterly for granted.

Turning to the driver, she rattled something at him in Spanish.

'Juan,' she said, reverting to English, 'will bring up your cases. The driver will tell him.'

She shepherded us between the palm trees and up a short flight of steps onto the terrace of an imposing villa, double-storied, pink, with wrought-iron balconies at each of the upstairs windows.

'Pretty, no?' She had seen the expression on our faces as we approached the balustrade that ran round the edge of the terrace. 'The best view, this terrace, which is why I've put you here.'

I turned my back on the sea to study the house. At its centre was a vast double door in weatherbeaten oak.

'When Carlos came,' said Zeynep, 'this was the only house. Until he built the Casa Nueva. That you will see later.'

'Magnificent,' I said.

Zeynep shrugged. 'It belonged to Picasso. He spent some summers here. His studio was at the back. I show you later.'

I remembered what my father had told me about the Lorca production. Did this explain how Tarifa had started?

Jed had wandered to the far end of the terrace, which was covered by a canopy of vines. I heard a mocking whistle.

'Aha!' said Zeynep. 'He's found Larry's bird. Come.'

Hanging from the vines was a wooden cage, and in the cage, a small grey bird with beady, distrustful eyes. As we approached, it let out another whistle.

'Careful!' warned Zeynep. 'He bites. Last week Carreras.'

'José Carreras?' Jacqui made the question as throwaway as she could.

'My dear!' Zeynep chuckled. 'How many Carrerases are there? *Ahora*! Your rooms.'

The double door led into a living room that stretched the entire length of the villa. To the left of the door, four white sofas were set in a square round an imposing fireplace, and on the wall above the fireplace, in niches, was a collection of colourful pottery. To the right was a grand piano, two massive, rather sombre wooden sideboards and a tall cupboard with its doors open which contained the nativity: the holy family, the three wise men, some shepherds, all fashioned out of porcelain and fabulously dressed in rich brocades. The walls of the room were whitewashed, the floor tiled, giving it, despite the magnificence of its furnishings, an aspect of austerity.

Feeling as if I'd entered a museum, I crossed to the fire-place to inspect the vases.

'Beautiful, no?' Zeynep had followed me, and was standing by my elbow.

'They look so old!'

'Over two thousand years. The best collection in Spain.'

It *is* a museum, I was thinking, a showcase for the owner's taste and wealth.

'Come!' Our guide had crossed to the staircase in the far wall. We fell into single file and followed her up to a dimly lit corridor that ran the length of the upstairs floor. She opened a door. 'For you, Jed.'

He hesitated a moment on the threshold; then, with a quick, unbelieving look at Jacqui, vanished into the room. Zeynep smiled at Jacqui. 'You are next to him.' She led us on down the corridor and, with a flourish, threw open a second door and stood back so we could enter first.

Again the effect was of austerity mixed with opulence: two narrow single beds set against the far wall, an assortment of oppressive mahogany furniture – a cupboard, a dressing table, a marble-topped chest of drawers – and hung across the window, a brocaded curtain that kept light to a minimum. The walls were bare and white, the ceiling vaulted and painted a contrasting shade of green. A gaudy chandelier hung from its centre.

Zeynep crossed briskly to the window, drew back the curtain, threw open the shutters, then crossed to a door in the opposite corner of the room.

'Your bathroom!' The room thus indicated was in stark, almost futuristic contrast to the bedroom. Its gleaming tiles, generous basin, bidet and shower cubicle consorted oddly with the Victorian mahogany. 'We have terrible problems with the water pressure, and sometimes, well, you have to wait for the hot water. But eventually it comes.' Zeynep returned to the window and stepped onto the balcony. I followed her. Below us the terrace basked undisturbed in the afternoon sun; below that I could see the domed roof of another building, below that the sea.

Zeynep pointed to the domed roof. 'Casa Nueva,' she said. 'Where Carlos stays. But for me,' she caressed the railing, 'this is the best house. A house for lovers.' She darted me a sly look. 'Tom Cruise and Nicole Kidman. You know, from Hollywood.' She gave the name a dismissive inflection. 'Carlos lent them this villa for part of their honeymoon. She stood here every evening and brushed her hair. She likes her hair. How long have you and Jacqui—?'

Before she could finish her question, Jed appeared on the balcony to our right. 'Neat, huh?' His eyes were shining.

'You like?' Zeynep transferred her attention to him.

'There's a shower and a bath and two toilets.'

She laughed. 'A bidet. One's a bidet. Wait. I show you.'

I followed her back into the room, and when she'd gone, looked enquiringly at Jacqui, who was emerging from the bathroom.

'So we're a couple, are we? In name only, or am I expected to perform?'

Without meeting my gaze, Jacqui threw herself full-length onto the nearest bed.

'He'd better bloody well get the part. That's all I can say.'

I sat down next to her and ran an exploratory finger the length of her arm.

'Know who's fucked here?'

'Who?'

'Assuming, of course, they do it.'

'Who?'

'Tom Cruise and Nicole Kidman.'

'You're not serious?'

'Zeynep told me.'

'Right here, you mean?'

'Apparently Carlos lent them the villa for part of their honeymoon.'

She frowned. 'Single beds, though.'

'Not much of an obstacle, surely? Except where you need it to be.'

She lifted my hand from her arm and began to toy with my fingers.

'It's all right,' she said. 'You can relax. I didn't say anything. About you and me. They're just assuming things.'

That was the moment at which our cases appeared, followed by Zeynep with a final set of instructions: dinner was at nine, on the terrace below the Casa Nueva; we'd hear a bell, we should wander down when we felt like it.

We unpacked, I helped Jed unpack, he bathed and took a shower, I showered, Jacqui showered, we changed, and then the bell rang. Tarifa time.

Whereas our villa stood proud on its terrace, spotlighted by sun, Casa Nueva was more subterranean. The sun had long since set, but even in the dark I had the sense as we felt our way down the vertiginous staircase up which, earlier, Zeynep had flown, that we were descending into a cooler, more cloistered domain. The staircase was canopied by vines and contiguous with a shallow gully in which murmuring water, tumbling the rapids created by the steps, splashed towards a pond that lay, silent and green, to the right of the terrace below. Everything here was green, green and moist: a miniature jungle of fern and vine.

Fronted by a further terrace that was subdivided by pillars into three sections, and roofed by a continuing complexity of vine, Casa Nueva was a mere suggestion of white against the verdure. We paused at the double doors that led into its deserted living room. With the exception of a palm that towered over the centre of the room, brushing the domed ceiling with its fronds, everything in it was white: the hexagonal tiles on the walls, the sofas, the cushions, even the coffee tables and the collection of shells on a shelf by the door. To our right was another, shorter flight of stairs, down which we ventured to find ourselves on a circular terrace that opened onto the night sky and, some two hundred feet below, the susurration of the sea. A large table, lit by candles and laden with food, stood in the centre of the terrace; and artfully arranged on the wicker chairs set in a semi-circle around its perimeter, a group of people, all impeccably attired in cocktail dresses or sharply pressed shirts and slacks, sat chattering softly. Zeynep, elegant in a sheath of emerald green, stood by the table.

'My dears! You found us. You have a shower? You feel more rested?'

We nodded dutifully.

'Come!' She placed a hand on Jed's shoulder. 'Let me introduce you.'

It appeared that with one exception, none of the people on the terrace spoke a word of English. First came an elderly woman in black with the forbidding, suspicious features of a peasant ('Quiepo's mother,' explained Zeynep, without explaining who Quiepo was), then a more or less homogeneous assortment of men and women who, with practised but subtly dismissive charm, nodded the briefest of greetings before returning their attention to their companions. Only one young man, whose name I didn't catch, broke off his conversation long enough to ask (in halting English) if we'd had a good flight, had we been to Spain before, did we like our rooms?

It wasn't his English, though, that made the impression. Or perhaps it was? He stumbled over his words as winningly as any Jean-Luís; and like Jean-Luís, would not have looked out of place in the pages of a fashion magazine. The

sculpted perfection of his face was complemented by a luxuriance of glossy black hair, the tan of his skin thrown into
burnished relief by the white of his shirt.

I was thankful when, introductions over, Zeynep led us
to the table, supplied us with plates, and urged us to help
ourselves to the cold meats, cheeses and salads displayed
upon it. Plates piled high, and in possession of wine from
the flagons that abutted the cutlery, we settled at one end of
the semi-circle of chairs and watched as the others stepped
forward to do the same.

'It's like a hotel,' whispered Jacqui. 'A very grand, very
select hotel.'

To my dismay, the young man whose name I hadn't
caught came and sat on my left.

'So,' he said, balancing his plate deftly on one knee, 'you
are teacher?'

My mouth full of potato salad, I could only nod.

'Perhaps you give me lesson? Carlos make joke of my
English.'

I managed to swallow my food. 'It sounds all right to
me,' I said quickly.

He shrugged. 'Carlos not like.'

There was a noise on the stairs, and two new players
arrived on the scene. The leading player was precisely that:
short and stocky, he had the air of someone accustomed to
commanding centre stage. A pair of glasses hung on a
leather thong around his neck, and as he muttered some
comment over his shoulder to the man behind him, he
rubbed the thong between the fingers of his right hand, as
if to test its quality. His face was surprisingly pale, so pale
that it blended with his outfit: a voluminous shirt and
baggy, almost ill-fitting trousers in frayed white cotton. His
hair was grey and crew cut. He looked to be in his sixties.

The man at his elbow was also pale, also in white, but

very tall and very thin: as if, in playing the shadow, he had decided to strike out on his own and give the viewer an alternative version of his leader.

No one acknowledged these new arrivals – they simply continued to help themselves to food and wine – but even so, a ripple of suppressed awareness went round the terrace, as if the house lights had been dimmed and the curtain raised.

Zeynep flew forward and steered the man and his shadow in our direction.

'Darlings!' he cried. 'Welcome. But all so white! You need the sun. My dear!'

He leant forward to kiss Jacqui briefly on both cheeks before ruffling Jed's hair.

'You like my humble abode?'

Jed nodded wordlessly.

'You must be Peter!' Up close, I was struck most by the intensity of his gaze. His eyes were an icy blue, as vivid as they were piercing.

'Very nice to meet you,' I mumbled, extending a hand.

He smiled delightedly. 'You English. So proper! So correct!' He threw an arm round my shoulder and shot something in Spanish to Zeynep, causing her to laugh embarrassedly.

'So this is our potential star.' The voice, which issued from Carlos's shadow, was archetypically American: it drawled the words, elongating them into a kind of lazy challenge.

'You see the eyes?' Carlos took Jed by the chin. 'And the colouring.'

'The name's Al. Al Bacardy. But you'll call me Al.'

He turned his attention smoothly to Jacqui.

'You must be Jed's mother.'

'And this is Peter.' It was Zeynep who came to my rescue, though I could tell from the perfunctory way in which Al allowed me his hand that I counted for nothing; markedly the lesser chaperone.

'After dinner,' Carlos was saying to Jacqui, 'we will talk a bit, yes, and look at the script?'

'All right, young man?' Al's question was directed at Jed.

'Fine!' Jed's voice was firm, but his eyes were on Jacqui, seeking confirmation that this was the correct response.

Carlos clapped his hands. 'I am famished!'

He crossed to the table and began to heap a plate with food. Al followed predictable suit. I sat down.

'You speak Spanish?'

It was the young man, who hadn't moved from his place at my side.

'I'm afraid not.'

'*Entonces!*' Coal-black eyes glinted mischievously. 'Maybe I teach you too?'

'Quiepo!'

The voice was Carlos's, and it caused the young man to leap from his seat and hurry across the terrace.

I turned for protection to Jed, who was in the process of swallowing his last mouthful of food.

'Good, huh?'

He nodded.

'Especially the tomatoes.'

'I liked the chips best.'

'You would.'

'Peter! Some more?'

It was the ever-vigilant Zeynep.

I held up my hands in laughing protest. 'I couldn't manage another thing.'

'Not even fruit?' She gestured towards the table, where the rather disapproving man who had brought our cases to our rooms was placing a bowl of grapes next to the flagons of wine. 'From Juan's own garden.'

I smiled. 'A real treasure.'

She looked at me blankly.

'Juan. Fetching and carrying, gardening . . .'

'My dear!' She slid into the chair vacated by Quiepo. 'If the truth be told, this house belongs to Juan. He was here when Carlos bought it. He was born here. He cooks, he cleans, he grows the vegetables, the fruit. Without Juan . . .' She let her hands finish the sentence.

'And Quiepo?'

She shot me a surprised look. 'Quiepo?'

'I was just wondering – well, how he fits in?'

She laid a jewelled hand on my arm. 'What is it you English say? A gentleman's gentleman?'

'You mean his valet?'

She shrugged. 'Assistant.'

'I thought. . . .'

She smiled enigmatically. 'What did you think?'

'I thought you . . .'

She chuckled. 'My dear, a man like Carlos, he has many assistants.' She leant forward and lowered her voice. 'The person to watch is him.'

I followed the direction of her gaze, and saw that Jacqui, who had now been joined by Jed, was deep in conversation with Al. As I watched, Jed insinuated himself between the two adults, fitting himself to the contours of Jacqui's body. Without pausing in what he was saying, Al patted Jed absentmindedly on the head, whilst Jacqui took him firmly by the shoulders and moved him aside.

'Why him?'

She made a moue with her mouth and felt in her bag for a cigarette.

'American men. Like hamburgers, my dear. Not proper food at all. But everywhere.' She lit her cigarette – a very long, very thin, almost anorexic cigarette, quite unlike any

I'd ever seen – and inhaled deeply. 'Tell your girlfriend to be careful, that's all. I've already told Carlos he's mad to be working with him, but when someone has the money . . .' She shrugged. 'It makes whores of us all.'

I was wondering how best to reply – should I explain about Jacqui and myself, or would I, in time, be thankful for this protective colouring? – when Carlos brought our intimacy to an end by calling Zeynep from across the terrace.

'My dear, excuse me.' She hurried over to where Carlos stood talking to Quiepo. The three of them began a rapid altercation in Spanish. Carlos described a vigorous circle in the air with his hand, then turned abruptly and, flinging a few tart words over his shoulder, vanished up the steps towards the Casa Nueva. Zeynep looked at Quiepo and shrugged, then they both started after him, as indeed did Al, Jacqui and Jed.

The party was beginning to break up. People had finished their fruit and were returning their plates to the table. I stayed where I was and watched as, in twos and threes, they wafted elegantly away. Juan, looking surlier than ever, appeared with a tray, on which he began to pile the detritus of our meal.

I got to my feet and made my own way up the stairs. Five of the dinner guests had colonised the table on the terrace opposite the door to the Casa Nueva, and were dealing cards. Another group had settled on the sofas in the living room and were watching television. I toyed with the idea of pouring myself a drink from the bar under the mirror at the far end of the room, but where would I take it? To whom could I talk? Besides, there was the danger that Quiepo might again seek me out.

I turned away, and as I approached the steps leading up to our villa, heard shouted laughter. I crossed to the pond

and saw that on the same level as the terrace on which we
had eaten, but tucked away to the right of it, and reached
by a flight of steps beyond the pond, there was another terrace on which, brilliantly lit, stood a ping-pong table. The
man I was avoiding stood at the far end of the table, face
towards me. I took in the flash of his arm as he hit the ball,
the speed with which he hunkered down to meet its
return; then, scared that I might be observed, fled upwards.

Safe on the top terrace, I stood by the balustrade and
gazed across the bay. Not far from the shore, and aglitter
with light, there was a yacht set like a jewel in the water;
and all about it, scattered like lesser jewels on the velvety
darkness of the sea, the subtler, warmer lights of a small
flotilla of fishing boats. In fact, everywhere I looked, the
darkness was pierced by light: the white brilliance of the
yacht, the yellow glow of the fishing boats, and on the
coast, in a zig-zag, the multi-coloured lights of a nearby
town, and high above the town, almost on a level with the
stars, a final, isolated cluster of red where the deeper darkness of the mountain softened into sky.

There was a low whistle behind me. I swung round.
The terrace, however, was empty. The whistle was
repeated. Only then did I realise what it was: the little grey
bird.

The next morning I woke to discover myself alone in the
bedroom. I looked at my watch. It was 10.30. Jacqui and
Jed had started the day without me.

Padding to the window, I drew back the curtain to test
the weather. The sky was a limitless blue, the sea a sun-
sparkled band of ripples. No sign of the yacht whose lights
I'd seen the night before, nor of the fishing boats. The terrace, too, was empty, empty and quiet. Mediterranean
vacuity awaiting the next chapter.

I pulled on a T-shirt and shorts and went outside. There was the inevitable whistle from my left. Another night's imprisonment had done nothing to lessen the bird's belief in its superiority over the merely mortal.

The Casa Nueva was as quiet and deserted as the villa above, also the dining terrace, though here at least there was evidence of earlier occupation: a bowl of fruit, the remains of a basket of toast, a thermos of tepid coffee. I helped myself to what was left and crossed to the balustrade. At the foot of the cliff that dropped from the terrace into the sea was a rocky outcrop, and on the last of the rocks, a small splash of colour: someone sunbathing. I heard a noise behind me, and turning, found Juan emerging from the kitchen with his tray.

'Good morning.'

He nodded curtly, then began to clear the table.

'Where can I find Zeynep?'

'Zeynep *abajo*.'

'I beg your pardon?'

'*Abajo.*'

He pointed past the kitchen. I handed him my cup and followed the direction indicated, passing along a narrow terrace planted with a plethora of exotic blooms until I came to a set of steps. They were of roughly hewn stone and divided into two flights, one curving to the left, the other to the right. I chose the right flight, and, turning the corner at the bottom, discovered that built into a grotto beneath the steps was a circular jacuzzi with a changing room and shower to one side of it. The terrace here had been balustraded by an arrangement of stone benches on which, colourful as cushions, were scattered a handful of towels.

Continuing along this terrace in the direction of the rocks, I passed beneath an avenue of vines, and, at the end of the terrace, came to an iron gate set in a stone archway, through which a final set of steps wound down to the sea. Now I could see that it was indeed Zeynep on the rocks, occupying a red square of towel.

'So!' I said, coming up behind my target. 'The siren herself.'

'Peter!' She showed no sign of being startled by my approach, and with the warmth of her smile, quite eradicated any feelings I may have entertained about being too much a stranger in this unfamiliar world. 'I was beginning to think you'd stood me up.'

She patted the rock and I sat down next to her.

'Swum yet?' I asked.

'My dear! For me it's too early. Maybe June. For you it's different. For you it's warm.' Her low, rather gravelly voice – combined, of course, with her accent – imbued even the most mundane of her utterances with a tinge of exoticism.

I shook my head. 'Tomorrow perhaps. Now it's enough to feel the sun.'

She glanced at her arms and frowned. 'I like the sun too much.'

'It doesn't seem to have done you harm.'

She laughed, and resting that jewelled hand of hers briefly on my wrist, said: 'My dear, since I know we are going to be friends, I can let you into a secret. I am not as young as I look.'

She was interrupted by a beeping noise from the bag that lay by her side. Grimacing, she rummaged in its depths and produced a mobile phone. Punching a button, she said sharply: '*Digame*!' There was a pause, then, from Zeynep, a flood of Spanish, after which she listened in silence for a while, let loose a second burst of Spanish, then clicked the phone off and returned it to her bag.

'People!' She reached for one of her slim cigarettes. 'They tell you one thing, they do another.'

'Problems?'

'You know Illusión Grande?'

I shook my head.

'Hats, my dear. Hats.'

'Hats?'

'They make hats. Pablo and André. My oldest friends. Pablo's Spanish; André, well he's from South Africa. Very expensive. Very chic. They have a shop in Barcelona, clients all over the world. Your Lady Di, Cher, Queen Sofia. They were coming for lunch today. Now they come tomorrow.' She flicked her ash into a crevice in the rock. 'You will like them.' She lowered her voice. 'Carlos, of course, hates them.'

'Hates them? Why?'

'They upstage him.'

'Tell me,' I said. 'You and Carlos. Have you worked for him long?'

Angling her body to better effect against the sun, she let out a sigh. 'My dear. An eternity.'

'How did you meet?'

There was a pause, and I had the sense that perhaps I'd asked the wrong question.

'He's a monster, of course,' she said eventually. 'But what artist isn't? You cannot create like an angel and also be an angel. It isn't possible.'

'I'm sorry,' I said. 'I didn't mean to pry.'

'He is also very loyal.' It was as if she hadn't heard me. 'I was born in Istanbul. My father was in government there. Life can get very complicated in a Muslim country. Not like England. I came to Spain when I was a young girl. I got a job in the Opera House in Barcelona. I met Carlos. He needed someone to organise his life. I needed someone to organise.' She smiled. 'The perfect marriage.'

Her account of herself, imprecise though it was, had been oddly moving. There was, I sensed, a sadness at the back of it, a sadness which only the richness of her chuckle kept at bay.

She sat up. 'But my life is boring. What about you? You and Jacqui. Will you marry? That would be nice, I think. For Jed.'

The moment had come to attempt the truth. I picked at a piece of flaking rock. 'We're only friends.'

'So? Friends can marry. Rare, I know, but not impossible. After all . . .'

I didn't let her finish. 'We haven't known each other long.'

'But what about Jed? Jed looks to you like a father.'

I smiled. 'Ah! But do I look to myself like a father?'

She stubbed out her cigarette. 'Fathers come in many sizes. Your father, for example. Tell me about your father.'

Perhaps it was because I hadn't expected the question, or else that I was being asked it here, in Spain, where he had spent those crucial years, but to my surprise I found myself telling her in some detail about his stint with the International Brigade, my mother, my mother's death, the house in Winterbourne Road, even the lodgers.

'Maybe this,' she said when I'd finished, 'is why you're good with Jed.'

I shot her a startled look.

'You know what it's like to be ignored.'

My eyes were caught by a shape in the water some thirty feet from the rock. A swimmer was cutting through the swell towards us.

'We have a visitor,' I said.

Zeynep followed the direction of my gaze, then consulted her watch.

'Every morning,' she explained, 'Quiepo swims into

town to take a coffee, and when he comes back, then it is lunchtime.'

'Even in May?'

'Like the song. May to September.'

The human clock had reached the rocks, and as Zeynep got to her feet, he pulled himself sleekly from the water. He had the body of a swimmer: sculpted chest, sturdy legs, tiny waist encased in a triangle of black. I looked quickly away.

'*Buenos días!*' He shook the water from his hair like a dog, then – asking permission with only his eyes – reached for Zeynep's towel.

'My dear! Please! Help yourself!'

He grinned at her. 'I do.'

I too got to my feet, and with Zeynep leading the way, the three of us began the ascent to the villa. As we mounted the first set of steps, I felt a hand on the back of my leg.

'The sun,' said Quiepo, nodding at my calves. 'You have sun.'

Virulent as any allergy, a pink flush had infected the whiteness of my skin.

'You must be careful, no?'

'Obviously,' I said. 'Very.'

If dinner the night before had been a performance, lunch was the rehearsal. With the exception of Quiepo's mother, who was still in her costume of funereal black, we were all more casually dressed – shorts, T-shirts, sarongs – and only the minor characters had been called. No Carlos, no Al, no Jacqui and no Jed.

'Where are the others?' I asked Zeynep.

'My dear, they didn't tell you?'

'Tell me what?'

'They're in Barcelona.'

'For the day?'

She shrugged. 'However long it takes. Have more fish. It's very good.'

'To do what?'

'A screen test, of course.'

'I see.'

Her mobile phone made another of its demands, and she removed herself to the far end of the terrace where she could talk without interruption. Quiepo, too, left me to myself, choosing instead to join another young man with a clipboard, over which the two of them pored. A further link, no doubt, in the chain of assistants with which Carlos fenced himself in.

As we finished the first course, Juan put in his usual appearance with fruit and coffee, then the party began to break up. Quiepo went off with the second assistant, Zeynep vanished into the kitchen, and I was left alone with Quiepo's mother, who'd taken a length of knitting from her bag and was concentrating on the interplay of her needles.

I put my cup on the table and went upstairs. As I passed the Casa Nueva, I heard a phone ringing somewhere in the bowels of the house, and on the terrace of our villa, I was greeted by the predictable whistle of the bird. In the welcoming gloom of our bedroom, I kicked off my clothes and fell on the bed. When I'd bought Jed his game at the airport, I'd treated myself to a trashy novel, and now I turned to it for consolation.

The world it opened up was a carbon copy of the world into which Jacqui, Jed and I seemed to have stumbled. People dressed in designer labels, one of the characters even wore a hat from Illusión Grande, and the hero bore more than a passing resemblance to Quiepo. He had the same perfection of body, the same mischievous eyes, the same luxuriance of hair.

I must have fallen asleep, because I'd gone swimming with the hero, and as the two of us cut through the water, he slipped a hand between my legs. I wasn't wearing a swimming costume, and now, as I lay across the rocks, the sun hot on my skin, his expert hands explored the geography of my groin. I opened my eyes and found that the hand belonged to a naked Jacqui, who had fitted herself to the curve of my libidinous body.

'Sshh!' She put a finger to my surprised lips, then guided me between her legs. Suddenly desperate, I buried my face in her breasts. Orgasm was swift and wordless.

'There!' Her fingers still fluttered between my legs. 'Quite banal, wouldn't you say, as a bodily function? But such fun!'

I wriggled free of her.

'What?' Very gently, she brushed the hair from my forehead.

'Nothing.'

I escaped into the bathroom and splashed my face with water.

'It needn't make any difference.' She had propped herself up on one elbow. 'Not as far as I'm concerned.'

'I know that.' I crossed to the chest of drawers and helped myself to one of her cigarettes. 'How was Barcelona?'

She continued to regard me; then, with an infinitesimal shrug of her shoulders, allowed my question.

'A dream.'

'What did he have to do?'

'Learn a page of the script and say his lines to camera.'

'He wasn't fazed?'

'A real pro.'

'Have they made an offer?'

She snorted. 'Don't be ridiculous. We won't hear until

we get back to London. I don't even know who else they're seeing. But this much I do know . . .' She smiled smugly. 'We're in with a chance.' She swung off the bed, subjected me to another searching look, then reached for her T-shirt. 'I need a shower.'

Next door, Jed was lying on the floor, intent on his game.

'I hear the camera likes you.'

He waved an admonitory hand to indicate I shouldn't break his concentration. I sat on the edge of the bed and peered over his shoulder. From a miniature boat, a miniature Popeye was fielding the pineapples which an energetic Olive Oyl was hurling from the shore.

'Two hundred and thirty,' he said. 'Level Two.'

'Two hundred and thirty what?'

'My score.'

The game beeped, and with a sigh, he threw it aside.

'Last night I could only make a hundred. Do you want a go?'

I shook my head. 'Jacqui says it went well?'

He shrugged. 'It was okay.'

'But did you enjoy it?'

He grinned. 'It's better than school.'

'And Carlos?'

'He's nice.'

'And Al?'

'Nice too.'

Everything, it seemed, was nice; everything was going according to plan. The fly in the ointment was me.

'You should have come,' he said suddenly.

'I should have? Why?'

'It would have been fun.'

That word again. I placed a hand on his head.

'How about a shower?'

He made a face. 'Do I have to?'

'I'll play you ping-pong afterwards.'

'Promise?'

'But only if you're clean.'

He leapt to his feet. 'Okay.'

We played until eight, then went to join the laughter emanating from the living room of the Casa Nueva. Jed made a predictable bee-line for the television. I crossed to the drinks cabinet and poured myself a gin and tonic.

Zeynep, in buttercup yellow, was standing by the double doors.

'I hope you realise,' she said, 'that if he gets the part, you will have to come too.'

'I have a job. I couldn't.'

'This would be a job. You teach. Jed will need a tutor. And if I speak to Carlos, it will be a job that pays.'

'You're very sweet, but really . . .'

She stepped into the room. 'I'm afraid, my dear, that Carlos will insist.' She thrust her evening bag at me. 'Hold this while I get myself a drink.'

The thing about ointment, I was thinking, *and being a fly, is that there's no escape. You are well and truly trapped. Unable to buzz off.*

'My dear!' Zeynep was back with her drink. 'Shall we sit on the terrace?'

We settled at the empty table alongside a group of card players.

'Do you play?'

I shook my head.

'After supper I teach you.'

There was a flurry of movement in the living room, a burst of laughter, then Carlos appeared in the doorway, dressed as the night before in the same voluminous shirt and baggy trousers, glasses still hanging round his neck.

'Carlos cheats, of course,' whispered Zeynep. 'Also Quiepo. You have to watch them like hawks.'

'What is the old witch saying?' Carlos came to stand behind Zeynep's chair. She laughed something to him in Spanish, whereupon he cuffed her lightly on the shoulder.

'Women!' he groaned. 'If it hadn't been for Eve, we'd still be in paradise.'

I smiled. 'Right now I feel like I am.'

I had said the right thing. Beaming broadly, Carlos pulled up a chair and sat between us.

'When I came here, there was only the top villa. All this I built, and the terrace where we eat. All the terraces, in fact, between here and the sea. You've seen the jacuzzi?'

I nodded.

'Next year I shall build another villa, down by the rocks, where I will live by myself, away from people.' He waved his hand at the card players. 'People tire me.'

'You'd go mad,' said Zeynep. 'You know you would.'

Ignoring her, he leant forward and fixed me with a probing look.

'You're a teacher, no?'

'Yes.'

'You teach Jed?'

I shook my head. 'English. I teach English to foreigners.'

He fell back in his seat and let out a delighted laugh. 'And now you're the foreigner! How do you like it, being the foreigner?'

I twisted in my chair.

He had begun to rub his leather thong between his fingers. 'De Vega. Cervantes. Lorca. Machado. It's not all Shakespeare. By the time we have finished with you, Don Pedro, you will be a proper teacher. Universal. To be English is very limiting.'

I was rescued by Al, who appeared in the living-room door and called in his American drawl: 'Carlos! Phone!'

No sooner had Carlos left than Zeynep laid a hand on my arm.

'You see? I told you he'd want you to stay.'

I took a reflective sip of my drink. 'Was that what that was about?'

She shrugged. 'Okay, so he's a little touchy about Spain.' She lowered her voice. 'The fact is, he wishes he were English. He admires the English too much.'

It was my turn to shrug. 'You could have fooled me.'

At that moment Jacqui appeared in a swathe of burgundy velvet, and from the terrace below, as if to mark her arrival, the bell tolled for dinner.

The meal was a replay of the night before. The same abundance of food, the same candles, and out to sea, their echo in the lanterns fixed to the little fishing boats scattered upon the water. I sat by the balustrade with Jed and let myself be soothed by their gentle movement. Talk I left to Jacqui, who ignored me completely, gravitating instead towards Al.

'What are those?' asked Jed at one point.

I followed the direction of his arm. He was pointing at the cluster of red lights on the mountain above the town.

'Search me.' I handed him my plate. 'Put this on the table and bring me a banana.'

'Can we have another game?'

'All right. But just the one.'

We were barely into our ping-pong game when Jacqui came swaying down the steps, glass of wine to the fore.

'So! This is where you are!'

She leant against a palm tree and watched as, for the second time that day, I let Jed beat me. Then, having accepted my self-imposed defeat, I put down my bat, and, relieving Jacqui of her glass, took a sip of her wine. Jed came to hang on her dress.

'Now you, Mum!'

'Me? You must be joking!'

'Please!'

'Give me back my wine, cheeky!' She retrieved her glass, then consulted her watch. 'Bedtime, young man.'

'Ah, Mum!'

'You've had a very busy day, and we don't know whether Carlos will want you tomorrow.'

'Ah . . .'

'No arguments!'

With a final 'ah', Jed began dragging his feet towards the stairs.

'I'll be up in a minute to tuck you in. Say goodnight to Peter.'

'Goodnight, Peter.' He flung the words gracelessly over his shoulder.

Jacqui was about to remonstrate, but I put a finger to her lips, and we watched in silence as, with continuing reluctance, Jed mounted the steps and vanished from sight. I let the finger I'd put to her lips trace a path along her jaw.

'So! In with our producer, are we?'

She looked at me oddly. 'Of course. The mother's job, wouldn't you say?'

'And mine?'

'Peter. . . .'

'Zeynep tells me that if he gets the part, they'll want me too.'

'So?'

'You mean you knew?'

She shrugged. 'Of course. Al said this morning . . .'

'What? What did Al say?'

'That if Jed gets the part, because naturally they want him to feel secure, it'll be best to have us both around.'

'And you said?'

She took the comb from her hair, shook her hair loose, then began rearranging it. 'I said that you and Jed got on really well and I thought you'd be delighted. Was I wrong?'

'Jacqui . . .'

What was it, though, that I wanted to say? That we weren't exactly a nuclear family, that I had a life of my own, that she couldn't co-opt me like that? Or that I was indeed there for the taking, but that it frightened me?

She polished off the last of her wine. 'Now, what about a jacuzzi?'

'A jacuzzi?'

'Carlos says it's on, and when I've put Jed to bed, I'll come down too.' She chuckled suggestively. 'Just you and me and a whole lot of bubbles.'

I should have said I'd promised to play cards with Zeynep, but instead – the memory, perhaps, of being in her arms – I found myself agreeing: 'Okay. You win.'

She darted up the steps to attend to her maternal duties. I picked up her glass, switched off the light and began to follow her. I half expected Zeynep to be at the card table, and was wondering how I would wriggle out of my promise, but luckily the terrace of the Casa Nueva was deserted. Something on television had drawn the entire party into the living room. I crept past without being seen.

On the terrace below I ran into Al, prowling outside the kitchen, mobile phone in hand.

'Goddamn Spain!' He waved the phone in the air. 'Ever tried phoning out of this dump?'

'Having trouble?'

He snorted dismissively. 'The more I get to know this country, the more sympathy I have for the old generalisimo.

Unless you crack the whip, nothing gets done.' He looked at me with sudden intensity. 'I hope *you're* not gonna let me down? I can see the kid depends on you. And let's face it . . .' He gave another snort. 'She wins in the looks department, and I admire her tenacity – but as a mother . . .' His phone beeped faintly and he lifted it to his ear. 'Yup?' There was a pause. 'Yeah, yeah, it's me. Who the fuck do you think it is? The man from La Mancha?'

He had turned his back on me, and I took the opportunity to melt away.

There was no noise coming from the jacuzzi, except of course the hum of its motor, and I literally leapt when, rounding the bottom of the steps into the grotto, I was greeted by name.

'Quiepo!'

He was alone in the pool, arms hooked over the metal bar at its edge, body pressed against one of the jets, causing the water to boil up over his shoulders in a frenzy of bubbles. He let go of the bar, allowing the jet to propel him into the centre of the pool, where he floated lazily.

'You join me?'

I managed what I hoped was a nonchalant nod.

He was floating on his back, buoyed up by the water, and I couldn't help but notice that he wasn't wearing a swimming costume. Turning my back on the pool, I began to undress.

He let out a laugh. 'You English. So shy. Why? We all have one.'

I was down to my underpants, which I peeled off quickly and threw onto my other clothes before lowering myself as quickly as possible into the water. Swimming past me, Quiepo gave my hair a flick, then kicked away to the jet at the far side of the pool, where he re-attached himself to the bar.

'So! You have a good time?'

I affected another of what I hoped were my nonchalant nods. 'It's a very beautiful place.'

'Carlos likes beauty. Beautiful things. Beautiful people. When the world is ugly, Carlos make it beautiful. You know his work?'

I shook my head.

'Like a painting. Rich.'

'Have you worked for him long?'

He shrugged. 'Two years.'

'And you're on the film?'

'*Si*. I – how you say? – I find locations. For *Murillo* we need a village. Very small, very, old.'

'Have you found one?'

'I think. In the mountains. South of Tortosa. Very small, very old. When tourism come, all the young people, they go to the coast. Waiters, chefs, barmen. In the mountains there are only olives and almonds. Is very hard. So now only old people. The houses are empty. Carlos, he comes next week. If he like, then Quiepo is good boy.'

He let his body float to the surface again, making no attempt, as he regarded me down the length of it, to hide his nakedness.

I swallowed. 'So when does shooting start?' To my relief, my voice didn't betray the terror I was experiencing.

Quiepo shrugged. 'Two weeks. A month. As soon as Carlos finds the boy.'

He kicked himself away from the wall, frothing through the water towards me. Despite myself, I flinched – though thankfully, before he could make contact, he had twisted away again, his attention caught by a sound on the stairs. Carlos was standing behind us, the suddenness of his appearance making it seem as if he had materialised out of thin air.

'Eat your heart out, David Hockney!' He was wearing his glasses, and they caught the sparkle off the water as he regarded first Quiepo, then me. 'I trust Quiepo is looking after you?'

Before I could frame a reply, Quiepo said something in Spanish and there followed a brisk exchange of words; an exchange that had me wondering whether something wasn't amiss between them. There was an edge of exasperation to Carlos's voice, an element of the placatory in Quiepo's.

A minute into the exchange, Carlos turned towards the balustrade, and, snatching up one of the towels that lay on the stone seat, began to fold it neatly. Quiepo pulled himself out of the water, and, padding past Carlos, wrapped himself in another of the towels. At least I no longer had to worry where to turn my eyes.

Carlos continued his peroration, then – slapping Quiepo suddenly on the rump – nodded him towards the stairs. Without so much as a backward glance, Quiepo vanished. Carlos reached for a second towel and began folding that. I waited for him to say something, and when he didn't, pulled myself out of the pool and struggled into my clothes.

'It's very soothing,' I ventured. 'The jacuzzi.'

Carlos was staring out to sea, where, I now saw, another yacht – or perhaps the same one – glittered seductively against its backdrop of night.

'Whose is it?' I asked. 'The yacht?'

Carlos snorted. 'Friends of Zeynep. Two awful old queens. Tomorrow they come for lunch. I advise you to avoid them.' For someone who was supposedly not simply her employer, but also a friend, the dismissive emphasis he gave Zeynep's name was almost shocking.

'Tell me,' I said, changing the subject. 'Those lights up there on the hill, the red ones. What are they?'

'The cemetery.' He didn't seem to mind my change of

subject. 'They're all fishermen along this coast, they spend their lives at sea, and when they die, they want to be buried where they can see it. In all the villages along the coast, it is always the cemetery that has the best view.' He picked up the last of the towels. 'Why do you ask?'

'Jed,' I said. 'He wondered.'

An expression of unexpected sadness flitted across Carlos's face. 'He is very lucky, that boy, to have you. Carlos knows. Carlos knows what it's like to be without parents.'

'He has Jacqui.' Something in his tone made me spring to her defence.

'All this.' Ignoring my last remark, he gestured up the hill behind us. 'And my work. I sometimes wonder who I do it for. Who's watching. Maybe no one.' He clapped a hand on my shoulder. 'But you must be tired. And tomorrow you fly back.'

I was being dismissed.

'Yes,' I said. 'Right. Well, goodnight.'

From the safety of the steps, I stole a final look at him. All the towels had been meticulously folded and placed in a pile on the edge of the balustrade. With his left hand, Carlos was smoothing the nap of the uppermost towel.

The other guests were still in the living room of the Casa Nueva, and at first glance it looked as if the terrace was deserted – except that I heard voices to my right, urgent, heated. Peering into the gloom, I could just make out the twin shapes of Jacqui and Al at a distant table.

'But you said . . .' Jacqui sounded as if she might burst into tears.

'I know what I said.' Al's drawl had contracted into a rapid, gun-like delivery. 'But this is the movies. It isn't up to me and Carlos. There's LA too.'

'Then you shouldn't have raised my hopes. It isn't fair.'

'Fair? What's fair? This is the real world, honey, not

some fairy tale. There's a lot of money riding on this picture.'

I didn't wait to hear more. Slipping quietly past the open door of the living room, I darted upstairs and, as instructed by Carlos, put myself to bed.

I didn't, however, go to sleep. I couldn't. Instead, I re-entered my book with its improbable plot and improbable characters. Except were they? Viewed dispassionately, Jacqui, Jed and I were enmeshed in a tangle of events no less highly coloured, no less unreal.

It was gone midnight by the time I heard the clack of her heels on the terrace outside, the whistle of the bird, her echoing progress through the silent villa and up the stairs.

'You're still awake.'

I laid the book on the bedside table.

'So it would seem.'

She crossed to the window and drew aside the curtain to stare at the night.

'Anything wrong?'

'Should there be?'

'We were going to have a jacuzzi, remember? You never showed.'

'Oh, Peter!' Suddenly she was crying, and, flinging back the bedclothes, I leapt to my feet and went to her.

'What is it?'

At first she didn't answer. Then, relaxing into my embrace, she said softly: 'I don't think he's going to get it.'

'The part?'

'Al and Carlos think he's terrific. They said so all day. But Al's been speaking to Los Angeles, and apparently they're insisting on someone with experience.'

'But surely Carlos, if he's the director . . .?'

She escaped from my arms and went to sit on her bed. 'It's the money men who have the final say. Apparently.' She slammed the pillow with her fist. 'Shit, Peter! He was so good. And it would have meant . . .'

'What?' I took up position on my own bed, facing her. 'These people are all very nice, Jacqui, all very charming, but they're in a different class. Sure, it would have been fun. You would have made some money. But afterwards?'

'Afterwards I could have coped with.' She looked at me with tear-stained eyes. 'Better some afterwards, wouldn't you say, than no afterwards at all?'

'Jacqui, we don't belong here.'

'Only in Kilburn?' She turned away, defeated. 'Shit!' I reached for her hand, but she evaded my grasp. 'You would have benefited too,' she said. 'You could have told Gloria to go stuff herself.'

I stood up decisively. I didn't want the conversation to turn on me. 'Sleep!' I commanded, and yanking her upright, unzipped her dress, turned back her sheets, then guided her into bed. 'Let's just enjoy tomorrow. Some friends of Zeynep's are coming for lunch. Perhaps we can walk into town.' She'd buried her face in the pillow, and now, very gently, I stroked her hair. 'We've had a wonderful couple of days. Let's just remember that.'

She didn't reply.

'It will all feel different in the morning.'

I switched off the light and crossed to the window. Pablo and André's yacht was still ablaze with light. Coming off it, teasing as perfume, was a suggestion of music. Illusión Grande. None grander. I closed the curtain, plunging the room into darkness.

Six

I'd never seen Jacqui depressed before. I'd seen her
moody, I'd seen her abstracted, I'd seen her angry, but
not depressed. Certainly not as she was on our return to
London. Her vivacity, her recklessness, her resilience, all
were doused, as if a plug somewhere had been pulled,
depriving her of current. She moved about the flat in a
daze, managing to cook a little, to drag the coverlet over
her bed, to do some shopping, but only with a monumental effort, as if even such trifling chores were so exhausting
she needed all her energies to accomplish them.

I did what little I could to help (I stopped at the shops
on my way back from school, I fed and bathed Jed, cooked
our evening meals, poured wine, kept up a stream of
inconsequential chatter), but I was facing problems of my
own. My little scam to get away for the weekend had
resulted in over a hundred essays on Trafalgar Square,
Piccadilly Circus, the parks, Buckingham Palace, Waterloo
Station, the underground, Wembley, even such urban
niceties as council estates and the Kentish Town High
Road. Added to which was the insistence with which the
weekend – the Sunday in particular – replayed itself in my
mind until I felt my head was a hall of mirrors in which

the various characters were endlessly reflected and super-imposed: Carlos on Al, Zeynep on Jacqui, Pablo on André, Jean-Luís on Quiepo, myself on Jed. And in combination, too: Carlos and Al on Pablo and André, myself and Jed on Jacqui and Zeynep, on Jean-Luís, on Quiepo. A myriad versions of each and every one of us, cut and inter-cut, and so many facets of myself that in the end I didn't know where to look.

It had started electronically, that final Sunday, with the beep of Jed's game – the sound it emitted each time Olive Oyl threw a pineapple at Popeye. Opening my eyes, I'd found the dedicated player ensconced on the foot of Jacqui's bed. Jacqui was still asleep.

I fumbled for my watch. It was gone eleven.

'How long have you been up?'

'Four hundred.'

Time, for Jed, was measured not against the clock but against his rising score. At least someone, I thought wryly, is turning the weekend to good effect. Swinging out of bed, I shook Jacqui awake.

'Breakfast time.'

In the event, we were too late for breakfast. Juan had already started to lay the table for lunch, though when he saw us, he did have the grace to usher us into the kitchen (a large, square room, dominated by an aluminium table) and make us some tea and toast.

Then, because there was nothing else to do, and because I guessed that was where we'd find the others, we made our way down to the rocks.

Either Quiepo took Sundays off, or else he followed an earlier schedule, but his was the first body I saw, sunning itself on the rock alongside Zeynep. The rest of the party, the people whose names and functions I still didn't know, were also in evidence, some playing their eternal card game, others lazing on a concrete platform to the left of the rocks.

'*Buenos días!*' Teeth flashing, Quiepo had propped himself up on an elbow.

'My dears!' Zeynep had also levered herself upright. 'Did you have breakfast? If not, I speak to Juan.'

We assured her that Juan had in fact fed us, then sat down next to them. Jed had brought his game, Jacqui was still subdued after the revelations of last night, and I was set on making it clear to Quiepo that our moment in the jacuzzi was as unimportant to me as I hoped it had been to him; mere horseplay, youthful high spirits. So, after a brief exchange of pleasantries, and with me taking care to avoid staring at that skimpy triangle of black nylon, we let Quiepo and Zeynep pick up the threads of their lazy, intermittent conversation.

Si. Digame. Por favor. The Spanish words made a kind of music, their melody underscored by the beep of Jed's game, the sucking of the sea at the rocks. Then all of a sudden, in mid-sentence, Zeynep stood up and waved both arms in the air. A motor launch was approaching across the water, and as it came closer, I made out two figures in the bow, one holding a miniature poodle under his arm, the other semaphoring like Zeynep.

Adjusting his costume, Quiepo leapt to the edge of the rocks, and as the boat swung up, caught the bow and steadied it whilst handing the two men ashore.

The one with the poodle got off first, then placed the dog on the rocks. It immediately began to run around in circles, barking ecstatically. It was a very dainty dog, perfectly manicured, and on its head, held in place by means of an extravagant bow, was a quite extraordinary confection of velvet, sequins and rhinestones.

'An example of their work?' I whispered to Zeynep, but

she had already stepped forward to greet the new arrivals.

The man who'd been carrying the poodle was tall, thin, and severely elegant. He was dressed in navy-blue slacks and a white satin shirt which opened at the neck to reveal a segment of skin as alabaster as his garb. His companion, by contrast, was short, fat and garishly attired in a purple caftan.

Whilst Quiepo helped the boatman push the boat off the rocks, Zeynep embraced this startling couple enthusiastically, then ushered them forward to meet us.

'My dears, I want you to meet my oldest friends. Pablo and André.'

Pablo was the thin one, André the butterball. Pablo, as his name suggested, and as Zeynep had told me, was Spanish, and he greeted us with a formal '*Buenos días*', bowing with old-world elegance as we shook hands. André, the South African, was altogether less formal, kicking away the excited dog and telling us not to mind her as he threw a careless 'Hi!' at each of us in turn.

'Poor little Nunu!' Shooting a reproving look at André, Pablo bent to fuss the dog. 'Is the horrible man bullying you?'

By this time Quiepo had joined us, and the four of them transferred into Spanish and began to move towards the concrete platform. Jacqui, Jed and I took up the rear. On the platform there was a further flurry of greeting, then the entire party started to wend its way upwards, the poodle Nunu dancing in frenzied attendance at our heels. On the first terrace, André dropped back to join us.

'So,' he said, ruffling Jed's hair, 'you must be the budding star. Zeynep's told us all about you.'

I shot a look at Jacqui, and decided it would be wise to change the subject.

'You're from South Africa, is that right?'

He nodded.

'What part?'

'Hideous place called Durban.'

I risked another look at Jacqui. 'You know Durban.'

'Do I?'

Her tone was so defensive that for a moment I thought André might comment on it, but happily his attention was distracted by the dog, which darted a dizzying circle about his legs.

'Nunu was in a film once,' he said, 'but she kept upstaging everyone. Didn't you, darling?'

Jacqui smiled acidly. 'Not for the money, I take it? She doesn't look as if she needs the money.'

André cackled. 'If you've got it, flaunt it. That's her motto.' And breaking into Spanish, he shouted Jacqui's joke ahead to the others.

'That dog,' Zeynep laughed over her shoulder, 'is to hats what Imelda Marcos is to shoes.'

As we approached the jacuzzi the bell rang, and by the time we got to the table, it was already laid out with food. Before I could ask her where she was going, Jacqui had vanished up the stairs to the Casa Nueva.

'Is Mummy all right'?' It wasn't like Jed to notice the moods of others – like most ten-year-olds, he lived in a parallel world – but Jacqui's lack of equilibrium that morning had been hard to ignore.

'She's fine,' I said. 'Just a headache.' I led him to the balustrade, where we were instantly joined by Nunu.

'She likes you.' It was André, two glasses of wine in his pudgy hands. 'Want some?'

I accepted the proffered glass.

'So,' he said, settling himself next to us, 'how are you finding it?'

There was something overly suggestive about the way he asked the question. I looked at him warily.

'It has to be one of the most beautiful places I've ever been.'

He shrugged. 'But at a price.'

'What do you mean?'

He laid a hand on my leg. 'You don't have to be coy with me. We all know what a monster he is. If it wasn't for Zeynep, we'd never come. And as for this film business!' He rolled his eyes. 'He's an opera director, for Christ's sake. A Spanish opera director. But is that enough for him? Oh no, now he has to conquer Hollywood.'

I was rescued by Pablo, who suddenly appeared at André's side and said acerbically: 'Not wasting time, I see.'

Without removing his hand from my leg, André turned to look at his partner. 'I'm filling him in on you know who.'

Whereupon, as if on cue, Carlos burst down the steps with the ubiquitous Al at his elbow.

'I mean,' whispered André, 'pure Laurel and Hardy.'

'Maestro!' Pablo forsook us to embrace his host.

André shot me a mischievous look. 'Time to pay court. See you later.'

One would never have guessed, from the effusiveness of the greetings that followed, that these people didn't like each other, and I wasn't surprised when Jed whispered in my ear: 'Who's a monster? I don't understand.'

'No one,' I said. 'Why don't you get yourself some water?'

Having bestowed his kisses on Pablo and André, Carlos crossed to the table and began encouraging people to help themselves.

'Chips!' Jed was back with his water. 'They've got chips again.'

'No ketchup, though,' I said.

'What's this?' Carlos, who had been passing, overheard

this last remark. 'Ketchup? You want ketchup?' And turning to the assembled guests, he segued into incredulous Spanish.

'Come on,' I said quietly to Jed. 'Let's eat.'

When we returned to our places, plates heaped with food, a smiling Zeynep was hovering nearby. Positioning herself in front of Jed so that the others shouldn't see what she was doing, she surreptitiously produced a ketchup bottle from her sleeve.

'As much as you want,' she commanded conspiratorially.

Hardly daring to believe his luck, Jed reached for the bottle and emptied a good quarter of it onto his plate.

'Me too,' Zeynep whispered, returning the bottle to her sleeve. 'I also love ketchup.'

Across the table from us, Pablo was telling a story – or rather, in the manner of a Beerbohm Tree, he was declaiming it melodramatically, using over-expressive hands to illustrate his words. He was in mid-sentence, arms outstretched, when suddenly Carlos got to his feet – he'd been sitting to the left of Pablo – and, helping himself to more wine, said something that cut across Pablo's story, leaving the orator speechless. He just stood there, looking as if he'd dried, mouth still ajar, whilst Carlos capitalised on his silence to make a crack that had the entire terrace in stitches.

Drawing himself up to his full height, Pablo issued a riposte, to which Carlos, picking up a chip and stuffing it carelessly into his mouth, made a dismissive reply. Now André, who'd been giggling with Quiepo in the far corner, entered the fray, quietly at first, though when he too caught Carlos's tongue, he was also on his feet and all three of them were shouting at once. Carlos waved his hands in the air, like a conductor bringing the movement to a close, and with a final retort at Pablo, vanished upstairs. For a moment there was silence, then André put his hand on Pablo's shoulder and steered him towards a chair whilst in the background there started up a low, uncertain buzz of conversation. I looked at Jed. Seemingly oblivious to the incident, he was polishing off the last of the ketchup with his final chip.

'More ketchup?' It was Zeynep, behaving as if nothing untoward had happened.

Jed shook his head.

I plucked at her sleeve. 'What was that all about?'

She looked over my shoulder and out to sea, and her voice, when she answered, was oddly strained.

'Pablo is great friends with Juan Carlos. Well, Sofia actually. Some Spaniards think that what the king has done to the country is not so good. They remember the old days.'

'You mean Franco?'

'Speak to your father. Didn't you say he was in the Civil War? It was a big thing, the Civil War. Your father would understand.' She looked at her watch. 'But it is almost three. Your car will be here at four. Where's Jacqui?'

'She had a headache.'

'Have you packed?'

I shook my head. 'But it won't take long.'

'I don't think Carlos will come out again this afternoon, so I'll say goodbye to him for you. Shall we meet by the gate at four?'

'Right,' I said, 'Fine. The gate at four.'

And that had been that: a complexity of innuendo and mismatched desire which, had it been Jed's game, would have defeated me at Level One.

Pushing aside my fourth Trafalgar Square of the evening ('Good sentence structure, but watch your punctuation'), I ventured a glance at Jacqui. She was staring dully into her empty glass.

'Shall I open another bottle?'

She let out a bitter laugh. 'You want me frightened, lonely and depressed?'

I attempted a laugh of my own. 'It would make a change.'

'All right, then,' she said strangely – in reply, I thought, to my question about the wine, until she continued: 'You explain about that commune, I'll tell you what's happening to me.'

'Jacqui!'

She slammed a fist on the table, causing her glass to jump. 'Don't patronise me!' She pushed back her chair. 'Your life isn't any more worked out than mine.'

'I never said it was.'

Any impulse I might have felt to lecture her, to tell her it didn't matter, that it was madness to look for a deus ex machina to solve one's problems, that wherever one travelled, one still took oneself, and that anyway, it wouldn't necessarily have been to Jed's benefit to be in a film, better that he enjoyed a stable childhood; any such impulse was held in check by the way in which she'd thrown the fact of the commune at me, thereby implicating me in the general malaise.

All I said was – and stiffly – 'Give it time.' Pompous as any teacher. 'Time heals all wounds.' Clutching at cliché.

'Heal yourself!' was her instant riposte, flung over her shoulder as she banged out of the room to collapse in front of the television, leaving me to wonder ruefully whether she'd meant the words in the sense of healing or of being a heel. Either would have been appropriate. Both had me dreading the days ahead.

My solution was to phone my father from school the next day and invite myself to Sunday lunch. If I went shopping on the Saturday and spent the Sunday in Norwood, that at least was the weekend taken care of – and who knew, by the following week perhaps my prescription would prove Jacqui wrong; maybe time would heal the wound?

'All three of you?' my father asked warily.

'No, no!' I said quickly. 'Just me.'

The only previous meeting between my father and Jacqui, in the week before I moved into the flat, had been such that the prospect of a return match wasn't something to be countenanced.

I hadn't suspected, when Jacqui suggested the meeting ('He sounds intriguing, this father of yours') that it would turn out as it did, though because I had known it wouldn't be easy, I'd tried to engineer it on neutral ground, in a restaurant in town. My father, however, wouldn't hear of this. He'd never held with eating out. In his eyes, it was an entirely unnecessary extravagance.

'Don't be ridiculous,' he'd said. 'I'll cook.'

I'll never know whether he planned it like this, or whether it was serendipity, but whatever the case, my decision to move into Jacqui's flat coincided with the arrival into my father's house of Barbara, angular Barbara of the aubergine-tinted hair, she who found hedges unnecessary.

'And anyway,' my father continued, 'I have a new lodger. I'll invite her too. You can tell me what you think.'

Me to pass judgement on Barbara, my father on Jacqui – and the two women, presumably, on us and each other: home-catered, we had all the ingredients of a show trial.

Looking flustered, my father greeted us at the door, and, using the potato-peeler he happened to be carrying as a baton, conducted us through to the kitchen.

'I was going to do a chicken,' he explained, 'but Barbara pointed out you might be vegetarian, so I'm trying some lentil cutlets. The problem is they keep disintegrating.'

It was a good thing my father was walking ahead of us and couldn't see the look on Jacqui's face.

The kitchen was its usual chaos of unwashed crockery, old newspapers, and on the floor by the sink, an off-licence worth of empty beer and wine bottles. Standing over the sideboard in critical attendance on my father's culinary experiment was the incisive form of Barbara.

'I think I've got them to stay together,' she said as we entered the room. 'They needed more flour.'

My father effected the introductions, then hurried to inspect Barbara's handiwork. The way in which this new lodger seemed to shadow his every move as he began to ease the cutlets into a frying pan made me think how like a court it was, this house of my father's, the court of an eccentric monarch in exile, a monarch surrounded by men and women in waiting, all doing precisely that – waiting: waiting for a better world, for revolution, for the day they would come to power.

'Don't forget the potatoes!' Barbara was, I divined, a courtier with an eye on the throne.

'The potatoes,' muttered my father. 'I'd forgotten the potatoes.'

'Please,' said Jacqui. 'Let me.'

Barbara waved a lentil-encrusted ladle in the air. 'You sit down and put your feet up. Why shouldn't the men do it?'

There was a slight pause.

'Politics and food,' smiled Jacqui sweetly. 'Never a good combination, I don't think.'

I banged our bottle of wine on the table.

'Where's the bottle-opener?'

'Hang on a minute.' My father started to shuffle through the papers on the table.

'Give here.' Jacqui deftly relieved him of the potato peeler and positioned herself alongside Barbara at the sideboard.

In the lull that followed, Barbara remained intent on the lentils, my father washed up two more glasses, I dispensed the wine. Jacqui peeled the potatoes and asked about the house, my father asked about her; Barbara told us she was doing a course in political literature and gathering notes for a book on women in the English political novel.

Eventually, after I'd cleared the table of newspapers and laid out the plates, we sat down to eat – which was when the evening came into its own.

'So you're a single-parent family?' began Barbara, addressing Jacqui in the tone of someone chairing an encounter group.

Jacqui shot her a surprised look. 'You make it sound like a disease.'

'Well, it isn't easy, is it?' queried Barbara.

'It would be if the English weren't so awful about children.'

'Exactly,' said Barbara. 'That's exactly what I mean. We don't have enough creches. This government . . .'

'It's nothing to do with the government,' said Jacqui. 'The English have always hated children. They much prefer dogs or horses. Things on four legs.'

'You were a single-parent family,' I remarked to my father, hoping to steer the conversation in his direction.

'It's easier for men,' dismissed Barbara. 'If a man brings up a child, people fall over themselves to help him. He's practically canonised. Women, on the other hand, are expected to get on with it.'

'Well,' said Jacqui mildly, 'we are the ones with wombs.'

'That tired old argument!' The bit now firmly between her teeth, Barbara was not to be deflected from developing her thesis.

'Don't you like your cunt? I certainly do. Hours of pleasure it's given me.'

The results of Jacqui's apparent non-sequitur were, to say the least, unfortunate. There was a moment's frozen silence, then Barbara pushed back her plate and got to her feet.

'I'm very sorry, Edward,' she announced, 'but I can't eat with a gender enemy.'

'Not even lentils?' Having gained, as she saw it, the upper hand, Jacqui was beginning to enjoy the encounter.

'I'll see you tomorrow.' And snatching up her bag, which I'd put with the papers on top of the fridge, Barbara deserted the room.

'I think,' said my father slowly, 'it would be best if you left as well.'

And that had been that. I'd returned a few days later to endure an evening of Barbara ranting that it was precisely because women allowed themselves to be ruled by biology that they were so oppressed. I didn't argue – I hadn't come to argue, I'd come to make peace – and after Barbara had vented her hurt and indignation, things finally calmed down. Shortly afterwards I took Jed on a visit and, no doubt because she pitied him for being vulnerable to all the wrong influences, Barbara ignored the fact that he was a male child and made him effusively welcome – as indeed, though for the simpler reason that he liked the child, did my father. A line was drawn under our dinner, and very few references were ever made to the fact that Jed had a mother.

I hadn't thought of taking Jed with me that Sunday, but when I woke and went through to the kitchen to make some tea, he was at the table, playing with his Lego, and he looked so alone, so small and so vulnerable, that my heart went out to him. If I was suffering at the hand of Jacqui's depression, then so was he; more acutely than me, and without the option of escape.

'What's that?' I asked gently of the complicated structure he was erecting.

'An inter-galactic shuttle.'

'Show me.'

Proud as any engineer, he explained the workings of his craft: which bit was the engine, where the passengers sat, how it docked.

'And which galaxies does it visit?'

'All of them.' His eyes were fixed not on the shuttle but on the worlds it opened up. 'It can go a trillion miles without refuelling. Further than anyone's ever been before. You could fly in this and never come back.'

I switched on the kettle. 'Would you turn up your nose,' I asked quietly, 'to a shorter trip? Lunch at the castle?'

The shuttle was instantly forgotten.

'Really?'

To a flat-dwelling ten-year-old, my father's house (nick-named the castle by Jed) was a place of immediate enchantment: the jungle garden, the pond, the cellar, the attic. Topographic wonders without end, requiring no flights of fancy to bring them within reach.

'Really.'

Eyes shining, he nodded assent.

I made my tea and took it to the phone. My father didn't flinch at the prospect of an additional guest.

'But of course,' he said. 'Of course there's enough for Jed.'

'See you later, then.'

I poured another cup of tea and took it through to the sleeping Jacqui.

'I've just rung my father,' I said as I put the tea on the floor by the bed. 'I thought I'd take Jed to lunch. Give you some peace.'

She stirred sleepily. 'When will you be back?'

'About five.'

'Okay.'

I leant forward and kissed her lightly on the forehead. 'Don't stay in bed all day.'

We arrived at the castle to find a mini army massing in the garden. Led by Barbara, who was carrying a placard emblazoned with the words READING IS A RIGHT, NOT A PRIVILEGE, it consisted of Jim and Roger, their respective girlfriends, plus half a dozen other recruits that were foreign to me. My father was hovering in the porch, distributing a pile of xeroxed pamphlets to the various army members.

'I can't believe it slipped my mind,' he was muttering apologetically. 'I must start keeping a diary.'

It turned out he'd forgotten about a rally outside the Town Hall to protest at cuts to the library services. When he should have been preparing to march, he'd been cooking Sunday lunch for the entire household plus Jed and myself; a lunch which he now couldn't leave, and to which the three of us were clearly never going to do justice.

'I must start keeping a diary,' repeated my father.

'Just as well, then,' I said, 'that Jed and I are here.'

'Family lunch,' said Barbara. 'Nice.'

It wasn't clear, from the tone of her voice, whether she intended this as a rebuke or a valediction.

'We'll save some for you,' said my father.

Roger shook his head. 'I'll grab a Big Mac.'

'Don't worry about us,' confirmed Jim.

Then, gathering to itself its weapons of cardboard and paper, the army set off down the road.

'Oh dear,' said my father, still unable to come to terms with his blunder. 'I really must keep a diary.'

We followed him into the house.

'Does it matter?' I asked gently.

'Of course it matters. I said I'd go with them. And if, as a teacher, you think what's happening to the libraries isn't important, then you're a bigger fool than I took you for.' We'd reached the kitchen, and he crossed immediately to the oven. 'Besides which, I've cooked an enormous chicken.'

'Jed and I will see to that,' I said. 'Now sit down and look what I've brought you.' I produced the bottle of Rioja I'd bought duty-free at Barcelona airport. 'A taste of Spain.'

I opened the bottle and poured us each a glass.

'Mmm,' I said. 'Nice.'

My father nodded cautiously. 'Indeed.' If, like Proust's madeleines, it brought back memories, he wasn't saying. Instead, he laid a familiar hand on Jed's shoulder. 'There's some Coke in the fridge. Just help yourself. And tell me about Spain.'

Jed was the one he'd asked, so I let Jed do the talking, and was amazed by how much he'd absorbed of the weekend.

'And you?' asked my father finally, transferring his attention to me. 'What did you make of it?'

I shrugged. 'They're different.'

'The Spanish?'

'The very rich.'

My father laughed. 'Fitzgerald.'

I looked at him blankly.

'The writer. Before your time. "The rich are different to you and me."' He took a sip of wine. 'To which, of course, Hemingway replied: "They have more money".'

I shook my head. 'It goes deeper than that. Not, of course, that it matters. To us, I mean.' And I told him that Jed hadn't managed to land the part.

His reaction, predictable though it was, still took me by surprise; the force of it, perhaps.

'Thank God for that!' He cuffed Jed lightly on the shoulder. 'You don't want to be doing with Carlos Tarifa. And nor, my boy, do you.'

I found myself parroting Jacqui. 'I don't know. It would

have been quite an experience. You know they wanted me
to go, too? As Jed's tutor.'

'And you would have gone? You would have thrown up
your job?'

'Why not? What's so terrible about Tarifa?'

I wasn't vouchsafed a reply.

'You travelled as a young man,' I continued. 'And anyway, I liked it. Spain. What little we saw of it. When they
start filming, they're going south. To the mountains. Near
Tortosa. What would that have been like?'

I was still not given a reply. Lost in his own thoughts, my
father was staring into his glass. I could smell the chicken.
I stood up.

'Time to put on the peas, I think.'

As we ate, my father asked Jed: 'Did they give you any
time off, or was it all script work?'

'Carlos showed me the church. That was nice.'

There was a pause in which we both stared at him.

'What church?' I asked eventually. 'When?'

'In the town. There's a church in the town. They have all
these statues round the walls. Jesus with the cross.'

'The fourteen stations,' supplied my father.

'And candles,' said Jed. 'Lots of candles. Carlos let me
light some. I lit one for you.' This to my father. 'And one
for you.' This to me.

'And Jacqui?' enquired my father.

'And Jacqui,' said Jed.

'You never told me this,' I said.

'You never asked.'

'When did you go?'

'On our way back from Barcelona.'

'With Al and Jacqui?'

Jed shovelled a forkful of peas into his mouth. 'They
went for a drink in a bar.'

I noticed that my father was smiling ruefully to himself. 'What?' I demanded.

'I told you,' he said. 'Remember? About Catholicism.' He put his knife and fork together on one side of his plate. 'We English think Spain is beer and Benidorm. Beaches and sun. *Viva España.*' He reached for his glass. 'The mountains, though,' he said softly. 'The mountains are different. You would have liked the mountains.'

I waited a moment to see if he meant to continue, and when he didn't, poured the last of the wine between our two glasses.

'They make good wine, at any rate,' I said.

'Can I play in the garden?' asked Jed.

My father stood up. 'You can help me cut back the grass round the old pond. Come.'

'Your wine,' I reminded him.

He shook his head. 'I shouldn't drink at lunchtime. It knocks me out. You finish it.'

I conflated the contents of our two glasses, then went to stand at the window. My father had his hand on Jed's wrist and was instructing him in the use of his rusty old scythe. They made a perfect picture; an advert for family harmony. Except, of course, that to his actual son, the man controlling the scythe was a virtual stranger. I ran through what I knew of him. That his father had been a clerk on the railways, his mother a char. That at the age of twenty he'd gone to Spain and fought for the International Brigade. Correction. I didn't know he'd fought. Only that he'd been there. That on his return to London he'd joined the Communist Party. Correction again. I didn't know precisely when he'd joined the party, only that for as long as I could remember it had been a factor in his life, even – presumably – during the Cold War, the complication of Stalin, the systematic dismemberment and colonisation of

Eastern Europe. Years when it couldn't have been easy – or wise, for that matter – to cherish the beliefs that he did. Or to square them with the jobs into which he was forced in order to earn a living: driver for a film production company, stage manager, something to do with newspapers.

Then had come his marriage to my mother, my birth, her death: a trio of events that sealed the sixties and led to the half-hearted seventies, the disappointing eighties, the compromising nineties. The need to organise his life around the demands of a child, the rise of Thatcher, the collapse of the Soviet Union.

I finished the wine. Even though I'd been an eye-witness from the mid-seventies onwards, the details of this latter half of my father's life were no more vivid than the early years. Indeed, in some ways less so. All I had witnessed was a gradual decline, a wilting, a certain drabness. Excitement in my childhood had come in the shape of a new lodger, a new coat of paint in this or that room, a new set of enthusiasms at the dinner table whilst my father continued his tortoise-like retreat into the impenetrability of disappointment.

If he were an assignment, I thought, such as I set my students, I would barely scrape a pass. His fault or mine? True, I'd never been made privy to his innermost thoughts, but then I'd never really tried. I'd taken his reticence at face value. Allowed it to shape my behaviour.

I turned my attention to the washing up, and when my father returned to the kitchen, leaving Jed to make a pile of the grass cuttings under the kitchen window, challenged him as follows: 'You never talk about Spain. Why?'

'The past,' replied my father, 'is past.'

'What exactly did you do there?'

He shrugged. 'Fought a battle which, sadly, it seems we have to keep on fighting. Maybe always will.'

'Against capitalism?'

He snorted. 'Human nature.'

'What did you mean earlier when you said we didn't want to be doing with Tarifa?'

He didn't, however, wish to pursue the conversation.

'As you get older,' he said, 'you learn that what you know is not always of use to others. Knowledge can be irrelevant. Now, what about some tea?'

I was forced to let the subject drop. 'Tea would be lovely.' I looked at my watch. 'Then we really must be off.' I wanted to avoid the return of the army.

As we were waiting for the bus, Jed slipped his hand into mine and left it there, letting go only when the bus drew up and I had to fumble in my pocket for change. We went, as usual, upstairs, to the seat at the front of the bus.

'You're lucky,' he said suddenly, 'to have a father.'

I looked at him, surprised. 'Fathers can have their draw-backs.'

'So can mothers.'

I smoothed his cow's lick.

'Well, if it's any consolation, there's always me. I'm not about to run away.'

And indeed I wasn't; not from Jed, at any rate. Events would see to that. Earlier that week I'd thought to tell Jacqui it was madness to look for a deus ex machina to solve one's problems. But there was, as it happened, just such a machina waiting to catapult us forwards, a modern machina of white plastic which, the following morning, the minute Jed had left for school, rang deliverance.

I was in the bathroom, and it was Jacqui who answered.

'Al!' I heard her say. There was a pause. 'You're not serious?' Another pause. 'You mean? God, I can hardly believe it! But that's fantastic! You really mean . . .'

I ran into the living room. She was facing the door, and as I came through it, she gave a thumbs-up sign.

'No, no, of course.' She was making an effort to sound businesslike. 'Yes, of course I'll do that. Yes, and I'll get him to ring you. No, that's no problem, really.'

She put down the phone and with a delighted whoop, threw herself across the room and into my arms.

'He's got it! He's got the part! Jed's got the part!'

I'm not sure if I swung her round, or she me, but a moment later we had fallen in a dizzy heap upon the sofa.

'Can you believe it?' She let out another whoop. 'They want him. They actually want him.'

She leapt up, and, going to the window, stuck out her tongue at the street. 'Fuck you, Kilburn.'

'But what about the money men?' I gasped. 'The guys in LA . . .'

She did a little dance. 'Carlos talked them round. Al sent across the screen test, and Carlos talked them round.'

'He was that good?'

'Obviously.' She stopped in mid-step. 'What is it with you?'

'With me?'

'Anyone would think you disapproved.'

I got up and crossed the room towards her.

'God, no! It's just . . .'

'Just what?'

I shrugged. 'Too sudden, I suppose. That's all. I mean, one moment . . .'

She finished the sentence for me. 'One moment we don't have a future, the next we do.'

'So now?'

'We get ourselves an agent. I'll ring Victor.'

Victor was another piece in the puzzle of Jacqui's past: an

actor and, I guessed, sometime lover who, when resting, would help at Parties Unlimited.

Jacqui skipped into the kitchen and retrieved her coffee. 'Al says he knows someone, but I think it's better I do this myself. Don't you?' She took a sip of her coffee. 'Shit! I can't believe it's happening!'

Again I shrugged. 'A fairy tale.'

She giggled. 'Some fairy tale.'

I came close and kissed her on the neck, nuzzling my face against her cheek.

'I think it's wonderful,' I whispered. 'Really, I do.'

I stepped back, and as I did so, she let out a further whoop, and with her left hand spun her saucer into the air like a frisbee. The sash window was open a fraction at the top, and we watched open-mouthed as the saucer spun through the air, and instead of crashing into the glass, sailed through the gap and into the street. Mrs Sargeson, the old woman from downstairs, was shuffling across the road, pulling a shopping trolley behind her. The saucer cleared the parked cars and landed neatly in the centre of the trolley. It must have made a noise, or else Mrs Sargeson felt the tremor of its impact, for she swung around nervously, fearing attack. Then, puzzled by the emptiness of the street, she shook her head and mounted the pavement opposite whilst Jacqui and I dissolved into hysterical laughter.

'Only in fairy tales,' I managed eventually, 'does the miraculous become commonplace.'

Jacqui handed me her cup. 'Make some more coffee whilst I ring Victor.'

I looked at my watch. 'I have a class in fifteen minutes.'

'They can wait.'

'They already will be.' I gave her a final kiss. 'Do your own coffee. I'll see you later.'

I got back to the flat at six to find Jed watching television with the sound off because Jacqui was on the phone to Suzy.

'Evening, kid,' I said.

He ignored my greeting. Jacqui's behaviour had obviously so incensed him that he wasn't talking to any adult. Jacqui put her hand over the receiver and mouthed 'In the fridge' before returning to her conversation.

I dumped my evening's marking on the kitchen table and opened the fridge. There was an open bottle of champagne in the door.

'So?' I said, indicating the contents of my glass when eventually she'd said goodbye to Suzy and come through to join me. 'Victor obviously came up trumps?'

She laughed derisively. 'God, no! No wonder he never works. He's always going on about his agent – my agent this, my agent that – then it turns out the guy's some creep who works from the back room of a council flat in Tufnell Park. I mean, really! So I talked to Julie. I don't think you've met her, but she used to work for Andrew Lloyd Webber. Anyway, she put me onto this guy called Agate. Peter-Jon Agate. Well, P.J. actually.'

'Who has a proper office?'

'*And* who knows Carlos. He's even had lunch at the villa.' She finished the remains of her champagne, and, opening the fridge to replenish our glasses, reeled off some of the people P.J. represented. It was certainly an impressive list.

'When are you seeing him?'

'We,' she corrected. 'We're seeing him Wednesday morning.'

'We?'

She pulled up a chair.

'Surely we don't have to argue about this?'

'Argue?'

'You know what I'm talking about.'

'I do?'

'Carlos rang after you'd left. We had a very long talk. About Jed. How this whole thing might affect him.'

'I thought that might be what we were talking about.'

'I also talked to P.J. I explained about the school. How it would mean you'd lose your job.'

'Jacqui!'

She held up a hand. 'And he said if they wanted you badly enough, not only would they pay you to be Jed's tutor, they'd reimburse you for the inconvenience. They'll pay us both. Me as chaperone, you as tutor. About two hundred pounds a day, P.J. reckons. Six thousand a month. If filming takes two months, that's twelve thousand pounds. Plus a sort of buy-out for the inconvenience. You could walk away with fifteen thousand pounds. That's a year's salary. Almost.'

I became aware of a movement in the doorway. Jed was there, regarding us solemnly.

'Bathtime,' said Jacqui briskly. 'Chop-chop.'

'Can't I listen?'

She clapped her hands impatiently. 'You heard. Chop-chop.'

'It isn't fair,' he muttered sulkily – though like his surrogate father, he knew when to admit defeat. Jacqui waited until he'd dragged himself out of earshot.

'The thing is this,' she continued quietly. 'Sure, I could do it on my own, but between the two of us, we could do it so much better. He does rely on you, you know. You ought to be flattered.'

Economics and need – Jed's need, but also mine – had dovetailed into an argument that was incontrovertible. I knew I could hold out for a while, but not indefinitely. Certainly not past Wednesday. So, thrusting my glass at

Jacqui, I decided to capitulate. Why waste time on the unattainable?

'Any more?' I asked. 'Where this came from?'

She stood up. 'You'll see,' she said. 'It'll be fantastic. For all of us.'

On the Wednesday morning I phoned in sick, and at 10.30 sharp, Jacqui, Jed and I walked to the High Road to hail a taxi. We made an unlikely trio. Scrubbed against his will into respectability, Jed was in a jumper that clearly prickled. Jacqui's outfit – turquoise with a plunging neckline – was as svelte as it was clinging. I was the schoolteacher still, un-remarkable in my tweed jacket and twisted tie, my baggy cords and dusty shoes.

The agency had its offices off Regent Street, on the third floor of one of those London buildings whose impe-rial grandeur remains unnoticed until you actually have occasion to stop and study it. We passed along a vaulted corridor to a lift which was out of keeping with the rest of the building – cramped, shabby and on its last legs – but which, on the third floor, disgorged us into a state-of-the-art reception area where, at a desk of gleaming black wood, sat a statuesque receptionist who looked as if she had been placed there less to answer the phone than to complement the single vase of vivid red tulips. Jacqui did the announc-ing, whereupon we were asked to make ourselves comfortable on the black leather sofa that ringed the recep-tion area whilst the receptionist dealt with an incoming call, then buzzed P.J.

'His assistant will be through in a moment,' she told us.

There was a pile of trade magazines on the low black table in front of the sofa, back copies of *Variety* and *Screen International*. My eyes, however, went to the posters on the walls. A roll-call of every West End hit of the last ten years, they established at a glance that this was an organisation that would never operate out of a back room in Tufnell Park. A young man with tightly curled hair and even tighter jeans sashayed through a door in the wall and threw a pile of letters onto the receptionist's desk.

'For the twelve o'clock,' he instructed, then graced us with a dazzling smile.

'You're here to see P.J., right? I'm Paul. Follow me.'

As I stood at the door to let Jacqui through first, she caught my eye.

'Did you say fairy tale?' she whispered.

'Sorry to keep you waiting,' Paul threw over his shoulder, 'but it's turning into one of those days. Still,' this to Jed, 'it means you miss more school, right?'

The entire floor had been gutted and given over to a maze of desks and filing cabinets, photocopiers and fax machines. Around the edge of the building, which was where we were headed, was a line of glass-fronted offices, the corner one of which had its door ajar.

'The nerve centre!' Paul stood aside so we could enter.

Whereas the rest of the floor had been done out in inoffensive shades of grey, so as not to draw attention to itself, the nerve centre had been designed to shout a statement. The walls were a bright canary yellow, the carpet an indigo blue, the furniture a series of arrestingly angled planes and textures: yellow chairs with triangular backs and seats, a hexagonal desk in Japanese oak, a Gaudi-esque standard lamp of fluted aluminium. Coming round the desk to greet us was a man in a white T-shirt and a pair of black tailored slacks. The T-shirt displayed to cunning advantage the fact that he worked out, whilst his deeply tanned face betokened equal devotion to the sun. It was a relaxed and sensuous face, a face that gave no clue to its age, though as he came closer, I saw that his hair was thinning and there was a scoring of lines around his eyes. Nearer fifty than thirty, I guessed, for all the sculpting of his pectorals.

'Jacqui!' he cried, clasping her hand. 'Good to meet you. And this is Jed! Well, well. I can see what Carlos is on about.'

He ushered Jacqui and Jed towards the yellow chairs, then turned to me.

'You must be Peter?' His handshake was surprisingly limp for someone so packed with muscle, but the eyes were hawk-like.

'Now! What about coffee?' He returned to his desk and fell into a black leather chair that reclined with his body.

'Coffee would be heavenly,' said Jacqui.

'And for you, young man?'

'Do you have any Coke?'

P.J. grinned. 'Sweetheart, even the kind with bubbles.'

'Two coffees and a Coke!' Paul pirouetted out of the door, shutting it behind him.

'So!' P.J. put his fingers together and regarded us over the pale expanse of his desk. 'Carlos has waved his magic wand!'

I don't know what I'd been expecting, but it certainly hadn't been anything as flip as this. I darted a look at Jacqui. She seemed totally unfazed by P.J.'s familiarity.

'Which is why we need you,' she laughed.

'Indeed.' P.J. picked up a pencil and drummed it lightly on the desk. 'The man is a monster. Charming, but monstrous. Though now you've spent time at the villa, you don't need me to tell you that. You just need me to keep the monster in check.' He executed a drum roll. 'He did a production once – Barcelona, I think – of *Sleeping Beauty*. He wanted Nureyev. I tried to talk Rudi out of it. I tried to talk Carlos out of it. I knew what would happen if the two of them got together. And boy, did it happen! The drama

was all offstage.' He put down the pencil and leant forward.
'The rules are very simple. Never let him steamroller you
into anything. Always tell him you need to discuss it with
me. He's bad enough in opera, I shudder to think what he
might be like on a film.'

The door opened and Paul appeared with a tray. He
handed Jed his Coke, Jacqui and me our coffee.

'Don't I get anything?' P.J. had picked up the pencil
again, and was rolling it between his fingers.

Paul let the tray fall against his legs, and, casting his eyes
ceilingward, put his free hand on his hip. 'I thought we
were on a diet?' Then, without waiting for an answer, he
made a face at Jed. 'When you grow up,' he said, 'work
down a mine. It's a doddle compared to this.'

'That will be all, thank you, Paul.'

With a final roll of the eyes, Paul left the office.

I took a sip of my coffee, and as I did so, noticed the
design on the cup. Grecian in feel, it featured a frieze of
priapic men, all clasping each other by their engorged gen-
italia. Startled, I looked up to find P.J.'s eyes on me. They
held a glint of amused enquiry.

'Well,' said Jacqui, 'having put the fear of God into us
about Carlos, where next?'

Suddenly businesslike, P.J. reached for a sheet of paper
and ran his finger along the writing. 'What I've agreed
with Al is basically what I told you over the phone. You' –
he looked at Jacqui – 'will act as chaperone, for which
there's a daily fee.' He transferred his gaze to me. 'It turns
out they've already hired a tutor, some Spanish priest, so
you, Peter, will work with him. On the same basis as
Jacqui. In due course I'll let you have details of the exact
requirements. In this country the law is that Jed doesn't
work longer than an eight-hour day, with an hour for
lunch, and a minimum of fifteen hours' tutelage a week.

I'm not sure about Spain, and on feature films – especially if they're shot out of the country – one has to be somewhat flexible, but I'll be proposing something along those lines. I'll let you have a copy, and if you find you're not getting enough time with Jed, or you think he's working unfair hours, you must let me know.' He turned over the sheet of paper, then returned his attention to Jacqui. 'Jed's fee we've already discussed, and I've asked that accountant to give you a ring. The monies have to be paid directly to Jed, though you will of course have signing powers.'

At this point the phone rang, and with a grimaced apology, P.J. snatched it up. 'Tell the old cow she's lucky to be offered the part at all. It's that or Butlin's.' He put down the receiver. 'The contracts should be ready next week, and when you sign them I'll let you have all the details about working hours, etcetera. My fee is a ten per cent commission, which I take off the top, and we can pay you your monies however you instruct me. In Spain if you'd like, or into an account here. Offshore, even. But that you should discuss with the accountant. Any questions?'

'How soon,' said Jacqui, 'will they want us?'

'The weekend after next.'

'What should I say to Jed's school?'

'Tell them he'll be away for two months. Try to get some books from them and a list of what Peter should be doing with him.' The phone interrupted him again. 'Shit! Yes, I'd better speak to him. Tell him I'll ring back in a minute.'

Jacqui stood up. 'We'll wait to hear from you, then.'

P.J. nodded. 'Tuesday at the latest.' He opened a drawer in his desk and began rummaging through it. When he straightened up, he was holding a black sweatshirt with a silver hook appliqued in a bold swirl across the front.

Turning it round, he displayed the legend on the back: 'We're hooked on Peter Pan'.

'Made specially for the crew,' he explained. 'Probably a bit big for you, but isn't that the fashion?'

'Wow!' Jed was open-mouthed.

P.J. came round the desk. 'Signed by Dustin himself.' He pointed out the signature, then laid the sweatshirt in Jed's arms. 'But in return, young man, you must promise not to let these film people mess you about.'

Jed was tracing the shape of the silver hook with his finger.

'What do you say?' prompted Jacqui.

'Thank you,' he said automatically. And then, unbidden: 'You don't have to worry. I like Carlos. He's interesting.'

'Well,' said Jacqui once we had attained the lift. 'What about that?'

Jed was tugging at her sleeve. 'Mum . . .'

'I haven't forgotten.'

'What?' I asked.

'You'll see.' We stepped out of the lift. I was given no choice but to follow her lead. Within minutes we were in Oxford Street and turning through the door of a McDonald's.

'I'm sorry,' she grimaced, 'but I promised.'

We took our trays downstairs, to where there was a seating area.

'Extraordinary,' said Jacqui once we had settled ourselves. 'But obviously on the ball.'

'He was nice,' said Jed. 'I liked him.'

'You,' I said, reaching for a chip, 'like everyone.' I didn't bring up the design on the coffee cups, nor the fact that I hadn't been given the chance to discuss my fee, nor even that I wasn't the only tutor.

'When will you tell Gloria?'

'Tomorrow, I suppose. If we're leaving next weekend.'

'How will she take it?'

'Badly, I guess. But I can handle that. And the school?'

'I might pop in this afternoon.'

'There's a lot to organise.'

'You're telling me. I haven't a clue what to do about the flat.'

'Do you need to do anything?'

'I'd rather not leave it empty. They're saying two months, but I reckon it could be longer. And we don't know what might happen afterwards.'

'Indeed.' I could see the way Jacqui's mind was working. For her, the film was only step number one.

We finished our Big Macs. Jacqui allowed Jed a second Coke, then looked at her watch: 'How about a film? To celebrate?'

'Yeah, man!' Jed's eyes glittered with excitement.

'In a month's time,' I said, 'you probably won't want to see another film in your life.'

'Then let's make the most of it now,' said Jacqui. 'Whilst we're still impressionable.'

I broke the news to Gloria and Ernesto the following day.

They were, unsurprisingly, in the midst of a row. I could hear their voices from as far away as the turn of the stairs, and it was only my knock on the study door that caused them to fall silent.

'Come!' To Gloria, who'd been brought up on a diet of post-war English films, that was the only way for a head-mistress to invite people into her sanctum.

Ernesto was skulking by the coffee pot. Gloria sat mag-isterially at her desk.

'Oh,' she said, 'it's you.'

Her glance returned to Ernesto, preparatory no doubt to

resuming their argument. I headed her off by literally blurting out my news, then waited for the explosion; which, to my surprise, never came.

'Tarifa? Carlos Tarifa?' she said. 'I never knew he made films.'

'He hasn't up to now.'

'But how fantastic for you! And for Jed. God, what an amazing thing. Tell me how it happened.'

I should have guessed, of course, that because of her background, she would see my announcement not as a defection – teachers are replaceable – but as an avenue of possibility that might, if she played her cards right, extend to her own front door.

'Ideally I'd have liked to give you more notice.'

She waved away my apology. 'My dear, you forget! I was brought up in showbusiness. I know how it works. Ernesto!' She nodded him towards the cupboard in the corner. 'And anyway, unlike most English people, I'm not against advancement. That's the problem with this country. Too little enterprise.'

Bearing a cognac bottle and three glasses, Ernesto turned from the cupboard.

'A toast!'

I could think of nothing I relished less than toasting my so-called advancement with Gloria and Ernesto. But there was no way out, so in between tentative sips of the burning brandy, I filled them in on exactly how the whole thing had happened. In return, I was treated again to the story I'd heard a hundred times before – how Gloria had been picked for *The Sound of Music*, the horrors and triumphs of being on tour, and then – as the brandy made her maudlin (she managed three glasses to my one) – how she'd made the terrible mistake of marrying Ernesto.

'But enough about me,' she concluded eventually. 'You have a new world ahead of you. Go out, enjoy! And who knows, perhaps we'll meet? We'll be in Spain this summer, if Ernesto gets his act together and books the tickets. Maybe we can join up for a day or two? Where exactly did you say the villa was?'

I swallowed the remains of my brandy. 'We won't be there. We'll be filming in some mountain village. I don't know where.'

'All the more reason to keep in touch, then.' Gloria poured herself another glass, then offered the bottle to me.

I shook my head. 'I must be getting home.'

'Well, don't forget. We mustn't lose touch.'

Ernesto clapped me on the shoulder. 'And when the film is finished, if you want your job back, it'll always be waiting.'

Back at the flat, Jacqui was experiencing less luck with her arrangements.

'Clothes!' she wailed. 'We have to get new clothes. I got through virtually my entire wardrobe in one weekend. I wish Zeynep had warned us they dress for dinner. What are you doing Saturday?'

She'd been unable to find anyone to look after the flat, so while she and Jed went shopping, I was delegated to visit Mrs Sargeson and explain about our departure, that we would leave her my key and that once a week she was to take in our post and put it on the kitchen table. Then there was more shopping to be done, bills to be settled, standing orders to be set up, another visit to P.J. to sign our contracts, tickets to be collected, leave to be taken of my students, and of Jean-Luís, whose class I left until last so he couldn't insist on a farewell drink. Also my father, who I put off ringing until the evening before our departure. I hadn't forgotten what he'd said about Tarifa, and now that we were going, the last thing I wanted was to know what he'd meant.

It was Catholicism, however, rather than Tarifa to which he drew my attention.

'When do you go?' he asked.

'Tomorrow.'

'For how long?'

'Two, three months. We don't really know.'

'Well, remember what I told you. Never take a Catholic at face value. They have a variety. Of faces.'

'Is this a warning?'

He laughed. 'Prescriptions I leave to the priests.'

'Well,' I said, 'thank you. I'll certainly remember that.'

His laugh abated to a chuckle. 'Innocents abroad.'

'Is that the plural?' I sought refuge in the word itself. 'Or an abstract noun?'

'Oh,' he said, 'both. Don't you think?'

His words were still with me when, the next morning at 8.30 precisely, our plane left the runway.

Seven

Returning to the villa was at once familiar and strange. The familiarity I'd expected – it was, after all, only three weeks since our first visit – but the strangeness caught me unawares.

It started at Barcelona Airport, where the figure holding the placard with Jacqui's name on it was not, as before, a professional driver, but a Catholic priest. Stout and severe in his simple black soutane, grey hair uncompromisingly crew cut, face less fleshy than the rest of him, black eyes circled by a pair of thickly rimmed spectacles, he put me in mind of a crow, and made me remember how Zeynep, as she'd flown up the steps of the villa to meet us, had also seemed like a bird, though of an altogether more decorative kind.

Tucking his placard under his arm, he bowed to Jacqui and announced: 'I'm Father Ricardo. I thought that since we'll be spending so much time together, we should get acquainted as soon as possible. You must be Jed.' Although his English was faultless, he chose his words with the deliberation of someone not wholly at ease with the language. 'You and I,' he continued, turning his attention to me, 'we'll be working together, yes? A chance to improve my vocabulary.' He gestured towards our luggage. 'I'll carry one of those.'

We followed him outside to a tiny, dust-covered Seat.

'Apologies for the car,' he said, 'but contrary to popular belief, the Catholic Church does not have unlimited funds.'

There wasn't enough space in the boot for all our suit-cases, so one of them had to go on the back seat, forcing me to put Jed on my lap, whilst Jacqui accommodated her-self in the front with our cabin luggage.

'I should have realised it was going to be such a crush,' said Father Ricardo as we swung out of the car park, 'and let them send the limousine. My selfishness. Forgive me.'

'Look out!' cried Jed.

'*Por Dios!*' Father Ricardo swerved violently to avoid the cyclist who only Jed had seen. 'Thank you, young man.'

I twisted in my seat to peer through the dust-encrusted rear window. The cyclist had pulled off the road and was shaking an angry fist at us.

'Worse than my English,' said Father Ricardo, 'my dri-ving. Now please, you have to tell me all about yourselves.'

He took his eyes off the road to smile encouragingly at Jacqui, causing her to intercept hastily: 'What do you want to know?'

'Everything.'

If I'd hoped, as a consequence of Father Ricardo's request, to learn more about her than I already knew, his driving put paid to that. Galvanised by the fear that if she paused, he might again be tempted to take his eyes off the road, she gave a rapid and decidedly perfunctory recital of her past.

'Now Peter!'

'Me?'

'Unless Jed would like to go next.'

Jed dug me sharply in the ribs.

'Well,' I began, 'my life is altogether less interesting.' Altogether more interrupted too, for now we were entering Barcelona, and my story was punctuated by a number of near misses as we cut across lanes and lurched across intersections whose lights had already turned red.

'*Lo siento*,' muttered Father Ricardo to Jacqui at one point as she flinched against imminent collision. 'Now Jed.'

I had finished my address and we were emerging from the city onto the road that ran northwards along the coast.

Jed squirmed reluctantly in my lap.

'No, let me guess. You like reading, you're good at arithmetic, even though everyone at school says it's boring, and your favourite sport is running.'

Jed's mouth fell open. 'Someone told you!'

Father Ricardo laughed. 'Being a priest is like being a detective. Your Sherlock Holmes. Have you read Sherlock Holmes?'

Jed hadn't, but that didn't matter. Father Ricardo had totally disarmed him. He recited the facts of his life in a slightly breathless, sing-song voice, every so often looking to me for confirmation.

'And you?' challenged Jacqui when Jed finally came to a halt. 'What about you?'

'My turn, you mean?'

'Fair's fair.'

We swooped out from behind a lorry, and for a nerve-wracking moment held our breath as the little Seat laboured to overtake it.

'Reasonable acceleration and faith!' laughed Father Ricardo, regaining our side of the road yards before a blind bend. 'That's all you need.'

His story turned out to be as much about Carlos as

himself. I hadn't realised that Carlos was an orphan and had taken his surname not from his parents but from the village in which he'd been born. Father Ricardo, too, was an orphan, and had grown up with Carlos in the same orphanage in Tarifa, graduating from there to a seminary in Seville. He'd returned to Tarifa as village priest, where Carlos, now a famous director, had become a benefactor of the orphanage. With Carlos's money and Father Ricardo's expertise, the two of them had widened the scope of the orphanage to include a retraining unit for homeless youngsters from the cities. And when Carlos had needed a Catholic adviser for a play he'd mounted in Madrid about Ignatius Loyola, founder of the Jesuits, he'd turned to Father Ricardo. And was using him again for *Murillo*.

'Do you always wear a dress?' asked Jed.

Jacqui coughed embarrassedly. 'I'm afraid Jed hasn't met many priests.'

'Pretty much always,' chuckled Father Ricardo. 'And when I celebrate mass, I have other outfits too. I will show you.' We took a corner too sharply. ' But then, as I'm sure you noticed, everyone at the villa likes to dress up. I come a poor second where dressing up is concerned.'

'Don't you get hot?' said Jed.

'So then I swim. Do you swim?'

Jed nodded.

'Perhaps this afternoon we can go together. There's a cove by the rocks where I like to snorkel. Do you snorkel?'

Jed shook his head.

'I will teach you.'

Father Ricardo was doing no more than he'd been hired to do: to make us welcome, to get to know Jed. His friendliness, however, was having an unexpected effect on me, one of alienation, and our arrival at the villa did nothing to lessen my sense of sudden superfluity. A seemingly familiar Zeynep was waiting to greet us at the gate, except that where her previous greeting had been elaborate and effusive, this time she was much more businesslike. Commanding Jacqui and Jed to wait with Father Ricardo in the courtyard, she took me briskly into the villa where we'd stayed before, and, crossing the deserted living room, led me down a short flight of stairs to a little cell at the rear of the house.

'No view, I'm afraid,' she said, crossing to a shuttered window high on the opposite wall, 'but it's very cool in here, also quiet. No one can disturb you.' She swung back the shutters. 'Carlos wanted Jacqui and Jed in the Casa Nueva, near his office, but we only have two rooms down there, and I thought that since you all have work to do, you'd rather have space to yourself.'

As an explanation it made perfect sense, and half of me wanted to believe she meant the arrangement kindly. I had, after all, tried to tell her on the last visit that Jacqui and I were merely friends. There was a part of me, though, that wondered if the person behind the contrivance couldn't have been Jacqui – and if so, why?

All I voiced, however, as I deposited my suitcase on the bed, was a bland: 'It's perfect.'

And indeed, for all its monasticism, the room had been exquisitely furnished. The bed was perhaps too narrow, but the bureau and cupboard were eighteenth century, there was what looked like an original Miro on the wall, and through a door to my left, I could glimpse a gleaming and well-appointed bathroom.

I set about unpacking. My jackets and slacks I hung in the prettily carved cupboard, my shirts, socks and underpants I distributed between the drawers of the dainty bureau, shoes went on the floor of the cupboard, books on the bedside table, toiletries in the marbled bathroom. The room began to feel marginally less cell-like. I was weighing up whether to have a shower or go for a swim when, from the living room, I heard the clear, sweet notes of the piano, and, venturing upstairs, was confronted by the grizzled, bear-like figure of a man with untidy white hair bent intently over the keys, alternatively testing the melody, then annotating the music in front of him with a pencil he kept clenched between his teeth. I stayed motionless at the head of the stairs, watching, fascinated, how he used pencil and key to unlock, as it were, the tune, until he himself broke the spell he'd cast by glancing up and noticing me.

I stepped into the room. 'Hello,' I said. 'I'm Peter.'

Returning the pencil to his teeth, he played the melody through without interruption, causing it to swell to its climax.

'What does that make you think of?' he demanded when he'd finished. After the euphony of the piano, his vocal instrument was gruffly Germanic.

'Think of?'

'What pictures does it suggest?'

I hesitated.

'Well?' he queried impatiently.

'Mountains,' I said. 'High mountains and empty plains.'

He nodded sagely. 'And this?'

He flipped over his music and executed a quick, trilling flourish in the treble clef.

'Children,' I said. 'Children playing.'

This time my answer didn't please him, and with a muttered curse, he scribbled angrily on the music. Then, discarding the pencil completely, he played a third melody, more haunting than the first two, less easy to categorise.

'Chopin,' he said. 'Unparalleled.'

Despite the fact that he'd made no attempt to introduce himself, only his music, I felt a sudden need to explain my presence; so, taking another step into the room, I said: 'I'm here with Jed.'

'Ah,' he said, 'the boy. I've yet to meet the boy.'

'I have the room downstairs.'

He stood up and rounded the piano towards me. 'Where is he, the boy?'

'In the Casa Nueva.'

'With Carlos?'

I shrugged.

'I have to see him. Please excuse me.' And with a curt nod of the head, he strode onto the terrace.

I crossed to the piano and looked at the music. The pencilled notes marched in impenetrable ranks across the staves, making sense only in terms of the occasional scribbled description: 'Murillo's studio', 'Confession', 'Street scene'. I hit a few experimental notes of my own. Plaintive as question marks, they hung unfinished in the air. Turning away, my attention was caught by the nativity scene in the cupboard against the far wall. The porcelain figures in their rich brocade looked frozen in time, perpetually present, and yet awaiting some offstage instruction to bring them to life.

'Beautiful, no? Such craftsmanship.' Father Ricardo had materialised at my elbow. 'Italian, I think. Turn of the century.' He stepped forward and readjusted Mary's veil. 'It starts with the family. Just the three of them. Mary and Joseph and the child. It ends with the three on the cross. Then the trinity. Do you ever wonder why it goes in threes?'

'Don't forget the onlookers.' I gestured to the wise men and the shepherds.

'Also three,' he smiled, 'in the case of the kings.'

'Not when you add the shepherds.'

'Now!' He slipped his arm into mine and steered me towards the door. 'I was on my way to find Jed and take him for that swim. Will you join us?'

It had been a toss-up earlier between a swim and a shower, but the prospect of attaching myself to Father Ricardo's coat-tails held little appeal. I disengaged my arm.

'That's very kind,' I said, 'but after the flight I think I'd prefer a nap.'

'As you wish.' He affected a little bow; then, pirouetting on his heels with surprising grace for someone so rotund, vanished onto the terrace.

I returned to my room, where I must have fallen asleep, because the next thing I remember was opening my eyes to discover an awestruck Jed running an exploratory finger across one of the painted panels of the cupboard.

'Well,' I said, 'stranger. And how are you?'

He turned to face me. 'What's through there?' He gestured towards the bathroom door.

'The bathroom. What's your's like?'

He came to sit beside me. 'I've got a double bed with nets around it.'

'Goodness.'

'Mummy too. And a balcony.'

'Very grand.'

'This is nicer, though.' He cuddled against me, and I ran my hand gently through his hair.

'How was your swim?'

'Good.'

'See any fish?'

He shook his head. 'It was too rough. We'll try again tomorrow.'

'He's nice,' I said, using Jed's word, 'don't you think? Father Ricardo?'

For once he didn't make use of the word himself. Instead he looked at his watch. 'I have to go.' He stood up. 'Father Ricardo's going into the town and he asked if I'd like to go with him.'

I sat up. 'See you later, then.' He'd reached the door. 'And whenever it gets too much down there, just remember you can always come up here.'

He made a face. 'The phone never stops ringing. And Carlos is always shouting.'

'What about?'

He shrugged. 'You'd better ask Mummy. It's all in Spanish.'

'All the more reason, then, to remember where I am.'

I waited until he'd closed the door behind him, then discarded my sweaty clothes and took the shower I'd been promising myself. Refreshed, I changed into cotton slacks and a cotton shirt and took up a book, which I read until, in the distance, I heard the bell for dinner. Someone had switched on a lamp behind the piano. Its curved, black back reflected the light as if from an undisturbed lake, whilst on the opposite wall, in their niches above the fireplace, Carlos's collection of ceramics kept silent witness to their owner's unknown past. How had he come by them, I wondered? And why? They belonged in a museum. Not a living room. I stepped onto the terrace to be greeted by the inevitable whistle of the little grey bird.

'Peter, my dear! Where have you been hiding?' As if to compensate for her earlier brusqueness, Zeynep was upon me the minute I appeared on the dining terrace. 'It's paella. Juan's best.' She thrust a plate into my hands and began to heap it with food.

I looked about me at the assembled throng. One or two of the faces I recognised either from earlier or from last time – Quiepo's mother in her garb of sombre black, one of Carlos's assistants, an elegant woman in a slash of designer red, Father Ricardo, the man at the piano – but there was an equal number of newcomers, most noticeably a veritable mountain of a woman whose slopes were swathed in what looked like a candlewick bedspread, and whose summit erupted in a chaos of hair and booming laughter.

'Where's Carlos?' I asked.

Zeynep cast her eyes heavenward. 'With Brett.'

'Brett?'

'The writer. You've not met him? Well, maybe you never will.' She lowered her voice. 'Al is in Los Angeles looking for a replacement.'

'There've been problems?'

'Problems? My dear, crises! Dramas! You could make another film.'

'And Quiepo?'

I'd purposely left his name until last.

'With Al in Los Angeles. They get back tomorrow. Now, my dear, find a seat, make yourself comfortable.'

I crossed to where Jed and Jacqui were sitting alone at the edge of the terrace.

'Zeynep tells me there are problems with the script?'

Like Zeynep before her, Jacqui rolled her eyes heavenward. 'You can say that again!'

'Eventful, then, life in the fast lane?'

She met my implied rebuke head-on. 'You should be thankful your room is where it is. I spent the afternoon in the jacuzzi just to escape the shouting.'

'Tell me,' I changed the subject. 'The old guy with the white hair?'

'Carl, the composer.'

'And the woman in the bedspread?'

Jacqui giggled. 'Costumes!'

We were joined by Father Ricardo.

'Jed and I,' he said, spearing his paella, 'bought some notebooks and pens in town, so I think we're fully stocked, and I've cleared it with Carlos that, barring emergencies, Jed will have the mornings for schooling. We just need to decide how to divide things between us. Arithmetic and geography are my specialities, and obviously English and history are best with you, but otherwise, well, perhaps we can get together in the morning to work out a schedule? After breakfast, say? Nine o'clock?'

Jacqui had lit a cigarette and now she exhaled a luxurious plume of smoke. 'Sounds like I'll be at a loose end.'

Father Ricardo smiled. 'Plenty of men,' he said, 'to look after you.'

There wasn't anything in his tone to indicate that the remark had been made with me in mind, but all the same, as with the separate room, it left me feeling there was something of a conspiracy to keep Jacqui and me apart.

'Mind you,' continued the priest, 'you'll need to keep your wits about you. A Spanish man can sometimes be one man too many.'

Jacqui flicked her ash over the edge of the parapet. 'There can never be too many men.'

Father Ricardo stared at her. 'Never?'

'Well, can there?'

'There were thirteen at the last supper,' he replied quietly. 'That was one too many.'

No surprise, I thought wryly, that arithmetic is your preferred subject. It's obviously an obsession. What I gave voice to, though, was another thought altogether: 'I've only just realised. That must be where the superstition comes from.'

'Absolutely,' assented Father Ricardo. He turned to Jed. 'Are you superstitious?'

'What's superstitious?' Jed stumbled slightly over the word.

'Avoiding black cats,' I supplied. 'Not walking under ladders. In case something awful happens. Silly things like that.'

'Silly?' Father Ricardo raised a sacerdotal eyebrow. 'Not silly, surely, to have respect for the ways in which the world can trip us up? The ladder, now. Not walking under ladders. Do you know why that is?'

I shook my head.

'The number three again.' He was smiling delightedly. 'The triangle that the ladder makes with the wall represents the Trinity, and if you walk through the triangle, then you're fracturing the Trinity.'

There was a sudden commotion at the head of the stairs.

'You know fuck!' The voice was Carlos's. 'Dialogue? You call that dialogue?'

The terrace fell briefly silent, and in the silence I heard a muttered expletive, followed by the sound of receding footsteps. I looked enquiringly at Jacqui.

'Must have delivered another scene,' she whispered.

Carlos came down the steps at a virtual run, right hand fiddling feverishly with the leather thong about his neck. Instantly Zeynep was at his elbow, steering him towards the table.

'God doesn't know how lucky He was,' said Father Ricardo quietly. 'Only the world to create. If it had been a film . . .'

Carlos, who had allowed Zeynep to put a plate of food in his hands, crossed the terrace towards us, eating as he came.

'That boy,' he spat between mouthfuls, 'is an imbecile.

One script they have accepted, and because it's Spielberg, they think they're Shakespeare.' He challenged me with a look. 'Who knows how to write? English! The language of Shakespeare and Milton. Oscar Wilde. George Bernard Shaw. Where are the giants of today?'

I felt myself starting to blush.

'The trouble with you English,' he continued unabated, as if I were responsible, 'is that you don't know how to preserve your heritage. You're too fucking liberal. You think it doesn't matter if you don't do your best. You think it will all come right in the wash.'

He was interrupted by Zeynep, scurrying up with a portable phone. Carlos put his plate on the parapet, and snatching the phone from Zeynep, took it in the direction of the kitchen, gabbling in Spanish as he went.

Jed was sitting bolt upright in his chair, staring sleepily into the middle distance. I stood up and took his hand. 'You look fit to drop,' I said firmly. 'Come on. Say goodnight, and you can show me your room. I haven't seen it, remember.'

'Right,' I said a moment later, as we were mounting the stairs. 'You'll have to show me the way.'

On the terrace above I caught sight of a figure in the shadows at the far end, a thin squiggle of a figure that looked as if it had been pencilled in against the sky at the last moment. The scriptwriter, I guessed, dreaming up lines to say in his defence.

Jed pulled me into the white living room and up the stairs into a wide hallway from which opened a number of rooms.

'That's Carlos's,' he said, pointing, 'and Mummy's.' He opened the door next to hers. 'And this is mine.'

It was a cool, airy room, painted a subtle shade of blue and boasting, as he'd indicated earlier, a massive bed festooned by swathes of net.

'Well, well,' I said, 'very MGM.'

'What's MGM?'

'A film studio. You know, the one with the lion.'

'There's a bathroom, too,' he said, taking me by the hand.

I duly admired the fittings, the bidet, the shower, the mirrors that hinged above the basin, then made him brush his teeth and get into his pyjamas. Once he was safely in bed, I started an impromptu story about my father's house and a dragon that lived in the attic. I hadn't got further, though, than describing the dragon when I saw his eyelids droop. I continued until they'd closed, then turned out the light and tiptoed from the room.

Downstairs, I came across the figure from the balcony helping himself to a slug of Scotch from the drinks cabinet under the mirror. In the light, the impression I'd had earlier of scribbled intensity was heightened. He was very tall and very thin, the face cadaverous despite its youth, the eyes sunk into their sockets, the whole body stooped over itself, like a vulture.

He glanced up as I came through the door.

'Fucking Spaniards!' he spat. 'Conquistadors and peasants, the whole fucking lot of them!'

And then he was gone, out onto the terrace to nurse his whisky and his battered ego. I beat a complementary retreat to my room.

Like a character in one of the Enid Blyton stories which, in defiance of political correctness, I sometimes read Jed, I fell asleep as soon as my head hit the pillow, drifting into a muddled dream in which my face, coming to meet me from the bathroom mirror before which I stood, became that of the eager, smiling Zeynep, the mountainous costume designer, the tortured scriptwriter, omnipotent Father Ricardo, then two points of a triangle

I'd sought to obliterate from my consciousness, Patsy and Dirk. I came half awake. A piano was playing somewhere, and I recognised the music of high mountains and empty plains.

'The mountains, though,' said my father. 'The mountains are different. You would have liked the mountains.'

Eight

*T*he fortnight that followed is best presented in the language of film, as a montage.

Thus, Jed careering round the upper terrace after the ball which Father Ricardo and I are throwing to each other whilst Carl provides the soundtrack: allegro vivace.

Or a hesitant Jed being taught by Quiepo to dive from the rock whilst I hover on the steps worrying for his safety, and Father Ricardo, from the comfort of a deckchair, looking up from his book to encompass all three of us. The music here being that of the sea, as soft as it is sibilant.

Jacqui approaching me along the avenue of vines, gift-wrapped in a brilliant sarong and humming to Al, who nods a hello as they pass.

Myself, reading on the top terrace, whilst at the gate Zeynep oversees the departure of the scriptwriter, his thin, curved body making me think him a curl of smoke from a snuffed candle, evaporating into our past and his future.

Jacqui and I strolling into town, shadow from the mountain snaking behind us, and on the soundtrack the two-tone blast of a busful of tourists as it hoots its way along the corniche.

Or Carlos and Jed at the far end of the lower terrace, pacing up and down, Carlos gesticulating vividly, Jed nodding wisely; pupil and teacher, but of another school to the one run by the priest and his acolyte.

All played out against the rhythms of life at the villa. The sun rising orange from the sea and setting purple behind the mountains. The sea itself, calm one day, frothy the next, now blue, now grey. The gathering heat and the gathering people, flocking to the villa in preparation for the journey south.

Or that, at any rate, is one interpretation of the images. There are others.

The way in which, whilst Father Ricardo and I play piggy in the middle with Jed, Jacqui walks by on her way to the rocks, and the look on her face as she watches the ball pass over her son's head, from Father Ricardo to myself.

Or how, as Quiepo teaches Jed to dive from the rock, I watch not only Jed, but the play of Quiepo's muscles, and how aware I am that Father Ricardo's eyes are as much on me as they are on Quiepo and Jed.

Me under the vines, looking back at Jacqui and Al to note the way he touches her shoulder as he ushers her up the steps.

Zeynep, having shut the gate on the scriptwriter, closing her eyes and taking a deep, determined breath before turning back to the villa to answer the call of the bell.

Jacqui and I on the road into town, having to jump aside as the approaching bus, horn tooting, erupts round the corner, and how she pulls away from the hand I place on her waist.

The replacement scriptwriter, a belligerent Yorkshireman with a pencil behind his ear, more carpenter than writer, watching with dour satisfaction as Carlos and Jed pace the lower terrace, practising his words.

All culminating, two weeks later, in the day of the festival.

Father Ricardo and I had managed, from the chaos surrounding us, to carve out a pretty unwavering routine.
Either separately or together, depending on what we were
teaching, we would give Jed his morning lessons in the
deserted kitchen of the top villa. There, at the vast oak table
strewn with books, we would take our pupil through his
paces whilst next door Carl worked on his score. Until such
time – usually around midday – that he was called by Carlos.

On the day of the festival, Father Ricardo was working
alone with Jed, I was reading on the terrace. There was a
breeze coming off the sea, a would-be thief of a breeze
which riffled the pages of my book and snatched at Carl's
melody.

I hadn't been reading long when Father Ricardo
emerged from the kitchen.

'Strange,' he said, settling on the stone seat that skirted
the edge of the terrace. 'He finds division easier than mul-
tiplication. It's usually the other way around, with children.'

I folded down the corner of the page and shut my book.

'He's desperate to know how things work,' continued the
priest. 'What lies behind them. The influence of your
father?'

'My father?'

'They get on well, I think.'

I nodded. 'Well, yes, they do. Not that they see each
other very often.'

'Jed listens, though, and it sounds to me like your father
is very definite, no? In his ideas.'

I smiled ruefully. 'You can say that again.'

'A moral man.'

'A believer in prescriptions, certainly.'

I was remembering what he had said in the course of our
final phone call: 'Prescriptions I leave to the priests.'

Father Ricardo leant forward and picked up a leaf from the terrace.

'Marx,' he said thoughtfully, 'had good reason to be frightened of religion.'

'I thought Marx disregarded religion?'

'To call religion an opiate is not to disregard it. To misunderstand it, maybe, but not to underestimate it.'

'Are you trying to tell me that thanks to my father, Jed's a communist?'

Father Ricardo was folding the leaf into ever smaller segments. 'I'm simply observing that your father has very set ideas about how things work, and that Jed has ears.'

'He's never spoken to me about this.'

The priest smiled. 'Ah, but he's your father. Perhaps Jed doesn't feel the need. Or else . . .'

He left the sentence hanging.

'Or else what?'

'The father,' he said, 'is seldom easy to approach. In the Church we need Christ. We need the son. Otherwise . . .' He'd folded the leaf into a tiny square, and now he unfolded it, and, dropping it over the edge of the terrace, watched as it fluttered onto the roof of the Casa Nueva. 'What about you?' he asked. 'What do you believe?'

I took an age to answer, and when I did, despised myself for the inadequacy of my response. 'To be honest, I don't know.'

To my surprise, Father Ricardo nodded encouragingly. 'That's good.'

'It is?'

'Belief can be a barrier. To have faith . . .' He paused. 'To have faith you need to start from nothing. *Nada.*'

'But if I choose a false god?'

He smiled. 'Ah, yes. Of course. And such a tempting array!'

Out of the corner of my eye, I became aware of movement. Jed was hovering in the kitchen doorway, exercise book in hand.

'Finished?' asked Father Ricardo.

Jed stepped onto the terrace.

'I can't do the last one.'

'Bring here.'

Father Ricardo took the book from Jed, studied it a moment, then proceeded to explain the problem in a couple of crisp, clear sentences.

'Right!' Father Ricardo rose to his feet. 'I'm off to the town. Over to you, Peter.'

'What about this afternoon?' asked Jed.

Father Ricardo ruffled his hair. 'Don't worry. I've not forgotten.'

He nodded a farewell, then swept off, his black outline etching itself sharply against the sun-bleached white of the terrace: ovoid negative to the villa's positive.

'This afternoon?' I queried lightly.

'The Festival of San Jorge,' said Jed solemnly.

'San Jorge?'

'Saint George. You know. And the dragon.'

'Saint George and the dragon?'

Delighted to know something an adult didn't, Jed nodded smugly. 'He's the patron saint of the town. Every year they have a festival. Someone dresses up as Saint George, he fights a dragon, then they burn the dragon and there are fireworks.'

'But Saint George is English!'

Jed became suddenly defensive: 'I'm only telling you what Father Ricardo told me.'

'Well, well,' I said. 'Who would have guessed!'

'Father Ricardo's promised to take me to the church this afternoon to watch them painting the dragon. He showed me a picture from last year. He's really huge. They make

him out of cardboard and paper. Then Father Ricardo
blesses him.'

'Tell me,' I said cautiously, 'when you and Father
Ricardo aren't doing sums, what do you talk about?'

'Lots of things.'

'Like?'

'Just things.' Jed scuffed at the terrace with his foot.

'God, for instance,' I persisted. 'Do you ever talk about
God?'

'Sometimes.'

'And you tell him what Edward says?'

'Edward doesn't like God,' said Jed. 'He thinks priests are
a menace.'

'And you? What do you think?'

We were interrupted by Zeynep.

'Jed!' She was crossing the terrace towards us in what I
thought of as her deckchair dress — a cotton shift in contrasting stripes of red and green. Over her shoulder was a
basket. 'Carlos wants you. He's in the studio.'

Clearly relieved to be thus released from history, not to
mention interrogation, Jed thrust his exercise book into
my hand and darted off. The little grey bird let out its
statutory whistle.

'A saint, that boy,' said Zeynep as his gangly frame disappeared from view.

'Indeed,' I said tartly. 'Or on the way to becoming one.'

She looked at me enquiringly.

'He and Father Ricardo have started a religious debate.'

She perched herself on the stone seat. 'And you don't
approve?'

'Did I say that?'

'You don't look as if you approve.'

'I'm just surprised, that's all.'

'And a little jealous, maybe?'

I was forced to concede a smile. 'All right. And a little jealous.'

She returned the smile. 'I've known Father Ricardo for many years. He's a good man. You can trust him.'

'Maybe,' I said, 'I'm more like my father than I know.' I parroted Jed. 'He thinks priests are a menace.'

Zeynep began to twist one of her rings round her finger.

'So delicate,' she said. 'Human relationships. Our need to be loved. When I was your age . . .' She paused. 'What is, is,' she said eventually. 'That's all.' She stood up. 'Now! Will you come to lunch?'

'Lunch?'

She gestured impulsively across the bay, and I saw that at some point in the morning, a familiar yacht had moored offshore.

'You don't have to worry about Jed,' she continued brightly. 'He's with Carlos, and this afternoon' – she grinned teasingly – 'your rival is taking him to see the dragon. I know because he told me. André and Pablo, they really like you.' Again the teasing grin. 'André says you see eye to eye on Carlos.'

I was about to remonstrate when she laid a quick hand on my arm. 'Just the four of us. No priests.'

'Well,' I said, 'in that case. Thank you. Yes.'

She clapped her hands delightedly.

'So get a swimming costume. In case we swim.'

'Tell me,' I said as we started down the stairs. 'This thing in town? This festival?'

'You didn't know?' She looked surprised. 'It's the Feast of San Jorge. They celebrate it all over Spain. Here, because San Jorge is their patron saint, they have a battle. Just pretend, you understand. Between the Moors and the Christians.'

We passed the kitchen and started along the avenue of flowers.

'And the dragon?'

'After the battle San Jorge must fight the dragon. Then there are fireworks. They always ask Carlos to light the first firework. If he's here, of course.'

We passed the jacuzzi.

'Afterwards we have a dinner. At the bar on the beach.'

We reached the rocks. Materialising through the glare on the water was the shape of the motor launch, and at its helm, the figure of the boatman.

'Enrique,' she explained. 'He's been with Pablo and André since he was a boy. Most faithful.'

The launch nosed up to the rock. Zeynep exchanged a volley of Spanish with the boatman, an urchin of a man in, I guessed, his early thirties. He was dressed in a pair of cut-off jeans as bleached by sun as his torso had been darkened. I took her basket and helped her into the boat, then handed the basket to Enrique, who extended a calloused hand to help me on board myself. He waited until we'd settled ourselves, then threw the engine into gear and cut away from the rock in a sharp curve, banking up water in our wake.

'Nice, no?' Zeynep shouted above the noise of the engine. 'To be at sea?'

I thought I might have to explain the involuntary smile her choice of words engendered, but she continued blithely: 'In Istanbul we had a house on the Bosphorus. I grew up with the sea. I need the sea. When we're in Madrid, in the villa there, I get very nervous.'

As if jealous of the power of speech, the wind tore the words out of her mouth, scattering them across the water. Zeynep lapsed into silence, and the wind turned its attention to our hair and clothes. We came alongside the yacht. A set of steps dangled from the side. Enrique cut the engine, and with it, the wind. Scaling the steps like a monkey, he lowered a hand to help Zeynep aboard. I followed more slowly with the basket.

André was on deck to greet us.

'Darlings! What heaven!'

He was dressed in another of his caftans, garish with sunflowers, that did little to mask his Falstaffian stomach. He kissed Zeynep extravagantly, then turned to me.

'And what's this?' he asked slyly. 'Not for me, is it? You really shouldn't. You know I'm trying to cut down.'

Zeynep laughed. 'Peter was all on his own.' Confirming me in my suspicion that the decision to invite me had been taken on the spur of the moment. 'So of course I ask him.'

'Heaven!' he said again, enfolding me in an ample embrace.

We were parted by the arrival of the poodle, who flung herself in a frenzy at my crotch.

'Down, Nunu!' commanded André. 'Down girl!' And when she wouldn't: 'That dog is anyone's.' He slipped an arm through mine. 'We're on the foredeck.'

He ushered us along the side of the cabin to the fore-deck, where white wicker chairs and a wrought-iron table had been set under a canvas awning. Enrique was at the table, pouring champagne, which he presented on a silver tray.

'Welcome to *Our Lady of the Flowers*!' said André, raising his glass.

Zeynep threw herself into one of the chairs.

'Where's Pablo?' she asked.

André became somewhat conspiratorial. 'Mercedes is here.'

Zeynep raised an eyebrow. 'They're going through his wardrobe?'

André shrugged. 'What else?'

Zeynep darted me a speculative look. 'I see.'

'Now, if you'll excuse me a moment.' André deposited his glass on the table. 'I was just finishing the salad. Help yourselves to more champagne.'

He waddled off down the boat.

'Mercedes?' I queried lightly.

Zeynep took a sip of her champagne. 'The costume designer. You know.' She allowed herself a smile. 'The one with untidy hair.'

'Of course. I'm sorry. So many new people. I can't remember all the names.'

She put down her glass, and, like André earlier, became suddenly conspiratorial. 'The thing is,' she said, 'Pablo likes to dress up.'

'Dress up?'

'In women's clothes.' She scanned my face keenly. 'Does that shock you?'

It certainly took me aback. Made me uneasy, too. A man in woman's clothing. The feel of satin, and of tweed, and of lace. Memories I struggled to suppress. Though all I said was, and lightly: 'Of course not. Should it?'

She shrugged. 'He has the most fantastic wardrobe. Dior, Balmain, Valentino. Mercedes loves it. It will be a fashion show.'

Whereupon, as if on cue, Enrique appeared with a large black ghetto-blaster, which he placed on the table. He pressed a switch. We were treated to the opening bars of 'New York, New York'. Zeynep laid a hand on my arm.

'The show begins.'

Round the corner of the cabin, tottering on a pair of perilously high heels and swaying with exaggerated elegance, came Pablo in a floor-length, sequinned dress of shimmering green. He had a feather boa round his neck, a little green handbag dangling from his arm, and from his ears, a pair of extravagant earrings. A pace or two behind him, clapping her hands in time to the music, came the mountainous figure of Mercedes, haphazardly attired in one of her candlewick smocks. Pablo reached the table, where he executed a rather unsteady pirouette to show off the line of his outfit. Then, grinning broadly, he advanced on Zeynep, who had risen to her feet.

'Darling!'

They kissed and she ran an admiring hand over his sequinned chest.

'Pablo, it's beautiful!'

'And you've brought a guest. How marvellous!' Gathering up the hem of his dress, he dropped me a curtsy.

Despite myself, I began to colour. 'It's very good of you to include me.'

He made another pirouette. 'Do you like? I wanted the Balmain, but Mercedes insisted on this. To start with, anyway.'

Mercedes, who had been greeting Zeynep, now favoured me with an apologetic nod of the head.

'Okay,' she said. 'Balmain next.'

And shooing Pablo before her, she steered him back the way he'd come.

'Quite an ensemble!' grinned Zeynep.

At a total loss for words, I merely nodded and took another sip of my champagne. Already it was going to my head. Or was that memory? I sank into a seat alongside Zeynep's.

'That's right,' she said. 'Relax. Enjoy.'

The music had changed to something bluesy – it was a compilation tape no doubt put together for the purpose of the show – and, slinking round the corner in a sheer black number slashed to an incongruously hairy thigh, Pablo now made a bee-line for my knee, settled himself on my lap and began to tickle my face with his feather boa.

'Darling!' he whispered, batting his eyelids. 'Can we have the next dance?'

'Leave the boy alone!' André had appeared, and, yanking Pablo to his feet, swept him into an impromptu tango. 'You're a married woman, remember.'

Enrique was at my elbow, replenishing my glass.

'*Salud*!' laughed Zeynep, raising her glass to mine.

Mercedes clapped her hands, bellowed something in Spanish, then led Pablo away for the next costume change.

'Such a child, that one,' sighed André. 'Do you think he'll ever grow up?'

'My dear,' giggled Zeynep. 'I sincerely hope not.'

The memories were beginning to crowd in on me: satin, tweed and lace. I took another gulp of champagne. It's just a game, I told myself. André is right. For all the hair on his body, for all the knowingness of his coquettish tricks, Pablo is simply a little boy dressing up in Mother's clothes.

'Now! For the finale I need a lady in waiting!' Pablo grabbed me by the hand.

'Pablo, no!' That last thought of mine had opened the floodgates.

'I insist!' He gestured dismissively at André. 'That one would split the frock.'

'Get you, dear!' murmured André.

'I cannot do the finale without a lady in waiting.'

I was yanked to my feet.

'Your colouring is perfect. You'll see. Just trust me.'

I found myself being dragged along a narrow corridor and into a spacious bedroom in the bow of the yacht, against the far wall of which, doors open, stood a built-in cupboard brimming with dresses.

Throwing aside his shoes, Pablo lifted a voluminous bridal gown off the bed and caressed its creamy surface. 'I shall wear this. And you, my dear Peter, you will wear this.'

Crossing briskly to the cupboard, he rummaged through the dresses and extracted a vivid red affair, the skirt of which, cut short in front, lengthened at the back into a flounced train. 'And this, of course.' With his other hand he felt along the shelf above the dresses and produced a lace mantilla.

'Now all we need are the shoes!'

'Peter, angel, you look divine.' By rights, the voice should have belonged to Patsy, but it was Dirk who spoke. 'I could really go for you. You know that?'

I plucked at the sheer white satin, as if to remove it.

'Don't fight it,' smiled Dirk. 'Surely, if we've taught you anything, we've taught you that?'

Then I was in the attic in Winterbourne Road, disinterring a suitcase of women's clothes. My mother's? Aged seven, I didn't register the difference between the severity of the winter suits and the lace mantilla wrapped in its shroud of tissue paper.

I lifted the mantilla into the air. A beam of light from the attic window spotlighted the lace, echoing its filigree with a stitching of motes that danced in the afternoon sun. I struggled out of my clothes, and, as I did so, became aware of an unfamiliar sensation in my groin. Looking down, I saw that my tiny member was protruding like a flagpole from the alabaster architecture of my legs and belly. I put on the jacket first, then the skirt, then the mantilla. The suit irked my skin, making me want to scratch, but the mantilla was softer than a kiss. Excited, I ventured out of the attic to inspect myself in the bathroom mirror, only to find my way blocked.

Standing now in the opulence of Pablo and André's bedroom, I could still see the look on my father's face: first disbelief, then horror, finally anger as, with a bull-like roar, he snatched the mantilla from my head and ordered me back up the attic stairs to fetch my clothes.

Out of the corner of my eye, I became aware of Pablo
taking a worried step towards me. Raising both hands to
fend him off, I shook my head violently, and turning tail,
fled the room. Halfway down the corridor, I spied a door,
and, bursting through it, found myself in a tiny, wood-
panelled toilet. Locking the door behind me, I collapsed
onto the toilet seat, and, burying my head in my hands,
gave myself over to the hot, unstoppable tears that had
begun to flood my cheeks.

I don't know how long I sat there, but my tears had run
their course, my shoulders ceased to heave, when I heard a
tentative knock on the door.

'Peter?' The voice was Zeynep's.

Getting to my feet, I splashed cold water onto my face,
ran a hand through my hair, then cautiously opened the
door.

'Peter! Are you all right?' She sounded breathless, as if
she'd been ransacking the yacht in search of me.

I nodded mutely.

'What is it?'

'I'm sorry. It's impossible to explain.'

Her eyes demanded that I try.

But how could I? How to explain with any coherence
that to spite my father I'd gone to live in a commune of
hippies, sad relics of the sixties. How Patsy and Dirk had
taken me under their wing. The production we'd mounted
of *Private Lives*. Why, for instance, *Private Lives*? Why not
Hair? Even at the time it had been puzzling. And the party
afterwards, at which Dirk had decreed the men should dress
in the women's costumes, and vice versa. 'Let's push back
the boundaries.' How Patsy had found me on the lawn, and
afterwards in my room. To be followed by her husband.
The feel of Dirk's forearm as it encompassed my neck, the
dusting of hair at the base of his spine. The pain of being

entered. The revulsion. The excitement. The discovery that during it all, Patsy had left the room. The memory of my mother's clothes, my father's face, that sensation in my groin, and the fact that when I'd gone back to the attic a few days later, the suitcase had vanished.

I cleared my throat.

'I think I told you,' I heard myself saying, 'about my mother. When I was seven, I found some of her clothes in a suitcase in the attic. I put them on. My father was very angry. That's all.'

She didn't reply immediately. Instead, turning towards the porthole on her left, she stared through it at the sun-sparkled sea.

'I lost a parent too,' she murmured eventually. 'Both parents, in fact. And a lover. You know Turkish history?'

I shook my head to indicate how little; then, realising that because she had her back to me, I'd have to say something, reeled off a short list. 'The Armenian massacre. Ataturk. *Midnight Express.*'

She let out a laugh. 'The usual clichés.' She ran a finger down the side of the porthole. 'The history of some countries is – I don't know – too strong. They imprison their people. Turkey is such a country. Also Spain. Only in England, I think, can you escape your history.'

It was my turn to laugh. 'Try telling that to my father.'

She raised a reproving hand. 'England is not like Turkey.'

I stood corrected. There was a pause, which I broke by asking softly: 'So what happened? To your parents?'

'It was in the fifties. I had just left school. There was a – how do you say – a reaction among certain Muslims to the reforms of Ataturk. These young Muslims, they didn't want Turkey to be like the West. They wanted Islam. They wanted purity. They were idealists. My father was in the government. He was old then, but in his youth, he'd fought with Ataturk. He was very worried by these Muslims. Their idealism frightened him.' She ran a hand through her hair. 'I loved my father very much. He was everything to me. A pillar of strength. I didn't like to see the fear in him. It made me doubt his power, and therefore my own security.' She twitched her shoulders in an ironic shrug. 'So I started to attend the Muslim meetings. I didn't like the fanaticism, but the idealism, the certainty, that was – how do you say? – very enticing. Better than my father's fear.' She paused. 'Then I met Raschid. Suddenly it wasn't politics at all. I was in love. We were going to marry. Have children. Make a life.'

She turned to face me.

'Okay, so he was young, he was stupid, but his heart was good. All he wanted was for the world to be pure. But the world isn't pure. And Raschid was impatient.' Her eyes, usually so piercing, filmed over with tears. 'There was a silly plan to blow up a statue of Ataturk. As a symbol of how Turkey had lost her way. Raschid volunteered to write a document explaining why the statue had to be destroyed. He asked a printer he thought he could trust how much it would cost to print the document. The printer told the authorities. They raided Raschid's house, and when he tried to escape, they shot him.'

'No!'

She shrugged. 'I said: Turkey is not England. Things happen differently.' She produced a small square of lace from her pocket and used it to blow her nose.

'And then?' Her account of herself had quite overshadowed my own concerns.

'Then they found my letters. In Raschid's room. They told my father. He wasn't, I discovered, a weak man at all. There were some things which, as a liberal, he couldn't allow. He threw me out of the house. He forbade my mother to speak to me. So I got on a boat. I came to Spain. I found a job in the Opera House. I met Carlos. The rest . . .' She gave another ironic shrug. 'The rest is history.'

'I'm so sorry,' I whispered. 'I had no idea.'

She laughed. 'My dear, how could you? Carlos is the only person who knows. Pablo and André, even they don't know. No one knows. But Carlos I can talk to. Carlos listens. We all need people who will listen to our stories.' She tucked her square of lace back into her pocket. 'But come! The others will be wondering where we are.'

We were back in the present, up against the fact of my strange behaviour. I felt the onset of panic.

'What will I tell them?'

She took my arm. 'Nothing. You don't say a thing. Nor will they ask. These are civilised people.'

Together we began to mount the steps to the deck.

'Thank you,' I said. 'For being so understanding.'

'My dear!' She was her usual, teasing self. 'What is there to understand? You think you're peculiar? What about Pablo?'

Nine

Zeynep had been right. They were indeed civilised people. At lunch no reference was made to my bizarre behaviour, and when we took our leave, genuine delight was expressed at the fact we'd meet again that evening at the festival. The only hint I was given that perhaps I could have conducted myself differently was when André squeezed my arm in farewell. 'Maybe,' he said, 'tonight you will do some of the talking and stop being such a delicious enigma.'

Which only increased my determination to talk as little as possible. In my present state, talking could be dangerous. Safety lay in silence, and it was silence I was intent on keeping when – after an afternoon spent squirrelled in my room – I ventured downstairs to find the Madame Defarge-like figure of Quiepo's mother alone on the terrace of the Casa Nueva, backlit by a sky turned flagrant pink by the setting sun and ravelling time into an ever-burgeoning complication of blood-red wool.

'*Muy bonito!*' The old lady came to the end of a row, and, with her knitting needle, stabbed at the horizon.

'*Si, si,*' I said lamely.

'*Lo mejor del día.*'

'*Si, si*,' I repeated, whereupon she broke into a positive torrent of Spanish. I was rescued by the appearance of Carlos, uncharacteristically attired in slacks and a blazer. Without drawing breath, Quiepo's mother transferred her vocal attentions to him, and, getting to her feet, stretched her jumble of wool against his back. Seemingly satisfied, she returned to her knitting whilst Carlos came to throw himself into the chair next to mine.

'For you?' I ventured. 'The jumper?'

He rolled his eyes. 'Every year she does this. I have an entire cupboard full. The sooner Quiepo provides a grandson, the better. Where's Jed?'

'With Father Ricardo. Being shown the dragon.'

'You will like,' said Carlos. 'The festival. It's very dramatic. Better, of course, if I had staged it. But even so. For a little town.'

'I always thought,' I said carefully, 'that Saint George was English. I didn't realise . . .'

I knew I was providing the perfect opening for another of his shots at the English, but to my surprise, he didn't rise to the bait. Instead, he favoured me with a different facet of his personality: that of teacher.

'San Jorge is celebrated all over Spain. And in the East. He's very important on the continent, San Jorge. You know who he was? A Christian martyr. Third or fourth century. And, as you say, patron saint of England. Also, I think, of soldiers and boy scouts. Martyred at Diospolis in Palestine. Or what was then Diospolis. Now Lydda.'

As if it were a rosary by means of which he could run a checklist of his answer, Carlos felt for the leather thong about his neck and began to roll it between thumb and forefinger.

'And the dragon?'

'That's a myth, of course. Started in the Middle Ages.

San Jorge is supposed to have rescued a maiden from the
dragon at Silene in Libya. It led to the baptism of thou-
sands. Different people interpret the story in different ways.
Some say the dragon represents evil. The Devil, if you like.
Or the triumph of Christianity over paganism. Others see
it as purely secular. Chivalry. A very mediaeval concept.'

As he spoke, I became aware of a movement at the far
end of the terrace, and, looking past his head, saw the figure of Quiepo materialise from the gloom. He was wearing
a pair of soft, white cotton slacks surmounted by a billow-
ing shirt, also white, within which halo of clothing the
dark chrysalis of his body was clearly, almost shockingly
etched. Indeed, given the darkness surrounding him, and
the darkness within, his clothes seemed like the most ten-
uous of afterthoughts; a filmy casing which, if removed,
would return Quiepo to the element through which he
was approaching.

Following the direction of my gaze, Carlos leant forward and tapped the arm of my chair.

'Others, of course,' he said mischievously, 'see the story
in sexual terms. The dragon as lust, which – ironically –
you kill by the insertion of a sword in the mouth.'

'*Buenas tardes.*' Quiepo had reached our chairs. Resting a
hand on Carlos's shoulder, he honoured me with a funny
little bow, oddly old-fashioned and formal, then consulted
his watch. 'What time the boat?'

'Eight-thirty.' Carlos levered himself upright. 'Did you
speak to Larry?'

Quiepo nodded.

'And?'

Quiepo nodded again, but warningly this time, and in
my direction. 'I tell you later.'

Quiepo's mother was calling softly to her son. He turned
to answer her.

'We meet at the rocks in half an hour,' said Carlos. 'The boat will take us into town.'

He moved towards the living room, pausing as he went to exchange a few words with Quiepo's mother. The old woman lifted the mountain of wool from her lap and gestured to Quiepo that he should drape it across Carlos's shoulders. Quiepo, however, chose to fling the shapeless garment over his own shoulders, and tossing back his head, paraded before them like a model on a catwalk, swaying his hips as he went. Carlos laughed; Quiepo's mother shook her head indulgently. For the briefest of moments, they made an unlikely but almost familial group, the director, the old woman and the old woman's son.

I slipped away to the terrace below. The sky had lost its hectic flush and darkened to a sombre purple. Leaning against the parapet, I stared across the bay at the bobbing lights of the fishing boats as they ventured into the darkness for another night's toil. With, at their centre, the vulgar, glittering jewel of Pablo and André's yacht.

I heard the bell, followed by the click of heels along the terrace above. Zeynep, I guessed, and no doubt the others, starting for the boat. I waited for them to get well ahead of me, then began my own, more lonely progress along the avenue of flowers, past the deserted jacuzzi, and down the steps to the looming outline of the rocks.

The boat was already there, and Quiepo was in the process of helping his mother aboard. Proud as a figurehead, Carlos stood in the prow, at his side an elegant Zeynep, neatly encased in a frock of midnight blue, silver evening bag tucked under her arm. The only other person in the boat, apart from the helmsman, was mountainous Mercedes, her swirling dress a battleground of colour. No sign of Jacqui and Al; nor indeed, of Jed and Father Ricardo.

'Come on, Peter!' Having helped his mother aboard, Quiepo now extended an impatient hand to me. Running forward so as to avoid making physical contact, I leapfrogged over the gunwale, landing slightly to the left of Zeynep.

'My dear!' She welcomed me with a dazzling smile. 'You almost missed us.'

'Where are the others?'

'They walked in earlier.'

'Even Jacqui?'

She felt in her bag for a cigarette.

'I thought you knew? She's with Al, in Barcelona.'

'And Jed?'

'Still in town with Father Ricardo.'

'Heavens!' said Carlos. 'What an inquisition.'

The helmsman had pushed us off from the rocks, and now he opened the throttle. The boat surged forward, rounding the headland in a dramatic sweep and heading for the distant lights of the town.

'I should have brought a jacket,' shivered Zeynep. 'It'll be cold coming back.'

I held out my jumper. 'You can use this.'

She shook her head. 'Later, perhaps.'

We had started to weave between the fishing boats and yachts moored inshore, and the helmsman was throttling back so we could glide the final distance to the jetty that jutted like a single, blackened finger from the yellow palm of the beach. The boatman leapt out and made us fast. Quiepo jumped with him, and the two of them began to hand us from the boat.

'*Venga!*' commanded Carlos, striding up the beach towards the esplanade and the trellised fairy lights of the nearest bar, where a delegation of suited gentlemen had gathered at the edge of the sand to greet us.

'The mayor,' grimaced Zeynep, 'and the town council. Now we have drinks with them.'

I hung back as kisses and handshakes were exchanged. We moved towards a large table outside the bar. I found myself a seat at the very end of the table, slightly away from the others. Almost immediately a waiter was at my elbow, demanding to know what I wanted to drink. I placed my order, then settled back to watch.

The bar was packed to overflowing, as indeed were all the bars along the beach, not to mention the esplanade itself. Brightly dressed children ran excited circles round their more leisurely parents, who were either strolling in groups, or else – like us – gathered boisterously at the waterfront bars. An air of expectation hung over everything; the sense that a drama was about to unfold.

Our group had finished their drinks and were getting to their feet.

'Time for the battle.' Zeynep detached herself from the others and took my arm.

'The battle?'

'The Moors versus the Christians. Remember?' She laughed softly. 'Me against you.'

I shook my head. 'Our forebears. You and I, we don't have any quarrels, do we?'

'My dear! What about the war of the sexes?'

'Ah,' I replied, patting her arm, 'but in that battle you have vanquished me utterly.'

We followed the delegation of suits through the jostling crowd, our progress made snail-like by virtue of the fact that every few yards someone would greet either Carlos or the mayor, both of whom would repay the compliment by stopping to exchange a few words. Never having followed a celebrity before, I found the attention we attracted almost alarming, certainly intrusive. What, for example, was being made of me? Did I, in the curious, questing eyes of the crowd, measure up to my companions?

'Where are Father Ricardo and Jed?' I asked. 'How will they find us?'

'In the square,' said Zeynep. 'We'll find them there.'

'And the others? André and Pablo?'

'The same.'

When we reached the square, however, having negoti- ated the labyrinth of narrow streets overhung by balconies bursting with people, washing and splashes of geranium, we didn't meet a soul. The square had been cordoned off, and a member of the Guardia Civil had to lift the rope that kept back the crowd to allow us to cross its empty expanse towards the Town Hall opposite. At the ropes on the other side, we were ushered by another official through the mass of people on the Town Hall steps and into the building itself. We crossed an echoing marble hall and mounted a sweeping staircase to a salon on the first floor in which, on a table against the far wall, stood an array of drinks. I lost Zeynep to Carlos, who, in the manner of a husband, put her on his arm and stepped onto the balcony. The rest of us followed suit, forming a loose, protective semi-circle around the matrimonial tableau provided by the com- manding Catholic and the one-time Muslim.

With a theatrical flourish, the mayor produced a red silk handkerchief from his pocket, which he handed to Carlos. Carlos stepped to the edge of the balcony and held the handkerchief aloft. An expectant hush fell on the crowd pressing into the floodlit square below, and showman that he was, Carlos held the moment for as long as possible before bringing the handkerchief down in a vivid slash. There was a fanfare, and from opposite ends of the square, two contingents of horsemen galloped into the open space. The horses of those on the left were a dazzling white, their riders gowned in the flowing robes of the desert Arab. The Christians, by contrast, muted and motley bunch that they were, had been given horses that were brown, and were garbed in an assortment of mud-coloured clothes ranging in style from the mediaeval to the seventeenth century. I heard a snort to my left. Mercedes was muttering under her breath to Quiepo's mother. Obviously she thought she should have done the costumes.

And I could see her point. The square below had become stage to a rather haphazard amateur theatrical. Whilst the men on horseback struggled to control their restless steeds, a second fanfare sounded, and from each side of the square an even more amateurish array of Moors and Christians – decidedly pedestrian – ran forward to lock each other in clumsily choreographed combat.

There was a third fanfare, and though neither side seemed to have gained any ascendance, the foot soldiers fell back and the horsemen left the square. The figure of a knight in shining armour, lance at the ready, cantered into the arena. A huge shout went up, which the knight acknowledged by raising an arm. On the balcony, as if under some spell cast by his lance, we all stepped forward. The crowd fell silent.

San Jorge reigned in his horse, lifted his visor, and bellowed his challenge to the dragon. In answer, a group of men dressed entirely in black trundled on a massive creature of papier mâché meticulously overlaid with scales, each painted a virulent green. From its gaping mouth there issued an unsteady cardboard flame.

There was a final fanfare. San Jorge dropped his visor, positioned his lance, and, with a blood-curdling yell, dug his heels into the flank of his horse and charged the dragon. The lance pierced the dragon's mouth, severing the flame, and a cry went up from the crowd. San Jorge withdrew his lance, returned his horse to the other side of the square, and began a second charge. This time he caught the dragon on its side, ripping through its scales and causing the creature to rock on its wheels. Another cry went up. San Jorge trotted towards the balcony, and, raising his lance, saluted Carlos and the mayor. Then, turning to face the dragon, he made another dash at it, going in under the wheels with his lance and bringing it up as he did so, so that with an almighty crash, the dragon keeled over. The crowd went wild. Lance erect, San Jorge made a triumphal circuit of the square before galloping off.

Carlos raised his handkerchief. The crowd fell silent. One of the men in black ran forward to crouch by the splintered dragon. The handkerchief came down, and as it did so, the man struck a match. It took a moment or two for the flames to take hold, but once they had, the dragon became an instant bonfire. The crowd gave voice to a final cry.

It was then, as the flames took hold, that I saw Jed. He was standing with Father Ricardo on the opposite side of the square, jigging on his feet. As the dragon flared, his jig flowered into a dance.

Carlos was once again brandishing the handkerchief, causing the velvet casket of the sky to swing open and shower us with multi-coloured jewels that exploded to earth in swooning trajectories of silver, red and gold. More vivid, though, than any firework, was the look on Jed's face as he feasted his eyes on the burning of the dragon. That and the way Father Ricardo's hand had come to rest so naturally on his shoulder.

The fireworks lasted perhaps ten minutes, by which time the dragon had been reduced to a pile of embers and the crowd was beginning to disperse. No longer in control of proceedings, Carlos turned and led us back into the building.

'So?' he queried a moment later. 'Does the Englishman approve of Spanish barbarism?'

I smiled. 'You forget. We also celebrate Saint George.'

'Not like that.' He deftly devoured a passing canapé. 'Mind you, when it comes to pomp, you English do it rather well. The opening of Parliament. The Trooping of the Colour. Royal weddings. I was at Diana's. Quite magnificent. Even Tarifa would have been hard pressed to equal that.'

Then it was Zeynep's turn.

'My dear! Did you like?'

'Well,' I confided once Carlos's back was turned, 'what puzzled me was who won the battle?'

'The Christians, of course. Don't they always?'

'But the Moors didn't flee.'

'Aha!' She tapped the side of her nose. 'Because next year we have to fight again. And the year after that. It's a battle without end, the battle for God. Like the battle of the sexes.'

The room had begun to empty. Zeynep was summoned by Carlos. Quiepo had taken his mother's arm. I joined the general exodus. Outside, in the now-deserted square, a tiny figure stood watch over the dying embers of the dragon.

'There you are!'

At the sound of my voice, he looked up, eyes still ablaze with excitement.

'Wasn't it great! I helped them paint it this afternoon, and wheel it down the street. They wouldn't let me into the square, though. They said that might be dangerous.'

'Where's Father Ricardo?'

'At the church. He'll be back in a minute.'

The group from the Town Hall had reached the opposite side of the square.

'Wait here!' I ran after them, catching up first with

Quiepo who, in keeping pace with his mother, had fallen to the rear.

'Where exactly are we going?'

'The bar on the beach.'

'Where we were before?'

He nodded.

As I retraced my footsteps across the square, a phalanx of young men burst past me, then vanished down a side street, their easy laughter echoing against the canyon of its walls.

'Poor dragon,' I said. 'Well and truly vanquished.'

'Tomorrow they start building him again.'

'So soon?'

Jed nodded sagely. 'Father Ricardo says it's so they remember he's always there, always needs fighting. They keep him in a courtyard behind the church. Then next year, on the day of San Jorge, they get him out and paint him. Ready for the fight.'

'Poor dragon,' I repeated.

'It's only a symbol, silly.'

'Is that so? A symbol of what?'

I wasn't at all prepared for the nature of his reply: 'The things that separate man from God.'

'Who told you this?'

'Father Ricardo, of course.'

I heard footsteps on the cobbles.

'This young man' – the face of Jed's other teacher was beaming proudly – 'worked very hard. You know he helped wheel the dragon to the square?'

'So I heard.'

'But where are the others?'

'At the bar on the beach. They're expecting us. Come.'

Led by Jed, we made our way through the narrow streets, less busy now that the festivities were over, and onto the esplanade, which was where the entire town seemed to have congregated. Our group was at a table on the terrace of the bar, their numbers swelled by the addition of Pablo and André, the composer Carl and the bull-necked scriptwriter – without, for once, a pencil behind his ear.

'Over here!' André was indicating two empty seats on either side of him.

'You go,' said Father Ricardo. 'I'll sit with Carlos.'

I took Jed by the hand.

'You remember André? From our first time at the villa?'

Jed shook his head.

'Of course he doesn't,' said André. 'How can anyone be expected to remember an old fogey like me? But you remember Nunu?'

The poodle must have heard her name, for she was at our side, a cone of black velvet perched precariously on her head.

Jed let out a disbelieving laugh. 'Another hat?'

'Dogs like to dress up too,' said André. 'For special occasions. Don't you, darling?'

A waiter came up and asked what we'd like to eat.

'The chops!' instructed André. 'Luís cooks the best chops in Spain.'

'Two chops,' I told the waiter. 'And a Coke.'

'And for you,' said André, reaching over to fill my glass with wine, 'some nectar of the gods.'

'Thank you.'

'So!' André returned his attention to Jed. 'Wasn't that good? Better than last year. Last year they had a very poor knight. Couldn't topple the dragon at all. In the end some of the Christians had to run on and do it for him.'

I wouldn't have expected André to be good with children, but he was – very. He didn't just question Jed, he let him into secrets, cracked complicated jokes, treated him as an equal; which compliment Jed repaid, I noticed, by very ably holding his own. More ably, indeed, than his chaperone, who, in his isolation, had become uncomfortably aware that an adult knee was casually but persistently making contact with his thigh.

'Peter!' It was Pablo, leaning forward to catch my eye. 'You enjoy the fiesta?'

I grasped this conversational straw. 'Very much. And you?'

He grimaced. 'Too like the bullfight. Not an equal battle. Too much emphasis on death. But the fireworks were nice. They, at least, were pretty.'

'As pretty as me?' Zeynep propelled the question across the table in a jet of smoke.

Pablo blew her an answering kiss. 'Don't be silly!'

'Talking of dragons . . .' The voice in my ear was André's. 'What did you make of that charade on the balcony?'

'I beg your pardon?'

'Carlos and Zeynep.'

'What about them?'

His knee was still in contact with my thigh.

'You don't have to pretend with me. Zeynep's an old friend, remember.'

'I'm not sure I understand you.'

He made a face. 'Why do you think Carlos hates it so much when Zeynep visits us? Okay, so he's jealous of how much she likes us. But it's really how we live. Pablo and I. How openly.' He took a sip of wine. 'Catholic duplicity. I spit on it.'

Less sure than ever that I knew what he was driving at, I restated my ignorance. He looked at me in disbelief.

'London must have changed,' he muttered, 'if you can really be that innocent. Hampstead Heath? Those bars in Soho?'

I was still looking at him blankly. He lowered his voice even further. 'No one must guess the sexuality of our sainted director. One more task for Zeynep. Providing cover.'

'What are you saying?' Having heard her name, Zeynep was smiling pleasantly at André. He leant across the table: 'Darling! I'm telling this divine young man what a saint you are. Saint Zeynep.'

'Look around this table.' André had returned to the matter at hand. 'Who would you say is Carlos's fuck?'

I was remembering the jacuzzi, the tension I'd sensed between Carlos and Quiepo, the way Carlos had patted Quiepo's behind. Quiepo's mother and her knitting, the family group. The way Carlos had challenged me with his eyes when explaining San Jorge. *Others, of course, see the story in sexual terms.* A shiver of apprehension went down my spine.

'Catholics,' continued André smoothly, 'they laugh at us poor Protestants. But who laughs last, I wonder? At least I don't live a lie.'

At which point, mercifully, our conversation – my isolation – was interrupted by the sudden and boisterous arrival of Jacqui and Al.

'Fucking Barcelona!' Al made the announcement for the benefit of the entire esplanade. '*Mañana, mañana*! What is it about you Spanish that you can't do today what can be put off until tomorrow?'

Jacqui skirted the table in our direction.

'How was it?'

Before I had a chance to reply, Jed had launched into his practised account of the day. Borrowing a chair from a neighbouring table, Jacqui drew it up and listened solemnly.

'No wonder you look bushed,' she said when he'd finished.

He was instantly on guard against this hint of parental control. 'I'm not tired, if that's what you mean.'

'But Jacqui is,' I said, finally managing to lock eyes with her. 'Do you want something to eat?'

She ran a careless hand through her hair. 'We ate in Barcelona. But some wine would be nice.'

André, who had – thankfully – removed his knee, did the honours, refilling my glass in the process.

'And how was Barcelona?' I was intent on keeping the lines of communication open.

She pursed her lips. 'Dead boring. Al had these people to see. I just wandered up and down the Ramblas. I don't know why I went.' She laid a hand on Jed's head. 'You look ready for bed.'

'Aw, Mum!'

'Enrique's here with our boat,' said André. 'He'll take you back, if you like.'

The prospect of a ride in André's boat silenced Jed long enough for Jacqui to say: 'Now what about that? A whole boat to ourselves.'

'I won't be a minute.' André got to his feet – contriving, as he did so, to rest a hand on my shoulder – and disappeared into the bar. Jacqui swallowed the last of her wine.

'I'm bushed too,' she announced. 'All that walking. And your man there drives like a maniac. I thought the end had come.'

André reappeared with a beaming Enrique in tow.

'Ready when you are,' he said, indicating the boatman.

Jacqui stood up. 'Right, Jed, say goodnight.'

I stood up with her.

'I'll come too.'

'You don't have to.'

Was it my imagination, or was her tone discouraging?

'No, really, I'd like to.'

'But Peter!' It was André, who, as Jacqui led Jed away to say his goodnights, slipped his arm into mine. 'We're only just getting to know each other. And tomorrow we sail for Gibraltar.'

'I'm sorry. Jed isn't the only one to be tired by today.'

'Funny boy!' He pinched my arm, causing a stab of pain. 'Why are you so frightened?'

'Frightened? Of what?'

'You tell me.' Once again he lowered his voice. 'You don't have to worry about Pablo. He and I, we have an understanding.'

I managed to disengage myself.

'You're making a mistake,' I said. 'About me.'

'Am I?' He was a paradigm of wide-eyed innocence.

'Thank you for lunch,' I said. And to Pablo, who had risen from his chair: 'I hope we meet again.'

'Peter!' It was Quiepo, calling across the table. 'You're not going?'

'I'm afraid I must.'

'But later we dance!'

'I'm too tired.'

'Don't expect me to stay faithful then!' This from Zeynep. 'I might find another man.'

I shrugged. 'It's a risk I'll have to take.'

Jacqui and Jed had completed their circuit of the table, and after a final chorus of goodbyes, we crossed the beach to the pier, where Enrique was already waiting for us. Within minutes we were slicing into darkness, the fiesta a rapidly receding reality. Jed shivered.

'I'm cold.'

'Come here, then.' Enveloping him in her arms, Jacqui lifted him onto her lap. He nuzzled his head against her shoulder and closed his eyes.

'Sweet,' I said. 'Madonna and child.'

She shot me an enquiring look. 'Not had enough Catholicism for one day?'

I laughed wryly. 'Little do you know.'

We skirted a vulgar gin palace of a boat, ablaze like the town with light, then Enrique throttled back and we were gliding up to the rocks. Jacqui got to her feet, and once I'd leapt ashore, handed me the sleepy Jed.

'Here,' I said. 'I'll give you a piggy-back.'

I hoisted him onto my back, waved thanks to Enrique, and then, with Jacqui leading the way, toiled slowly up the stairs to the Casa Nueva. In the living room, I unburdened myself of my load, and whilst his mother led him to bed, poured myself a whisky and took it onto the terrace, where I leant against the parapet and stared across the water to the noise and light of the gin palace. Music was playing, music which, as I listened, assumed the lineaments of a song:

> A cigarette that bears a lipstick's traces
> An airline ticket to romantic places
> And still my heart has wings
> These foolish things
> Remind me of you.

I heard a sound behind me, and, turning, saw that Jacqui had joined me at the parapet.

'Strange,' I heard myself saying, 'how potent cheap music is.'

'Nasty, insistent little tune.'

Before I could express surprise at the speed with which she'd recognised the reference, she continued seamlessly: 'Whose yacht is that?'

I decided to make free with my reply: 'Adnan Kashoggi's, I expect. It always used to be.'

The moonlight fell at an angle across her face, high-lighting her smile and causing me to skip a section: 'You're looking very lovely you know, in this damned moonlight, Amanda. Your skin is clear and cool, and your eyes are shining, and you're growing lovelier and lovelier every second as I look at you. You don't hold any mystery for me, darling, do you mind? There isn't a particle of you that I don't know, remember, and want.'

'Don't!' she said softly. 'Don't say any more.'

Suddenly I wasn't sure we were acting.

'Where do you know it from?' I asked.

'I played it once. Durban, actually. And you?'

'Devon.' To say more than that would have been too revealing. The word 'commune' I left unspoken.

She picked at a piece of flaking plaster on the balustrade. 'Particles,' she said bitterly. 'Just particles. So much less than the whole. Funny how little we know each other. Really.'

I took a step towards her. 'We could remedy that.'

'Could we?' The look in her eyes was almost wistful. 'I don't think so. Not at this stage. Not in this production.' She gestured towards the gin palace. 'Even the song is wrong.' She pushed away from the parapet. 'But I'm whacked. I need a shower.' She crossed smartly towards the living room, then turned. 'I almost forgot. We leave in ten days.'

'Leave?'

'To start filming. It's a village in the mountains to the south of Barcelona. Al was telling me in the car. It sounds fabulous. Well . . .' She pushed back a lock of hair. 'See you in the morning?'

'Indeed,' I assented quietly. 'In the morning.'

Then she was gone. I remained by the parapet, staring across the bay into the uncertain darkness that was the future, and which – whether I liked it or not – it seemed I would have to face in continuing isolation.

> 'Some day I'll find you
> Moonlight behind you
> True to the dream I am dreaming.

Blocking out the thump of disco music that had begun to emanate from the gin palace, I felt for the song we should have been singing.

Ten

Y ou're making a mistake, I had told André. But wasn't
I the person making the mistake? A dangerous one, at
that: the mistake of suddenly wanting Jacqui, of not confronting my feelings, of those feelings being for someone
who, it turned out, belonged to someone else. The person
employing me.

I felt trapped. A proverbial rabbit caught in the glare of
approaching events, events which had started to speed up,
to speed up and show their other side. Heads one moment,
tails the next. Heads you win, tails you lose. Not a game for
beginners.

In the manner of birds gathering at the end of summer
for their migration south, there began a similar but non-
seasonal colonisation of the villa by the burgeoning film
crew. Bedrooms filled, terraces were seldom deserted, the
kitchen in the top villa, where Father Ricardo and I had
been schooling Jed, was commandeered by a plethora of
production assistants, forcing us into my bedroom, where
we could at least shut the door on the ceaseless clattering of
typewriters, the urgent conferences, the shouted conversa-
tions into mobile phones.

In the wake of the production team, in a second, more

leisurely wave, came a flock of actors. First, as Murillo's assistant, a crass Australian I'd never heard of, but who – Zeynep assured me – was the next Mel Gibson. Then Murillo himself, a regal Frenchman who, though I couldn't have named them, I'd certainly seen in countless roles. Then a handful of supporting players – English, Spanish, German – and last but not least, a latter-day Loren, all sunglasses and couturier clothing, who was to play the assistant's lover, and who, in addition to her wardrobe, had brought along a publicist and a Roman boyfriend.

Mealtimes took on the aspect of being at court. Centre stage sat the royal family – Carlos, Al, Murillo, Murillo's assistant, the Italian starlet – whilst grouped about them, deferring to their every mood, hovered the courtiers: the scriptwriter, Carl, Mercedes, the Roman boyfriend.

I began to long for the past: mealtimes when the only social hazards had been Quiepo's mother or Carlos's moodiness; when we had been a family of sorts; when the problems confronting me had not seemed insurmountable.

At dinner on the evening of our departure, in what was becoming an inviolate pattern of behaviour, I took my food to the far end of the terrace, where I could eat undisturbed, leaving Jacqui – who, by dint of perseverance, had easier access to the inner circle – to sit with Al, and Jed, who had become something of a mascot for the other actors, to cope unaided with the Italian starlet's eccentric English. To my surprise, I was joined by Quiepo. There was a look in his eyes that I hadn't seen before: a look of quiet desperation. He waved a fork at the royalty.

'Don't you hate? All these people.'

Whereupon, to my amazement, he burst into tears.

'Quiepo! What is it?'

He shook his head violently. 'Is nothing.'

Fumbling for his handkerchief, he turned his back on the gathering and leant on the balustrade.

'Has something happened?'

He managed a ragged smile. 'I guess.'

'Is it the film?'

We were interrupted by one of the assistants, clipboard at the ready, come to tell me how I was travelling to the village. Together with the scriptwriter, I'd been assigned to the car of the starlet and her Roman boyfriend.

'You leave at seven,' explained the assistant, consulting his clipboard. 'You are booked into the Reina Cristina. Smallwood, yes?'

'Al,' said Quiepo, blowing his nose fiercely once the assistant had moved on. 'He choose the Cristina.'

'It's in the village?'

He shook his head. 'Castres. Not far. Fifteen kilometres.'

Perhaps it was the contrast he made with the inner circle, who chose that moment to laugh at a joke of Carlos's, or the fact that even among so many, one could still be alone, or that his sudden, perplexing isolation echoed mine, or simply the touching paucity of his English; whatever the case, and to hell – for once – with the consequences, I put down my plate, stood up, and gave him a quick hug.

'I'm always here,' I said. 'If you need to talk.'

He gave my hand an answering squeeze.

'Nice,' he said, using that word again. '*Simpático*. Thank you.'

He took up his plate and moved away.

Over coffee, I was joined by Zeynep.

'Is everything all right?' I asked

'How do you mean? All right?'

'I was talking to Quiepo earlier. He seemed upset.'

'My dear.' She laid a confidential hand upon my arm. 'This afternoon we hear that Larry is in the hospital.'

'Larry?'

'You know – the bird. He used to work for Carlos at the opera.'

I recalled that Carlos and Quiepo had spoken of a Larry the evening of the festival; and that indeed, on our first visit to the villa, that was how the bird had been introduced: as Larry's.

'Serious?'

She gave vent to a bitter laugh. 'How old is Larry? Twenty-three, twenty-four? And in six months, like a skeleton. I hate it, that disease.'

It had been implicit in my last question, what disease? Now I knew. And when she added 'So what if he likes men?' there was no doubt at all. I thought of the bird in its cage, mocking our freedom of movement.

'Tonight,' continued Zeynep quietly, 'Carlos goes to Barcelona. To say goodbye. I would like to go too, so would Quiepo, but Al . . .' She shrugged. 'It isn't always possible to do the things we want.'

The party began to disperse. I chose to stay where I was, staring out across the bay at the lights of the fishing fleet, and, on the hill above the town, the pinpricks of red that denoted the cemetery. I was remembering how lonely Quiepo had looked when we talked, and the feel of his arm when I had touched it. The warmth of his flesh, and how, though he hadn't been expecting my gesture, he hadn't pulled away. That and, at the other end of the terrace, the confident sound of Carlos's voice.

The next morning I was woken by a peremptory rapping on my door.

'Yes?' I managed sleepily.

'Car's ready,' came the gruff, impatient tones of the scriptwriter.

Squinting at my watch, I realised I had overslept, so, throwing back the sheets, I stumbled into my clothes, and, thankful I'd had the foresight to pack the night before, snatched up my bag and made a dash for the courtyard. The scriptwriter, ginger hair still spiky from sleep, was squatting on his case, face buried in a Spanish newspaper.

'Where are the others?'

He folded the paper with a sigh. 'Probably hiring a trailer. You should see madam's luggage. Just as well we English have the sense to travel light.'

From the stairs behind me came the sound of laboured breathing, and, struggling into view under the weight of two enormous suitcases, a tortured Juan, followed at a suitable distance by the immaculate, sunglassed figures of boyfriend and star.

'*Avanti*!' grinned the boyfriend, by-passing Juan and clicking open the gate. In dutiful unison, the scriptwriter and I reached for our bags, and, with Juan bringing up the rear, began our ascent to the road.

At the car, low-slung and sporty, it took Juan all his remaining strength to heave the cases into the boot. There wasn't room for English luggage, however modest, so the scriptwriter and I had to squash our bags into the back. The boyfriend gave Juan a tip, the starlet made good the ravages of the climb by fussing over her hair in the mirror, the boyfriend opened the sunroof, and then, with a final wave at Juan, hit the accelerator and catapulted the car into the road.

'Is okay?' shouted the starlet over her shoulder, hair unravelling in the wind. I nodded numbly.

On the motorway, the boyfriend thankfully closed the sunroof, then counteracted his kindness by putting on a tape of disco music that caused a sonic boom in the rear. The starlet began, if such a thing is possible, to break-dance in her seat, and with such compelling absorption that for a while I feared she might encourage the driver to follow suit. The scriptwriter took refuge in some crumpled pages of script.

'How soon,' I shouted above the cacophony, 'before filming starts?'

He shrugged. 'Tomorrow.'

'Why are you still working on the script?'

He slapped the pages with the back of his hand. 'Thanks to that fuckwit of a Canadian, I'll be working on this till we wrap.'

'You mean Brett?'

'If that's his name. Myself, I've erased it from memory.'

'Some of it must be ready, surely?'

Rather grudgingly, he agreed. 'They can do the early scenes. The ones with Jed.'

There was a break in the music, allowing me to lower my voice. 'Funny. I always imagined the script would have to be ready before you started. Isn't it chaos, otherwise?'

He chuckled. 'This film is chaos anyway. Okay, so Carlos is one of the world's leading opera directors, but what he knows about film . . .' He cast around for an appropriate comparison. 'It's like asking me to run the economy.'

'But isn't that Al's job? To keep things under control?'

'Al?' The scriptwriter snorted. 'Al's too busy fucking his piece of English ass. He wouldn't notice if Carlos started making a film about Picasso by mistake.'

Had my life depended on it, I don't think I could have mustered a response. Not that my life did depend on it, or even our conversation; the mention of Al had caused the scriptwriter to mount what was clearly a hobby horse: 'Which is why Carlos uses him, of course.' He lowered his voice. 'You probably think it's the money. That the Americans have the money. Let me tell you, it's got fuck all

to do with money. The Americans are in awe of the
Europeans. Carlos may be new to film, but he isn't a fool.
He knows that with someone like Al, he can do what he
likes. Al's so cunt-struck by Carlos's artistic credentials, he'd
let him rebuild Seville if he wanted to. The only people
who can handle the Europeans are the English. We know
their game. We're not in awe of their shit. You can't beat an
English producer. Or an English writer. We know our
European. And I don't mean the paper.'

I was only half listening, my mind intent not on his
words, but on a series of images: Jacqui in the moonlight,
asking me not to say any more. Quiepo in his whites,
emerging like light out of darkness. Myself in my own
sheath of satin, Dirk's arm on my waist. Pablo's wedding
dress. My mother's clothes. André's knee against mine. Jed
and the burning dragon. Father Ricardo. Carlos on the
terrace by the jacuzzi, folding those towels. A skeleton in
the cupboard called Larry.

'Are you all right?'

The scriptwriter had broken off his peroration and was
staring at me worriedly.

I nodded quickly. 'A little carsick, that's all.'

In support of which hasty excuse, I rolled down my
window and turned my back on him.

'Sitges!' said the starlet, pointing to a sign. 'Very beautiful, Sitges.'

'This coast horrible,' opined the boyfriend.

'Not Sitges,' said the starlet. 'Sitges beautiful. *Bellissima.*'
She kissed the tips of her fingers.

Although it ran parallel to the coast, the motorway was
sufficiently inland to mask the fact; only at intermittent
intervals did it curve towards the sea and grant us a glimpse
of water fringed by the inevitable holiday apartments. To
our right, also running parallel to the road, was a line of

mountains, etched purple against the paler backdrop of the sky, and in the central reservation, a profusion of oleander.

The boyfriend turned off the motorway, and, as we stopped to pay the toll, reopened the sunroof. We headed inland along a secondary road that ran straight for the mountains, dissecting a plain planted with oranges and olives, the orchards of the one as lushly green as the fields of the other were drably dusty. Every so often we would come to a village, small clusters of whitewashed houses each boasting a gathering of men sitting at a pavement café. We began to climb. The plain fell away behind us, the air became cooler. No oranges now, only tiny terraces cut zig-zag into the foothills, and in them farmers who, as we passed, would raise an acknowledging hand. We were trav-elling back in time, into a world that measured itself solely against the seasons.

We came to a ravine where the road ran alongside a river. The landscape here was almost alpine; extravagantly green and fed by the rushing water. Then we began to climb again, in earnest this time, emerging from the ravine onto a twisting pass that tricked its way upwards until sud-denly, without any warning, the terrain had flattened and we were entering a town. Castres.

A veritable Don Quixote, the boyfriend tilted at the narrow streets until, by dint of automotive audacity, he swung us into a sizeable square scattered with pavement cafés and dominated by the crumbling façade of the Reina Cristina.

Watched by a group of mildly curious old men at a nearby table, the boyfriend threw open his door, ran round the car and ceremoniously handed the starlet from the vehi-cle. She emerged as if into a spotlight, magnificently aware of her audience, before flinging her bag over her shoulder and striding up the steps of the hotel. The old men, brandies forgotten, stared after her in unconscious parody of their younger selves.

Like the starlet, the foyer of the Reina Cristina had been designed to seduce, though in the building's case, a long time ago. The floor was of cracked and faded marble; the tiles on the walls, once vivid, were overlaid by dust; dispirited palms wilted on either side of the Moorish arches that opened into a bar and dining room; and the lift, a baroque confection of overwrought iron, would not have looked out of place in a museum. At a wooden desk against the far wall, a dark-haired man in an ill-fitting suit was rustling nervously through an array of keys whilst the boyfriend and starlet, still wearing their dark glasses, watched impassively.

'*Et in Arcadia ego*,' grinned the scriptwriter.

'I beg your pardon?'

He gestured towards the desk. 'Even in paradise, the ego of the star must be satisfied. Needs to know she's getting the best room.'

'And where does that leave us?'

He shrugged. 'In the attic, probably.'

He wasn't far wrong. Once the actress and her boyfriend had been assigned a key and a bellboy not much taller than their suitcases, the scriptwriter and I were altogether more peremptorily signed in, and, without the benefit of a bellboy, pointed in the direction of the lift and told that we were on the top floor.

To be precise, on the top floor and at the back. I don't know about the scriptwriter – he was at the other end of the corridor – but my room was no bigger than my bathroom at the villa, and had a view to match: a section of drainpipe and brick that wouldn't have looked out of place on the set of *West Side Story*.

I emptied my bag onto the narrow bed, then discovered that because there were only two hangers in the wardrobe,

both wire, I had to hang all my trousers on one, my jackets on the other, praying that neither would collapse under
the weight. There was a basin under the window, cracked
and plugless, from which I would have splashed my face
with water had I not decided to find the bathroom and
treat myself to a proper shower. Not that you could call the
trickle of lukewarm water I managed to coax from the
encrusted shower-head a proper shower.

Impelled by the scriptwriter's revelation to stay on the
move – for if I didn't, I ran the risk of imploding utterly –
I returned downstairs. Except for the manager, the foyer
was deserted. I handed him my key, glanced into the empty
bar, then went outside to the nearest café, where I ordered
a coffee.

I don't know how long I sat there, but when I looked at
my watch, it was after one. The old men had long since left
their table, and the square was deserted. I made a circuit of
the cafés, then struck off to the right, down what looked
like the town's main street. Even this was more or less
empty – a smartly suited businessman, a handful of women
in plain cotton dresses, two or three children, and one old
crone dressed entirely in black who every few yards would
stop to lean on her stick. There were shops, though not as
many as I would have expected in a town this size; more
houses, in fact, than shops, in addition to which the shops
were in the process of withdrawing, tortoise-like, into their
shells for the siesta. A vegetable merchant was covering his
pavement stall with a tarpaulin, shutters were coming down
in the *farmacia* and the bakery. There were a couple of open
bars, then only houses, then, at the edge of the town, an
abrupt succession of terraced fields cut into the stark continuation of the mountain. I retraced my footsteps to the
nearest bar, where – in the company of two other customers – I ordered myself an omelette and a beer.

Emerging later, I found that the town had surrendered itself entirely to silence and the sun. Of people there was now no trace at all; the only movement that of a cautious, feral cat. I returned to my room, where I fell onto the narrow bed and into the merciful oblivion of sleep.

I awoke at four to the sound of voices in the corridor, and, splashing my face with water, pushed open my door. Father Ricardo was standing outside the room next to mine, talking into it.

'Aha!' he said. 'We wondered where you were. Jed!'

Almost immediately, Jed appeared at the open doorway.

'Peter!' He was so transparently pleased to see me that I felt ashamed of my earlier self-absorption. I was, after all, here on his account; his were the emotions that should be exercising me. 'Where have you been?'

'Sleeping. And you?'

'To the village.' He turned to Father Ricardo. 'What's it called?'

'Beniplacar.'

'And what's it like?'

He made a face. 'Ancient. Over a thousand years.' Again he looked to Father Ricardo for confirmation. 'And zillions of cats.'

'Cats?'

'All over the place. Really wild. They won't let you stroke them.'

Father Ricardo interrupted. 'In the sixties, when tourism started, all the young men and women went down to the coast. To work in the hotels. It isn't easy making a living in the mountains. The village died. Now maybe two hundred people, all old of course, in a place that used to be two thousand.'

'I see.'

'Look at this!' Jed vanished into his room, reappearing

seconds later with a huge key, which he thrust into my hand. It was pitted with rust and weighed about a kilo.

'Neat, huh?'

'What is it?'

'For the house where I'm supposed to be living. In the film, I mean. Al said I could keep it.'

'Twenty-one already.' I returned the key to its owner. 'And you don't look a day over ten.'

Father Ricardo raised an interrogative eyebrow.

'You don't have that custom? The key to the door?'

'You should see the house,' continued Jed, entirely uninterested in the provenance – or indeed providence – of keys. 'They used to keep their animals in the downstairs room. There's a trough for their food, and one for their water, and big iron rings on the wall where they tied them up. The people lived upstairs. Weird, huh?'

'Poor,' corrected Father Ricardo. 'For these people, their animals were very valuable. You didn't leave them out on the mountain.' He consulted his watch. 'But what about that bath? Otherwise there won't be any hot water. I can't imagine the Reina Cristina enjoys an unlimited supply.'

Without so much as a murmur of dissent, Jed turned back into his room.

'Heavens!' I laughed. 'What's your secret?'

'Secret?'

'I have to bargain with him over baths.'

A self-effacing smile traversed the priest's placid features. 'He's a trifle overwhelmed, I think. Hungry too, I wouldn't be surprised.'

'What time's dinner?'

'Eight.'

'And tomorrow?'

'You haven't got a schedule?'

I shook my head.

'Quiepo has them. He'll give you one at dinner. I'm afraid that for the next ten days Jed is filming more or less continually. I suppose we can fit in a little, but it might be better to wait until he's not needed so much. Don't you think?'

Jed reappeared, toilet bag at the ready, and, ducking past us, streaked across the corridor. 'Me first!' he yelled. 'Baggies me first!'

'That child,' said Father Ricardo, shaking his head indulgently. 'More energy than Carlos.'

What the allocation of rooms had already indicated in terms of filmic importance, dinner that evening underlined. Beaten to the bathroom not only by Jed, but the entire crew, it was almost eight by the time I managed to grab a shower, and quarter-past when I appeared in the Moorish arch that separated silent foyer from sound-filled dining room. The hotel management had left a scattering of tables in the far corner for passing trade – a whispering couple, a travelling salesman – running the rest into a single horseshoe, at the head of which sat the luminaries (no Carlos, I noticed, but a preeminent Jacqui), with everyone else ranged along the sides, technicians and production assistants to the left, Quiepo, Zeynep, Mercedes, Father Ricardo and Jed to the right.

Father Ricardo noticed my arrival and raised an arm to indicate that he had kept a seat for me. I skirted the technicians and slid into my chair. The others were already on their first course.

'The soup,' suggested Father Ricardo. 'It really is excellent.'

Breaking into Spanish, he gave my order to a passing waiter.

Quiepo leant across the table to fill my glass with wine. '*Salud!*'

Zeynep, who was sitting next to Quiepo, intercepted my tentative smile. 'Now tell us. Is your room as awful as ours?'

'Worse, I would think.'

She lowered her voice. 'Already he's saving money. Not good.'

'Who?'

She gave a surreptitious nod in the direction of the luminaries. 'Mr Producer.'

Quiepo brought his head into frame with Zeynep's. 'He knows – how do you say? – that Carlos will step over budget. He takes . . .'

'Precautions.' Father Ricardo supplied the missing word.

'I'm glad,' said Zeynep, 'I go back to the villa.'

'You're not staying?'

'My dear!' She indicated the technicians and assistants with a sweep of her jewelled hand. 'How many slaves does a genius need? I have other things to do. When he finishes here, there's a new production of *Carmen* in Barcelona with Carreras. And in January he goes to the Met. Here, thank God, I am redundant.'

'Like all of us,' interposed Father Ricardo with a rueful smile. 'Momentarily, at least. I have a copy of the schedule. Look.' He produced a sheaf of xeroxed papers and laid them between us. 'It's now the sixth. Jed is on set every day until the fifteenth. Then, on the sixteenth, Sean Connery arrives, and until the twenty-fifth, Jed is hardly needed at all. We can catch up then.'

'Plate away from you,' I said automatically, reaching over to tip Jed's soup plate in the required direction. 'Like so.'

'*Bueno!*' Quiepo was grinning at me across the table. 'You and Father Ricardo have holiday. What will you do?'

'Look after Jed, of course.'

'Jacqui can do that, no?'

'Mummy's going to Los Angeles,' said Jed casually.

'I beg your pardon?'

'With Al.' He looked at me pityingly, as if to say: surely you knew?

'When?'

He shrugged. 'Tomorrow or the day after. Al has some meetings, and he's asked Mummy to go with him.'

'Are you sure?'

'That's what she told me.'

I darted what I hoped was a casual look at the subject of our conversation. Head back, she was laughing uproariously at some crack of Al's.

'Do not worry.' Quiepo had followed the direction of my eyes. 'We amuse ourselves.'

'You,' said Zeynep quietly, 'have work of your own to do.'

I was rescued by Father Ricardo, who – seemingly oblivious to any undercurrents – said blithely: 'There's a Carthusian monastery near Beniplacar. Perhaps you'd like to visit? They have an excellent cellar.'

After dinner, Quiepo was first on his feet.

'*Ahora!*' he said to Jed. 'Show me.'

It transpired he'd promised Jed a turn on some fruit machines which Jed had spied in a café off the square.

'I shall take a coffee outside,' said Father Ricardo. 'Will you join me?'

I shook my head. The party broke up. Zeynep replenished her glass and came round the table to claim the chair next to mine.

'Poor Peter!'

There was no need to pretend I didn't know what she was talking about; no need and no point.

'It won't last,' she went on, patting my wrist. 'The man is married. He has a wife and children in Santa Barbara. It's like being on a ship, being on a film. People have affairs. The ship docks. The affair ends.' She regarded me quizzically through a screen of cigarette smoke. 'Anyway, I thought you were only friends?'

'Of course,' I said. 'Absolutely. Just friends.'

'And maybe . . .' She picked at a breadcrumb. 'Maybe this gives you freedom?'

'Freedom?'

'My dear, let me tell you a story.' She took a sip of wine. 'You may not believe this, but when I was young, I was very beautiful. Also sad, of course. I hadn't got over Raschid. Beauty and sadness . . .' The ghost of a smile flitted across her face. 'Very appealing. I was at the Opera House. Carlos had a young assistant. We became lovers. He was a great support to me. He helped me forget Raschid. And then, because he didn't want to hurt me – he was, as we say, *muy simpático* – he couldn't bring himself to tell me he also loved men. He thought that might destroy me.' She prised my fingers loose of the napkin I had been in the process of smoothing and then folding. 'Except he did tell me, of course. I read it in his eyes, the way he looked at me, the way he looked at men. You can deceive yourself. That's easy. Others are more difficult.' I let my hand stay in hers, taking comfort from the subtle pressure of her fingers. 'So one weekend I asked a friend of mine, a male friend, very handsome, to come and stay in our apartment. I went away. And when I came back, it was – I don't know – like birds when you open a cage. We could fly again. Yes, it hurt. No, it wasn't easy. But it didn't hurt like the other.' She relinquished my hand. 'He was only being honest. You can't hate honesty.'

There was a pause in which, without meeting her eye, I crumpled the napkin back into a ball.

'And if I don't know what I want?' I asked eventually.

She laughed. 'What priests are for, perhaps?' Then she pushed back her chair. 'Now! I too would like a coffee. *Si?*'

I shook my head. 'Will you forgive me if I don't?'

'My dear!' She stood up. 'You won't find a better companion in all Castres.'

'That I know. It's just . . .'

She patted my shoulder. 'Tomorrow,' she said. 'We will have coffee tomorrow. Tomorrow we are all still here. The sun will shine, Al will save money, Carlos will spend it, you and I will have coffee.'

She brushed my forehead with her fingers before crossing smartly to the door.

At the main table, Murillo was indulging in a story that had his audience in stitches. I noticed that Jacqui had one arm extended along the back of Al's chair, and that at regular intervals she would curl a tendril of his hair about her little finger. I stood up, and under cover of a prolonged burst of laughter, escaped into the foyer, where I turned into the hotel bar. To my surprise, it was deserted. The technicians and assistants were either in bed or on the town. I advanced upon the solitary barman, who forsook the paper he had been reading to flick his napkin over the counter in honour of my approach.

'*Buenas tardes.*'

I levered myself onto a stool and ordered a cognac, which the barman splashed into a snifter before returning to his paper.

'You can deceive yourself,' Zeynep had said. 'That's easy. Others are more difficult.'

Was it deception, though, to think I wanted Jacqui? Or to be fearful of Quiepo? Carlos too. Did I want to become like Pablo and André? And if there was a part of me, a very specific part, that seemed determined to seek the inappropriate, then wasn't it my duty – San Jorge with his dragon – to disarm the worm?

'Señor would like another?' The barman had finished his

paper and was seeking diversion. I nodded automatically.

There were voices in the foyer, amongst them Jed's. I slipped off my stool and went to the arch. Father Ricardo, his hand on Jed's shoulder, was ushering our charge towards the lift. Jed in his T-shirt of white, Father Ricardo in his outfit of black. Positive and negative. One proton, one electron. Making a neutron. Who was I to disturb or doubt their chemistry? I returned to the bar.

'Dragons,' I muttered. 'Dragons at every turn.'

I was on my third or fourth cognac, and still playing word games, when I became aware of someone behind me. I swung round, and there, in the arch, stood Quiepo, dark eyes fixed in my direction. I was about to beckon him over when Carlos appeared at his side.

'*Dos coñac,*' he called to the barman. He strode into the room. '*Y una más para el pedagogo.*' Was it my imagination, or did he give the word an ironic inflection? 'I take it you'd like another?' He ran a quick, impatient hand across his head. 'That road is a nightmare. Especially at night.'

'You've come from Barcelona?'

He nodded curtly. 'An old friend, he is dying. Maybe dead already. The doctors say it is only a matter of hours.'

Out of the corner of my eye, I was acutely aware of Quiepo remaining quietly in the arch.

'I'm sorry.'

He let out a sudden, harsh laugh. 'Sorry? You? Why? Did you know him?'

I felt myself start to blush. 'No, no, I meant for you. I didn't—'

He cut me short. 'You live, you die. There is no sorry. Only life. Only death.' He picked up his drinks and nodded at mine. 'Enjoy the cognac. It comes from the monastery. The best in Spain. Some things they do well in the mountains.'

At the arch, he was about to hand Quiepo his glass when Al spun into view with all the force of a tornado.

'Eleven-thirty!' he began, slapping his watch for emphasis. 'Fucking marvellous! Too late to phone Douglas and another ten thousand down the chute.'

Without pausing in his hand-over of the cognac, Carlos made a funny clicking sound in his throat.

'Why don't you,' he said icily, 'take your precious dollars and stuff them up your arse? You could do with a fuck.'

There was a momentary silence during which Al's elongated frame seemed to become even thinner, as if spiralling into the vortex of his own shock and anger. Then, tapping his watch again, he said stonily: 'Tomorrow morning I want you on that phone to Douglas. You can explain why some fairy in Barcelona is more important than this movie you're supposed to be directing.'

With which riposte he vanished, leaving Quiepo to put a hand on Carlos's arm and guide him into the foyer.

Outside in the square, a bell began to toll. I looked at my watch. It was twelve o'clock. Downing my cognac, I slipped from my stool, nodded goodnight to the barman, and went into the foyer, where I approached the reception desk.

'The English señora,' I said. 'Not Italian. English. With the black hair. Which room?'

The night clerk stared at me uncomprehendingly, and I had to repeat myself before he understood.

'Ah!' he said, beaming broadly. '*Si, si! Veintitrés.*'

Now it was my turn to stare uncomprehendingly. The clerk held up both hands, extending two fingers of the one, three of the other.

'Twenty-three,' I said.

'*Si, si!*' He nodded violently. 'Twenty-three.'

I'd expected to find her asleep, and to waken her by slipping between the sheets, but although the light was on, her room (the door of which I'd found unlocked) was empty. An orange dress lay on the bed, and there were other articles of clothing – scarves, blouses, a pair of jeans – draped over the chair and the open door of the wardrobe. An army of jars had been marshalled on the dressing table, and on the bedside table, next to a glass of water, there was an open paperback: the novel I'd bought at the airport on our first trip out.

Clearing my throat, I called her name. There was no reply. I crossed to the bathroom and pushed open the door. More clothes, and on the glass shelf above the basin, a further selection of jars. My face in the mirror looked oddly unfamiliar; that of an intruder.

I turned back to the bed, and throwing aside the covers, got between the sheets. At close quarters, the orange dress gave off a whiff of perfume. Drawing it close, I buried my face in its folds. Jacqui flickered like a flame in the recesses of my consciousness.

> And if my wings burn
> Then who am I to blame?

Quiepo was smiling at me, dark eyes collusive with desire. Then I was ten again, Jed again, and the bed I'd crawled into belonged to my father. The hair on his arms tickled my cheeks.

'Why don't I have a mummy?'

'You do,' he said, pulling me into his warmth. 'She's gone away, that's all.'

'Who's taken her?'

'God,' said Father Ricardo.

Then I slept, to be woken moments later by the movement of silk across my face.

'Dirk?'

I opened my eyes. Jacqui, swathed in a hotel towel, a second towel wrapped turban-like about her hair, was disengaging her orange dress from my grasp.

'What time is it?'

'Four-thirty.'

I sat up, and saw that a pale wash of light was filtering through the inadequate curtains; saw also that the dressing table had been cleared of bottles and was now home to an open suitcase.

'You're packing!'

'We leave in an hour. Our plane's at ten.' She had folded the orange dress, and was laying it into the suitcase. 'Why are you in my bed?'

'I had rather a lot of cognac last night. I came looking for you.'

'Charming!' She began to rummage in the wardrobe. 'You certainly know how to make a girl feel wanted.'

My mouth felt as if it had been on fire. I took a drink of water from the glass on the bedside table.

'I could say the same about you.'

'Peter, please.' She turned from the wardrobe, her arms full of clothes.

'Why didn't you tell me? Instead of leaving me to find out from someone else.'

She gave a quick, dismissive laugh. 'What's to tell?'

'Quite a lot, it would seem.'

'All right, so he interests me. Why shouldn't he? And if I interest him, where's the harm in that? He has his troubles too, you know. It isn't all roses, being a producer.'

I was sorely tempted to ask whether she knew he had a wife. Wasn't it my job, after all, to protect my fellow travellers? But I knew that if I said anything, it would only be to spite her. All I allowed myself was: 'And a girl has to get on.'

She looked at me sharply. 'Is that a crime?' She deposited the clothes on the chair and came to sit on the bed. 'You and I, we both want different things. All right, there was a moment when perhaps we didn't know that, when perhaps . . .' She left the sentence unfinished. 'But aren't you glad we didn't? At least now, with each other's help, we can both get what we want. Allies!'

I gestured towards the open suitcase. 'Aren't allies supposed to keep each other informed?'

'You didn't know we were going to LA?'

'Only thanks to Jed.'

She stood up. 'As it happens, I only found out myself yesterday. And I haven't seen you since then. Have I?'

I stared at the sinuous curve of her back as she bent over the suitcase and began to fill it with the clothes from the chair.

'No,' I said finally. 'I don't suppose you have.' I threw back the covers and got to my feet. 'I need the loo.'

She had straightened up, and now she intercepted me, pulling me into her arms.

'Don't spoil things,' she whispered. 'Remember. We're only young once.'

'And Jed?'

'What about him?'

'Doesn't he need you here?'

'It seems to me,' she said slowly, 'that of all of us, Jed is the best equipped to look after himself. He's doing fine. Everyone says so. And anyway, I'm only away for a week. You'll be here. And Father Ricardo.'

Now that I was in her arms again, and had said my piece, I wasn't sure it was where I wanted to be. Jacqui was right: it wasn't her I missed, only security. I took a step backwards.

'*Bon voyage*, then,' I said softly. 'To both of us.'

'I'll ring,' she replied. 'Every day. And by the way,' she looked at me teasingly, 'who's Dirk?'

An hour later, shaved, showered, and feeling more human, I ventured downstairs to find two transit vans parked outside the hotel. Various crew members, clipboards to the fore, were milling about on the steps, shouting instructions. I found Jed in the second van, on the seat immediately behind the driver.

'Where's Father Ricardo?'

'At mass. He's coming later.'

'Do you know what you're doing today?'

He fumbled in the pocket of his shirt and handed me a section of script.

'On your own, huh?'

He nodded.

'Have you rehearsed?'

'Yesterday, when we arrived, Al took me up to the village and showed me the house. You saw the key. But I only have to walk out the door.'

As Jacqui had said, he was taking it all in his stride, miraculously so. Who needed the chaperone?

'You'll have to be my guide,' I said. 'When we get there.'

In the event, he was my guide all the way. As the van pulled out of Castres and began its assault on the mountain, he gestured to our left: 'That's where the postman used to walk.'

'The postman?'

'From Beniplacar. All down the mountain to Castres to get the post, then all the way back again. Over twenty kilometres. Now they use a bus.'

To begin with the vegetation was quite lush: pine trees and a tangle of undergrowth in the ravines at either side of the road. Then, as we began to climb, the vegetation fell away and the landscape became more arid: small terraces of olive and almond trees, or else just mountain slope tufted with grass and skewered by the occasional tree.

We came to a narrow bridge that straddled a plummeting ravine.

'In the Civil War,' said Jed solemnly, 'they blew this up.'

'Who did?'

He frowned. 'The people from Beniplacar. I don't know. I can't remember. Father Ricardo will tell you.'

As we came off the bridge, the ravine opened out into a dam.

'Quiepo says we can go swimming there,' pointed Jed. 'It's five kilometres long. It supplies the coast with water.'

The water in the dam was a greyish green, as sullen and uninviting as the mountainside that hemmed it in.

'I'm not sure I'd want to,' I said. 'It looks rather ominous.'

'There's a village,' said Jed, 'under the water at the other end. They flooded it to make the dam. On a clear day, says Quiepo, you can see the houses through the water.'

The road began to climb again, and the dam fell from sight. Up here there was hardly any vegetation, just rock and scrub. We rounded a bend, and Jed pointed to a large, square building set all alone on the crest of a ridge. The rising sun had suffused its blank façade, accentuating its prominence over the shadowy mountain.

'That's the monastery. Founded in thirteen hundred.'

'You are a mine of information!'

'Father Ricardo,' said Jed. 'He knows everything.'

The road curved sharply to the left, and instead of continuing to climb, began to drop as it hugged the side of a peak. The peak rose stark and sheer above us, whilst to our left the landscape gentled into a steeply sided valley terraced with the ubiquitous olives and almonds.

'Valliguera!' Jed indicated a ridge in the middle of the

valley on which I could just make out a huddle of white-washed houses. 'It's the nearest village to Beniplacar.'

'Lonely.'

'The people here want that, Quiepo says. That's how they are. When the Moors invaded the south, they never controlled these mountains. Not properly.'

'Hence the monastery?'

He frowned. 'I think the monks just wanted to be nearer God.'

Now whose interpretation is that, I wondered. Quiepo's or Father Ricardo's?

The van rounded a corner, and as it did so, the sun crested the mountain ridge across the valley and a finger of sunlight pointed along the valley floor to the village nestling under its overhang of rock at the far end.

'Beniplacar,' said Jed.

The houses looked as if they'd been thrown, like clay, against the mountainside. Their roofs were tiled in red, their walls were white, and, at the top of the stack, outlined against the sky, there was a church, pregnant with dome.

The van laboured up the last stretch of road, pulling over as we came to the first of the houses.

'Cars can't drive into the village,' explained Jed. 'The streets aren't wide enough.'

The crew tumbled out and began to form into various groups.

'Come,' said Jed, taking my hand. 'I'll show you.'

He led me into the village. To our right, though both were shut, was a bar and a pension; to our left, also shut, a grocer's and post office. Or rather, since there was nothing except the rusted signs above their doors to distinguish these buildings from the whitewashed houses between which they stood, and because the doors were bolted, and none of the buildings had windows except for shuttered squares on the first and second floors, this is what I assumed them to be. In reality, they could have been deserted years ago.

Beyond the post office the street widened into a hint of square from which a flight of steps led past a fountain and up the side of the mountain into the heart of the village.

'This is where they get their water,' said Jed. 'Here and in the valley.'

The steps were lined by houses and overhung by a haphazard arrangement of balconies, on three of which were plants and washing, twin pointers to continuing occupation. We crossed a narrow street, deserted echo of the street below, and continued upwards. A cat appeared, though when Jed bent to stroke it, it vanished again.

'I told you they were wild.'

We breasted a third street, and, turning along it, came to the church. It, too, could have been derelict. It wasn't in bad repair, but its windows had been concreted up and its massive door looked as if it was never opened.

'Isn't it used?' I asked.

Jed shrugged. 'Search me'

He led me round the side of it, and suddenly we were in open countryside. No more houses, only terraces, rising in indefatigable, jigsawed unison into the mountain. I looked behind me, down the tumble of roofs to the valley below, and saw at last a sign of life: two women in black laying out their washing on a slab of stone by the side of a stream.

'Come.' I rested my hand on Jed's head. 'They're probably wondering where you are.'

On our return we passed an old woman emerging from one of the houses. I nodded a silent greeting.

'*Adios,*' she murmured from the depths of her shawl.

'Odd,' I said to Jed. 'To say goodbye when you meet.'

'It means "To God". That's how they do it in the mountains.'

'So? It's like goodbye. God be with you. The same thing.'

'God be with you.' Jed tested the words as if they were a new flavour of ice-cream. 'God be with you.'

We reached the fountain. A technician was struggling past under the weight of a spotlight. Seeing us, he shouted: 'Coffee in *fonda*.' And when we looked puzzled: '*Fonda*. There.' He indicated the pension, whose door was now open.

We stepped through it into a darkened room boasting a single, very long table, at which sat various members of the crew, drinking coffee.

'So there you are!' It was Mercedes, looking flustered. 'We thought we'd lost you.'

I apologised for both of us. 'Jed was showing me the village.'

'You're wanted in make-up.' She ushered him past the table and up a set of stairs at the rear of the room.

I pulled out a chair and helped myself to some coffee from the nearest jug. Around me, the crew eddied and flowed with a sense of subdued but urgent activity, each crew member intent on his or her task, making me – as someone without a task – feel increasingly superfluous. I swallowed the last of my coffee and wandered into the street.

The shop had now opened, and its owner, a wizened old man in a butcher's apron, was sweeping his section of street, pausing every so often to allow another technician to hurry past with a light or a cable, a stand or a square of poly- styrene. I walked as far as the fountain. The technicians were going down the street towards the lower end of the village. I turned to the right, and toiled instead back up the route Jed and I had taken earlier. I arrived at the open space behind the church, where – standing quite alone and staring towards the mountain – was the figure of Carlos, characteristically attired in baggy shirt and trousers, glasses strung by their leather thong about his neck.

'Don Pedro!'

He extended an arm to beckon me over. As we drew level, he threw his arm, which he'd kept extended, around my shoulder, drawing me into his space. With his other hand he gestured down the valley, along the line of tumbling, red-tiled roofs.

'Like a fortress,' he said. 'These mountains. Once they kept back the Moors. More or less. Now they keep back time. A thousand years ago, it would have looked exactly the same.'

Anxious to establish an existence of my own within his arena, I pointed to the wire protuberances on some of the roofs. 'Even the aerials?'

He frowned. 'There was a second invasion. The tourists. And this time, instead of staying in the mountains, the people went to meet the enemy. Make them welcome. The village died. And now we have the Common Market.' He spat the words. 'You had an English lord, I forget his name. They put the first railway line through his land. You know what he did when he saw it? Blew his brains out.'

'Good heavens! Why?'

'He knew what it meant.'

There was a pause. I wasn't sure I fully understood or fully welcomed the drift of his argument.

'These people,' I ventured, 'from what everyone tells me, they had to struggle for existence. Surely you wouldn't deny them the chance to get on?'

'Modernisation!' he replied. 'It's a virus. The greatest evil of our century isn't war. It isn't famine. It isn't greed.' He broke off, as if no longer sure of his conclusion, or as if the conclusion had suggested another, more troubling line of thought. 'Think of Harry Lime.'

'Harry Lime?'

'*The Third Man*. Your Graham Greene. Though it was Orson himself who wrote the speech. Six centuries of democracy, and what do you get? The cuckoo clock. Then look at the Medicis. Michelangelo. Leonardo.'

'All right,' I countered, determined to hold my ground. 'But going back to this century. What about Hitler or Stalin?'

'Tweedledum,' he said airily, 'Tweedledum and Tweedledee. There are worse dangers than that.'

'And Franco?' I asked quietly.

There was another pause, longer than the last one, and for a moment I feared I might have overstepped the mark. Then, in a voice as quiet as mine, he said: 'Franco knew Spain like the back of his hand. Better than anyone. Yes, he was harsh; yes he was cruel. But so are these mountains. Life isn't a fairy tale.'

Again I had the sense that perhaps, in his head, he was following a line of thought complementary but different to the one he was uttering.

'But surely,' I said, 'surely you can't agree with the Civil War? A country divided against itself?'

'If you want a tree to survive, you have to prune it.'

'My father,' I began, and then stopped. I didn't know how best to articulate what it had been on the tip of my tongue to say, nor whether it was wise.

Carlos smiled. 'Let me guess. He fought in the Civil War. The International Brigade.'

I nodded. Indeed, I was thinking, it's not impossible he walked these very mountains. He'd talked of mountains.

'And has he been back since?'

I was about to reply when he answered for me.

'Of course he hasn't. He didn't want to come under Franco.'

'Isn't that understandable?'

'Convenient, no? To fight when it suits you? And to walk away afterwards?'

If I'd had the courage, I would have asked him about Lorca. Butchered, as my father had said, for his politics and his poetry and being a lover of men. Hadn't Carlos worked with Picasso on a production of *The House of Bernarda Alba*? How did he square that with the history he was championing?

'Politics!' Carlos was saying. 'You young people, you think politics is only about right and wrong. Ideas. Systems. Politics is about countries. What's right for a country.'

There was, in his words, an unsettling echo of what my father had once said to me: 'Until you realise that politics are what happened, that politics aren't decoration, some sort of afterthought, but life itself, then I don't see the point.'

'In Barcelona,' Carlos continued, 'some of the critics, they like to sneer at me. They say my operas are sentimental. They say I prostitute my art. Make it too accessible.' He began to fiddle with his glasses. 'All artists are whores. We have to be. We take money, ideas, support, where we find them. If I was choosy, nothing would get done. And what I make, I make for this country.' He gestured towards the mountains. 'People you can forget. They come and go. Like ants. Like . . .' He swallowed. 'But Spain . . .' Suddenly his voice broke, and turning his back on me, he fumbled in his pocket for a handkerchief. 'You must go,' he said curtly. 'Find Quiepo. Tell him I'll be down soon.'

So strong, though, was Carlos's magnetic field, so unnerving our conversation – so fraught as well with undercurrents, with things left unsaid – that it was a full minute before I was able to pull away, and he had to repeat himself ('Ten minutes. Tell Quiepo') before I made off across the grass and rounded the corner of the church. A figure in black was mounting the street towards me. At first I thought it was Father Ricardo. Then I saw it was another priest. He nodded pleasantly.

'*Adios.*'

'*Adios.*'

I went on down the street, then stopped to look back. The priest had removed a large key, very like the one Al had given Jed, from the pocket of his soutane, and was inserting it into the door of the church. Carlos appeared. The priest pushed open the door, and, stepping sideways, raised his hand in greeting. Carlos took the hand and clasped it in his own. The priest put an arm around Carlos's shoulder, shepherding him into the church. The door clanged shut behind them. The street was empty.

Tearing myself away, I proceeded into the village to find Quiepo.

Eleven

Quiepo, when eventually I found him – upstairs in the *fonda*, in a small rear bedroom that had been commandeered as a production office – was on the phone, and I had to wait for a pause in his conversation before I could relay my message. He nodded curt thanks, then inadvertently supplied an answer of sorts as to what might have been on Carlos's mind during our recent exchange.

'Larry,' he said into the receiver. 'L-A-R-R-Y. Tillman.' He spelt the surname too, then put down the phone, which immediately began to ring again.

'Larry died,' he said quietly. 'We hear this morning. Carlos wants I arrange flowers.'

He snatched up the insistent phone. '*Digame*!' He listened intently for a moment, then dropped the receiver onto a pile of invoices and crossed to the door. 'Mercedes!'

'I'm awfully sorry,' I said as he turned back into the room.

'You know what I think?' He fixed me with a burning look. 'I think Larry ask for it. Carlos do everything for him. But Larry want to do himself. He tell Carlos go fuck. Then . . .' He shrugged. 'Too many boys. Is crazy. Is not Carlos. Is Larry. *Muy loco*.'

Suddenly he was crying, shoulders heaving painfully

with the sobs. I couldn't have said why – instinct rather than deduction – but I knew he was grieving less for Larry than for himself. Larry had flown the cage. Quiepo hadn't. Like my father, Carlos cast a long shadow.

In an action replay of the evening on the terrace of Carlos's villa, I went and put my arms around him. He managed a wry smile.

'You have nice eyes,' he said. '*Muy tristes.*'

'You too.'

He didn't withdraw from my gaze. Then, breaking free, he returned to the door: 'Mercedes!'

'Downstairs. Shall I call her?'

He nodded. 'Is Madrid. About Sean Connery.'

Before quitting the room, I touched him once more on the arm.

'Remember what I told you. You can always talk to me.'

Downstairs, I handed on my baton of information, then escaped outside.

Were it Satan himself who had stood on that incline by the church, pointing out temptation upon temptation, I don't think I could have been more unsettled. Not that it had come as a shock, Carlos's attachment to Franco. On our very first visit to the villa, hadn't he argued with Pablo and André over Juan Carlos? No, what concerned me was the power Carlos exercised over those in his employ; those in his shadow. What concerned me was Quiepo. How his existence had come to reflect my own. Carlos and Quiepo. Edward and me. Two sides of a coin.

'Peter!' I swung round to discover a cautious Father Ricardo advancing towards me. 'You haven't been at the filming?'

I took a deep breath. 'I was going to ask you. Would it be all right, do you think, if I went back to Castres? It seems rather pointless both of us hanging around.'

'Of course.' He didn't seem in the least surprised by my request. 'But how will you get back?'

'I thought I'd walk.'

'Walk?'

'This morning Jed was telling me about the postman. How he did the trip every day. I could do with some exercise.'

'But what about lunch?' Father Ricardo consulted his watch. 'They break in an hour.'

The thought of a communal lunch only increased my determination to be alone.

'I need some time to myself.'

The priest regarded me speculatively. 'You do,' he said eventually, 'what you want. I'll keep an eye on Jed.'

He raised his arm in a gesture identical to the one used by the unknown priest towards Carlos: a gesture of unconscious benediction.

To begin with I followed the road, until, just past Valliguera, I came to a path that cut into the valley, curving along its side towards the mountain at its easternmost tip. Forsaking the arterial securities of the twentieth century, I turned onto a route that could have dated from the Moors.

The sun was directly overhead, an eruption of light at the epicentre of a baleful sky. There was no breeze in the valley, just the cicada-like hum of heat in my ears, and I undid the buttons on my shirt, letting it hang loose. My handkerchief I knotted and placed on my head in parody of those middle-aged men you see on the sands at Margate.

Distant Valliguera looked as deserted as Beniplacar. There was no sign of life in its narrow streets, nor in the olive groves on its surrounding terraces – unless, that is, you counted the intermittence of a faint jangling bell strapped to the neck of an unseen goat.

At the end of the valley the path climbed steeply to the

crest of a mountain, where, out of breath and baking, I sat and rested on a stone. Overhead, a scattering of birds, black squiggles against the blue, rode the thermals with indifferent ease. To my right, atop another mountain, towered the monastery. Before me, dropping inexorably towards the coast, was an endless unfolding of valley and mountain, the one rising up to meet the other in a repeated clash of petrified waves.

'To be nearer God,' Jed had assumed of the monks' decision to build their home in these mountains. All I experienced, though, was an immense emptiness. Judged against the landscape, I felt of less consequence than the speck of bird riding its thermal opposite. Blink, and you would miss me.

I looked at my watch. Two-thirty already, and God knew how far to Castres. Beginning to regret my Garbo-like decision, I removed the handkerchief from my head, dabbed at my face and neck, replaced it, then set off briskly down the mountain, wanting now to escape its maw, to be among people again. I fell into an automatic, almost somnambulant rhythm, pacing myself on the downward slopes so I could manage the gradients, my eyes on the path, my thoughts on the goal of tea in the square at Castres.

I came to another rise, and through a cleft in the ridges to my left, caught a glimpse of sun-sparkled water. The sea. Heartened, I hurried into the next valley, and two hours later, hot, sweaty and light-headed with hunger, reached Castres. I was tempted to stop at the bar where I'd had an omelette and beer, but as I'd made the square my goal, I kept on going until, goal attained, I felt some justification in collapsing into a chair at one of the pavement tables, where I ordered a beer and a hamburger.

My attention was caught by a flutter of colour on the hotel steps at the far end of the square. Zeynep, wearing her deckchair dress, had emerged from the building. She held a handkerchief in one hand, and, as I watched, dabbed furiously at her eyes, then felt in her handbag for a pair of sunglasses. I stood up and waved, but she didn't see me. Head lowered, she darted down the steps and into a waiting limousine. The car drew away from the kerb. I stepped forward, hand still raised, and as the car drew level, called out her name. She looked up, but already the car was turning out of the square, and the last I saw of her, framed by the rear window, was the flash of her face as she turned to look back at me. Troubled, I returned to my table, where the waiter had laid out my food.

Because it was early evening, that period between siesta and dinner, the square was busier than usual. Women crossed and recrossed its centre, laden with shopping. Old men concentrated on their cards or their brandy, and a group of children, high-spirited and noisy, ran circles round the fountain.

An excited murmur from the self-same children announced the return of the film crew. Their white vans slewed into the square, pursued by the children, who hung back chattering as the doors swung open and the crew disgorged. Jed was in the first van, and as he stepped into the square, I raised my arm.

'Over here!'

He saw me immediately and came trotting across.

'Get it all done?'

He nodded.

'Well,' I said. 'Jacqui should have landed by now.'

He looked at his watch. 'She said she'd phone at nine.'

'And it's . . .?'

'Quarter to seven.'

'You'd better grab a shower before the hot water's finished.'

He hesitated.

'Off you go. I'll be along in a minute.'

Running across the square, he paused by the fountain to watch the children at play. It was only a fractional pause, but even so, the angle of his body made it abundantly clear how tempted he was to join them.

'Go on!' I shouted.

He continued his dash to the hotel, where he barrelled into the figure of Father Ricardo emerging from the foyer. The priest laid a restraining hand on his shoulder, whispered something in his ear, then patted him on his way.

'Do you mind if I join you?'

'Of course not. Please.'

Father Ricardo lowered himself into the chair opposite and beckoned the waiter.

'Will you have something?'

I nodded at my glass. 'Another beer would be nice.'

Order placed, Father Ricardo flicked a speck of dust from his lap, then looked at me speculatively.

'So how was the walk?'

I shrugged. 'Pretty tiring. And the filming?'

His turn to shrug. 'It seems all right. Not that I understand, mind you, how it takes so long to get one scene in the can. Is that the phrase?'

I nodded.

'All day it took, just to shoot Jed running out of a door. But then he always was a perfectionist.'

'Carlos?'

'You've never seen his operas?'

I shook my head.

'Attention to detail. It's what he's best at.'

'Well,' I said, 'at least Jed seems to be coping. Puts the rest of us to shame.'

'Indeed!' Father Ricardo smiled wryly. 'But at that age

he carries less baggage than us adults.' He lifted his glass to his lips. 'I have always envied children. For them – how to say this? – ideas are concrete. Emotions too. Pain, happiness, uncertainty. They're felt as simply as heat and cold, or an empty stomach. And so they pass.' He took a reflective sip of brandy. 'Children live in the present. We adults have the past. The past is a great complication.' He replaced his glass on the table. 'And, of course, the future. Perhaps the greatest complication of all.'

He'd kept his eyes on me throughout the above, and now he leant forward slightly in his chair.

'Jed has asked,' he said, 'if he can come to mass. In the mornings, before he starts filming.'

I tried to keep surprise out of my voice: 'And so?'

'I was only wondering,' said Father Ricardo, 'whether you'd mind?'

'Why should I mind?'

He shrugged. 'Both you and Jed have told me about your father. I don't wish to rock the boat.'

I managed what I hoped was a careless laugh. 'You forget. I'm not his father. Jacqui is the one you should be asking.'

'Ah!' he said quickly. 'But Jacqui isn't here. And it's very important to Jed, what you think.'

'It is?'

'You know holograms.'

'Holograms?' Now the surprise in my voice was palpable.

'Cut a hologram in half and you don't get half the picture, you get the full picture, but at half the strength. More blurred. Cut it into quarters, and you still have the whole picture. Even more blurred. And so on, and so on.'

I looked at him curiously. 'What are you suggesting?'

He threw up his hands. 'I'm merely saying that things are not always as – cut and dried, yes? – as they seem.' He ground to a halt. 'I'm being meddlesome. It's a priestly failing. You must forgive me.'

'Tell me.' I was determined to change the subject. 'I saw Zeynep just now. Going off in a car. It looked as if she'd been crying. Is everything all right?'

Father Ricardo frowned. 'She and Carlos had some argument. There's a man in Málaga she's been seeing. Carlos doesn't approve. I think she was hoping to spend some time with him. But Juan Carlos and Sofia, next week they visit the villa. Zeynep has to get things ready. So she can't go to Málaga.'

I stared at the priest in disbelief. Zeynep hadn't mentioned any man to me. Indeed, she'd given me to understand that as far as she was concerned, men were a thing of the past. And as for Juan Carlos and Sofia, Carlos didn't like the King. Why, then, play host to him?

'Will Carlos be there?' I asked. 'When Juan Carlos visits?'

'For a day or two.'

'And the filming?'

'He'll only be gone a couple of days.'

I ran an uncertain finger round the rim of my glass. 'You must forgive me, but I find all this very puzzling.'

Father Ricardo didn't need more in order to follow my train of thought. 'What you have to understand,' he said quietly, 'is that many people remember the old days.' He shrugged. 'Franco achieved a great deal for this country.'

'At a cost.'

'Nothing comes for nothing.'

'But surely things are better now? More democratic?'

'Democracy costs too. For instance, we have one of the biggest drug problems in Europe.' He said this very evenly, in a cool, dispassionate tone, giving little clue as to what he was actually thinking. 'The important thing,' he concluded, 'is forgiveness. God's forgiveness.' His tone was thoughtful. 'It's not for us to think anyone wrong. God is the only judge. Though if I may be allowed to say something.' He ran a quick hand through his hair. 'You make things difficult for yourself. You search for certainties where perhaps there are none. You shouldn't confuse ideology with life.'

'That's my father you're describing.'

Again he shrugged. 'So? Aren't we all our fathers' sons?'

I smiled. 'Or wish to be. Or wish we weren't.'

He too allowed himself a smile. 'Don't blame others for confusions in yourself.'

'Meaning?'

'Carlos, for example. It isn't given to us to see into Carlos's heart. Only God can do that.'

'Is that what you're teaching Jed?'

He looked put out. 'I don't teach. I merely facilitate. People come to God of their own free will.' Then, as if aware that he'd spoken too harshly, he concluded gently: 'What you must understand about Carlos is that he was an orphan. He didn't have a father. No one to tell him how special he was. And he is special. As we all are. But Carlos . . .' He paused. 'Sometimes I think he is harsh on others simply to prove his own worth.' He finished his cognac. 'Another?'

I shook my head. 'If you'll excuse me.' I tapped my watch. 'After all that walking, I need a shower. And if I don't go soon, there won't be any hot water.'

I had traversed the foyer and was waiting for the lift to make its clangorous descent when, at the reception desk, I heard the phone ring and, a moment later, my name being called. The manager was brandishing the receiver in the air.

'Señor! For you!'

I ran across and took it from him.

'Peter speaking.' All I could hear was a faint susurration on the line. 'Hello?'

A fragmented version of my voice echoed back at me, followed, after another pause, by the merest 'Peter?' from Jacqui.

'You're early.'

Again the pause, again an echo of what I'd just said, then: '. . . tail winds. We . . .'

'So where are you?'

'. . . in the hills above Los Angeles. It's absolutely fabulous. Al's gone to a meeting. I'm lying by the pool . . .'

'This line is terrible,' I interrupted. 'You keep coming and going.'

'This line is terrible,' I heard again. 'You keep coming and going.'

'I just wanted you to know we'd landed safely.'

'Hang on a sec!' I hit the receiver against my palm. 'Let me call Jed.'

There was no reply, just a continuing susurration on the line: electronic whale song.

'Jacqui? Hang on a minute. He'll be devastated to miss you.'

But the line had gone dead. I banged the receiver into its cradle. The manager looked suitably apologetic.

'I'm sorry, señor.' He shrugged. 'The phones in Castres . . .'

'The person who'll be sorry,' I said curtly, 'is Jed.'

I left it until after dinner to tell him. I didn't see any reason to spoil his meal, and in the event, I was glad, because dinner turned out to be something of a celebration – the result of completing the first day of shooting – and it would have been doubly unkind to blight the festivities.

Jed was given pride of place at the head table, between Carlos and Murillo, and a great fuss was made of him by all concerned, most notably the Italian starlet, more soignée than ever in a dress of vivid red. Quiepo, too, had been promoted to sit with Murillo's assistant – a promotion for which I was particularly grateful, since it meant I could concentrate on my food with only Father Ricardo and the scriptwriter to contend with. Not that either of them paid much attention to me. They'd discovered a mutual love of G.K. Chesterton, and spent most of the meal retelling Father Brown stories.

As coffee was being served, Carlos got to his feet and clapped his hands for silence.

'After dinner,' he announced, 'there will be dancing in the bar. Carl has agreed to play for us.'

He gestured towards the composer, who waved his hands in the air to fend off the catcalls and whistles from the intoxicated crew.

'For me bed,' said Father Ricardo firmly. 'My dancing days are over.'

'Mine too,' muttered the scriptwriter. 'How about a drink in the square?'

At the head table, the Italian starlet had yanked her boyfriend to his feet, and in mock flamenco style, the two of them stamped and whirled out the door. The party began to break up.

'It's quarter-past nine.' Jed was hovering behind me. 'Do you think she's forgotten?'

I pushed back my chair and took him onto my lap.

'They're having difficulty with the phones,' I said. 'She rang earlier, and was going to ring again, but I guess she couldn't get through. They had a wonderful flight and they're staying in the Hollywood hills. She sends buckets of love.' I planted a kiss on his forehead. 'Lots of these, too.'

He didn't say a word, just stayed in my lap, allowing me to rock him to and fro until, seconds later, we were interrupted by Quiepo.

'You coming?'

'You bet!' I eased Jed off my lap and fastened his hand in mine. 'We do a mean tango, don't we, pal?'

He nodded dutifully, and without protest, allowed me to lead him through to the bar.

The piano stood against the far wall, at it Carl, head bobbing in time to the waltz he was playing. The starlet and her boyfriend had modified their flamenco routine accordingly, whilst Mercedes, taking care to avoid their twirling figures, was organising some members of the crew to clear a proper dance floor. The barman was coping with an avalanche of orders. I put my other hand on Jed's shoulder.

'Right!' I commanded. 'One, two, three! One, two, three!'

He fell in with my instructions, trying, but never succeeding, to match his steps to mine.

'No, no! Is hopeless!' Mercedes had finished clearing sufficient space, and now she snatched Jed from me and swirled him off across the floor.

'We need Zeynep.' Quiepo sidled up to me, glass of wine in hand.

'We do?'

'She dances – how you say? – like a dream.'

'Zeynep's a stupid bitch.' We were joined by a glowering Carlos.

'Carlos, please! Forget it now!'

'The woman's sixty. Who does she think she is? A businessman in Málaga! I ask you!'

Quiepo sighed exaggeratedly.

Carlos laid a Zeynep-like hand on my arm. 'Years ago,' he said, 'when she came to work with me, she had another of these silly affairs. One of my assistants. Everyone knew the boy was gay. Only Zeynep couldn't see it.'

Really? I was thinking. *That's not how she tells the story.*

'What happened?' I asked, wanting to hear it from Carlos.

'What happened?' Carlos let out a dangerous laugh. 'What always happens when people are too stupid to see the evidence. She got hurt.'

'*Caro mio!*' The Italian starlet had deserted her boyfriend, and was demanding a dance from her director. Carlos thrust his glass into my hand and whirled her away.

'Carlos forgets.' Quiepo had sidled closer. 'That boy he liked. One night Zeynep found them, the boy and Carlos. It was . . .' He made a face. 'Not nice.'

'Come!'

Quiepo looked at me in surprise.

Impatient with stories, I held out my arms.

> 'We've just been introduced
> I do not know you well
> But when the music started
> Something drew me to your side.'

He looked at me, puzzled.

'Cheap music,' I explained. 'The very best.'

He placed a regretful hand on my shoulder.

'I'm sorry,' he said. 'Later, maybe. Not now. Carlos . . .'

'What about Carlos?' I challenged.

'Is not an easy day for him.'

I went in search of Jed, who I found at the bar, being bought a Coke by Mercedes.

'Right!' I said. 'Time for bed.'

'But, Peter . . .'

'No arguments!'

Mercedes turned from the bar, Coke in hand, but already I was pulling Jed away.

'Why?' he said later, as I tucked him in. 'We were having fun.'

'It's ten o'clock. Tomorrow you're up at dawn. You'll thank me then.'

'All right,' he conceded petulantly. 'But then you have to read to me.'

'It's too late.'

'Just a chapter.'

'Okay. Just a chapter.'

From underneath his pillow, he produced a battered copy of *The Lion, the Witch and the Wardrobe*.

'But we've already read that! We finished *The Last Battle* in London, remember?'

'I know. But I like it.'

'Very well.' I took up the book, and, settling myself on the edge of the bed, began again on the story of Peter and Susan and Edmund and Lucy and how, at the back of a cupboard in the Professor's house, they discovered a door that led into a parallel but enchanted universe.

Twelve

*T*he next day, much as my impulse was to be with Jed, who I knew was missing Jacqui, I cried off going to the village. Let Father Ricardo play chaperone. I needed a breathing space.

I spent the day in a field on the outskirts of Castres, in the grudging shade of an almond tree, discovering that to confront the truth is not as painful as might be expected – a process of recognition rather than revelation. At around four, mindful of the fact that I did have a job, I went into town to see if I could find Jed – who, as luck would have it, I met almost immediately. I'd taken a different route from usual, and before I reached the main square, came across another, at the head of which stood the white façade of a silent church. I was in the process of crossing the square when I heard my name, and, turning, saw Jed dashing into the road to join me.

'What have you been taught about crossing roads?' I asked sternly.

'I know,' he sighed. 'Left, right, then left again.'

'Precisely.'

'But in Spain,' he said, eyes triumphant, 'it's the other

way round. Right, left, then right again. And anyway, there's never any traffic in this square.'

'That's not the point.'

To pacify me, he slipped his hand into mine. 'Where have you been?'

'In the fields.'

'Doing what?'

'Thinking.'

He made a face.

'And you?'

'Father Ricardo's been showing me the stations of the cross.' He nodded his head in the direction of the church.

'I see. And tomorrow?'

'*Mañana*,' he said, 'we're filming by the dam. I have to go swimming.'

'Goodness! Well, I have to see that.'

'It means getting up very early.'

'Then you'll have to wake me.'

Which is what he did, with a rapid tattoo on my door, at just after five. By the time I'd dressed and shaved, the others were all in the square getting into the vans.

'No Father Ricardo?' I asked as I took my place behind the driver.

'He has to go to Barcelona for the day.'

I was expecting us to head straight for the dam, but instead we drove past it and on to the village.

'Make-up,' explained Jed. 'And costume.'

In the second van were a handful of other children – extras drafted in for the day's shooting – and at the village Mercedes marshalled them into the *fonda*. I helped myself to some coffee, then went outside to drink it. A moment later Jed appeared, swathed in a beach robe four sizes too big for him.

'Costume?' I queried.

'Don't be silly!' He undid the robe to reveal a loincloth.

'Aha! A mediaeval speedo.'

The other boys began to appear, similarly attired, and there was a general drift to the vans.

'Come on!' said Jed. 'We're ready.'

We approached the dam down a vertiginous path that dropped from the road in a series of startling bends before flattening out onto a patch of dusty earth the size of a football pitch. The camera was already set up on a track that ran parallel to the water, and there were lights placed at intervals along the bank, over which, like fretful parents, electricians fussed. Carlos was standing at the water's edge, and as the children tumbled from the van he called them over, Jed included.

The boys handed their robes to some waiting assistants, and, under Carlos's direction, began cavorting in the water. Jed was instructed to stand slightly apart, and, at a signal from Carlos, the others began to splash him. Jed waded further into the dam. Then, at a second signal from Carlos, he turned and emerged from the water, the expression on his face one of suitable isolation.

A car arrived, and with it Murillo, already wigged and costumed. Carlos, who had forsaken the boys to confer with the cameraman, led his star to the water's edge, where he explained the scene. Mercedes darted forward and began to fuss with Murillo's doublet. He was ushered to a slight rise. The camera had been rolled back along its track, various last-minute adjustments were made to the lights, a make-up girl dusted Murillo's face with powder, Carlos shouted at the boys to take up position, someone called for silence, and in the silence, the clapper boy snapped his board at the camera. Murillo watched the boys, the boys began to splash Jed, Murillo approached the water, the camera reached the end of its track.

They ran the scene maybe a dozen times. Each time
Carlos demanded some minor adjustment. Murillo was
walking too fast. Murillo was walking too slowly. The boys
were splashing too much, too little. Jed didn't look sufficiently unhappy. To me, the scene had seemed fine first
time around. I couldn't comprehend Carlos's need for alter-
ation. He dealt in subtleties that were beyond me. As Father
Ricardo had said, a perfectionist.

Finally the scene was played to the director's satisfaction, and whilst Murillo and the boys repaired to the
shade of a tree, the camera was lifted off its rail and carried to the water's edge. I went in search of some shade
for myself, which I found under an olive tree on the bor-
der of a neighbouring field. A farmer was working in
the field, a man as old, it seemed, certainly as gnarled, as
the trees which he tended. He glanced up at my
approach, shading his eyes against the glare of the sun
with the palm of an earth-stained hand. I nodded a greeting. He didn't reply; without the sanction of words, his
rheumy eyes assessed me with an acuity I would have
thought beyond them. Unsettled, I turned my back on
him and lit a cigarette.

At the dam they were ready to start shooting again.
Carlos was instructing Jed, Mercedes was fussing with
Murillo's costume. Some of the lights had been moved,
and a sheet of polystyrene had been erected over the
camera. I stubbed out my cigarette. The farmer hadn't
moved. Statue-like, he continued to stare at me. Running
a swift hand across my face, as if to erase whatever it was
the farmer found so remarkable, I returned to the filming.

The boys were back in the water, and at the call for
action renewed their splashing of Jed, who waded out of
the dam and into the arms of the waiting Murillo.

A hand alighted on my own shoulder. Turning, I found myself face to face with Quiepo. Smiling mysteriously, he plucked at my sleeve. 'Come!' he said. 'Is someone to meet you.'

He led me in the direction of the olive tree under which I'd been standing earlier.

'What is this?' I snapped.

He put a reproving finger to his lips. 'You see.'

Standing in the shade of the olive tree, as if rooted to the spot, was the old farmer. As we approached, he ran the back of his hand across his forehead, then extended it in a tentative handshake.

I took the calloused hand in mine, and was surprised by the forcefulness of its grip.

'*Si!*' he said, nodding his head violently. '*Si, si!*' He turned to Quiepo and burst into a torrent of Spanish.

'This man,' said Quiepo carefully, 'this man know you.'

'Knows me?'

The old man gave voice to a further bout of Spanish.

Quiepo lifted a hand to quell his volubility. 'Not you, someone like you. In the Civil War . . .'

It wasn't easy, between the old man's excitable Spanish and Quiepo's halting English, to be certain I was understanding things correctly, but in essence what I deduced was this: that not only had my father's unit fought in these mountains, but that the old man had a sister to whom something unpleasant had occurred at the hand of one of my father's colleagues, and that my father – yes, my father – had come to her rescue. As a result of which, an affinity had been established between the two of them. Well, something more than an affinity.

I saw the suitcase in the attic, the yellowing tissue paper, the lace mantilla. The past was unpacking itself.

The old man whispered something in Quiepo's ear.

There was a momentary silence. Quiepo looked at me.

'He asks you visit his sister.'

'Now?'

Quiepo nodded. 'She lives in Castres. He say . . .' He paused, searching for the appropriate words. 'Happy,' he said eventually. 'She would be happy.'

'He wants us to go there now?'

Quiepo laughed. 'He has car.'

The old man pointed proudly to a battered truck parked at the edge of the field. '*Mi coche.*'

I took a deep breath. 'All right,' I said. 'If that's what he wants.'

As if frightened that I might change my mind, the farmer hurried us in the direction of his truck.

'What about you?' I asked Quiepo. 'Aren't you needed here?'

He shook his head. 'You need translator. Carlos can wait. Anyway, is busy.'

We reached the truck. The passenger seat was piled with newspapers, and, with an apologetic shrug, the old man opened the back and gestured inside. Quiepo climbed in first and settled himself against one side, legs outstretched. I took up position opposite. The farmer shut the door and scurried round to the driver's seat, where only after a great deal of coaxing with the choke did he manage to get the engine to splutter into life. We lurched up the track that led to the road.

Faintly discernible through the whiteness of Quiepo's shorts was a triangle of black against which his hand inadvertently brushed. Underpants? Or was he, perhaps, not wearing underpants? The luxuriant vee of his chest and stomach hairs showed up just as dark beneath his shirt. Darkness and light. Darkness within the light. It was like the mountains, the very landscape: an element of darkness amid

the brilliance, enticing and mysterious. I turned my face to
the dust-smeared window in the back of the van and tried
to concentrate on the road as it unwound behind us.

I knew we had reached Castres because the truck slowed
and the view through the window became one of houses.
We turned this way and that through the narrow streets,
until finally we came to a juddering halt. The old man let
us out.

We were in a street on the very edge of the town,
parked before a pale blue house from whose first-floor
balcony there flapped the pennants of that day's washing.
We followed the old man to the heavy oak door and
waited at his shoulder as he knocked. Shuffling footsteps
were heard, and a querulous voice, demanding to know
who we were. The old man barked his name, whereupon – with agonising slowness – the bolts on the door
were drawn back. It opened to reveal a small, wizened
woman in traditional black, her thinning hair scraped into
the severest of buns. She had hawk-like features, and eyes
of a piercing blue; eyes which darted first to her brother,
and then – almost immediately – alighted on me, and, as
they did so, widened in shock. Her hand flew up to her
chest, and with a quick, bird-like action, she crossed herself. The old man put a steadying hand on her shoulder,
and in low, urgent tones, began to explain who I was. She
listened in absolute silence, then, pushing him aside, took
a step forwards, and very slowly, wonderingly almost,
touched me on the cheek before once more crossing herself.

'*Muy religiosa*,' whispered Quiepo. 'In all the mountains.
Muy religiosos.'

The old man took his sister by the arm, forcing her into
the house. We found ourselves in a sparsely furnished hall.
Chairs were set stiffly round the wall, as in a waiting room,

and in the centre there stood a small round table florid with plastic lilies. The floor was tiled, the walls were white-washed, and on each wall there hung a picture: two garish representations of Christ, two sombre photographs of Generalisimo Franco.

I don't know what I'd been expecting – an old woman, yes, and the black dress, the washing on the balcony, the sparseness of the furniture – but never the pictures. Unless, that is, the years since the Civil War had wrought a change in her. How could my father, he of the Communist Party and the unwavering ideology, have allowed a relationship, any relationship, with a woman so obviously steeped in what he had come to fight? It didn't make sense. Or rather, it made nonsense; nonsense of what my father was, what he had lived for, what he would have everyone – himself included – believe.

The old man led his sister to one of the chairs and sat her down. He took the chair next to her, gesturing Quiepo and I to seat ourselves on the opposite side of the room. For a moment there was silence, in the course of which all four of us regarded each other warily across the arrangement of plastic lilies. I spoke first. 'So,' I said to Quiepo, 'how exactly did she meet my father? You say he rescued her. From what?'

The question was duly translated. The old woman continued to stare at me, but without saying a word.

'What is it?' I whispered to Quiepo. 'Is anything wrong?'

Quiepo said something in Spanish to the old man, who leant forward and patted his sister on the arm. Fumbling in her pocket for a handkerchief, she blew her nose sharply, then stood up and left the room.

'What now?'

Quiepo motioned me to be patient, and almost imme-diately she was back, carrying a black cardboard box,

which she laid on the table. She took out a faded brown
envelope, which she thrust in my direction. Nudged by
Quiepo, I got to my feet and allowed her to put it in my
hand. Her eyes were on me all the time. The envelope
contained a rather blurred black and white photograph,
no more than four inches square. A young man, who I
recognised only because of his likeness to me, leant
against the wall of what appeared to be a look-out post.
The sun was in his eyes, and he was squinting at the camera. He looked slightly awkward – either that or he was in
pain.

The old woman took the photograph from my hand,
and, turning it over, indicated some writing on the other
side. 'For Maria,' it read. 'Love always. Edward.'

Stunned, I handed the photograph back, and, with a
weirdly coquettish toss of her head, the old woman raised
it to her lips, kissed it, then returned it to the envelope.

I cleared my throat.

'Tell her,' I instructed Quiepo, 'that my father is well.
That he often talks about his time in Spain. That he talks
about her.'

Quiepo raised an eyebrow.

'Just tell her,' I ordered.

The message was duly relayed. Raising both hands to her
lips, the old woman now kissed them, then pressed them to
my burning cheek.

'*Momento!*' The old man had got to his feet, and, waving
at me to stay where I was, shuffled into the next room. He
returned a moment later with another photograph, larger
this time, and in a frame. He handed it to me ceremoniously, then began explaining something to Quiepo.

The photograph was of a young woman in a white,
almost bride-like dress, smiling into the camera. Her small-
ness was less noticeable in youth, and her features, which

age had sharpened to the point of ugliness, were, in the photo, marvellously clear. She had been very beautiful. But that wasn't all. I hadn't seen many pictures of my mother as a young woman – there weren't that many in existence – and in none of them did she look like a bride. Post-war austerity for her: drab coats, drab hats, obligatory gloves and unwieldy handbags. But all the same, the resemblance was unmistakable. My father had looked like me. My mother had looked like Maria.

Quiepo had come to stand at my shoulder, and now he said: '*Que guapa.*'

The old man nodded delightedly.

'Indeed,' I heard myself echo. 'Very beautiful.'

The old man smiled. 'Very beautiful.' He gave the words an upward inflection. 'My sister. Very beautiful.'

Oblivious to our compliments, the old woman had resumed her seat and was staring into space, hands folded over her cardboard box.

'I think we should go,' I said to Quiepo.

Quiepo took the old man by the hand and pumped it. I followed suit. To the old woman we simply nodded. Her self-absorption discouraged physical contact.

Outside, Quiepo threw back his head. 'Amazing,' he laughed. 'Your father was – how you say? – a dirty dog?'

'So it would seem,' I said drily. 'A dirty dog and a liberator.'

'Liberator?'

'Not perhaps in the way he intended. But yes, a liberator.'

'Liberator,' repeated Quiepo. 'What is liberator?'

'A person,' I said, eyes on his, 'who allows you to be yourself. Rare, I know. Especially here. Maybe anywhere. But every so often . . .'

There was a pause.

'What?' said Quiepo.

'I feel like a beer. What about you?'

He looked faintly surprised. 'We go to the square?'

'In the hotel,' I said. 'I don't feel like people. Do you?'

There was another pause. Quiepo had lowered his eyes. Then, with an almost imperceptible shrug, he said quietly: 'Room three-one-four.'

Which details are crucial? The fact that we didn't say anything as we walked to the hotel? The fact that he went upstairs first whilst I ventured into the bar to buy the beers? The fact that by the time I reached his room, he was already on the bed, stripped to a towel? The whirr of his ceiling fan? The striation of light across his chest from the shuttered window?

I remember the tart, clean taste of the beer. I remember the chill of the bottle. I remember him telling me that the old man had said his sister had never married. After the affair with my father, the local boys had regarded her with too much suspicion. She'd become an outcast. Tainted by that which was foreign. I remember him laughing, 'Don't tell Carlos. Who would he cast? Richard Gere? Julia Roberts?' I remember him shifting slightly on the bed, and the way in which the towel rode up his thighs. I remember him following the direction of my gaze, and where I put my hand. I remember the dryness in my throat and the fear in my gut, the fear of Carlos, the fear of myself, the fear of what I was about to do and its result, the fear that it might not happen. I remember his lips on my nipple, I remember the softness of the towel, I remember him saying, 'Not so fast. Relax!' I remember being spread out, very tenderly, on the bed, I remember the play of light of the ceiling, the susurration of the fan, a change of rhythm. I remember feeling as if my inner self was being peeled open, layer by layer. I remember his gentleness, I remember his roughness. I remember excitement, pain, apprehension and pleasure. Then I remember 'Shit!' – and Carlos in the doorway, hand plucking at the leather thong about his neck.

The door banged shut. Quiepo grabbed his towel. I lay where I was, unable to move. Quiepo ran to the door, opened it, looked up and down the corridor, then closed it again.

'Shit! Shit! Shit!'

The hair on his legs ran up and over the globes of his buttocks, stopping short at his back.

'You must go.'

I managed to sit up.

'Go!' he spat. 'Go now.'

He scooped my clothes off the floor and flung them at me.

'And at dinner tonight?'

He took my arm and grasped it painfully. 'Normal! Act normal.'

'I'm not sure I can.'

'Is the only way.' He relaxed his grip and began to stroke my face. 'Weakness he hates. Come to dinner. Be normal. Promise?'

'Normal?' I could hear the incipient hysteria in my voice. 'What's normal?'

'Don't let him see.'

'I'm sorry.' I grabbed at his hand. 'This was all my fault.'

Suddenly he grinned. Lopsidedly, I'll admit, but a grin all the same. 'Mine too.' And, snaking a hand between my legs, he squeezed the cause of our troubles. 'Go now.'

I timed my entrance into dinner to coincide with the serving of the first course, and behind the smokescreen of bustling waiters, was able to slip unnoticed into my seat. I stole a glance at the head table. Carlos was deep in conversation with Mercedes who, in answer to whatever he was saying, was nodding her head vigorously. Quiepo was on the other side of the costume designer, head bent, also listening. I looked quickly away.

The English scriptwriter was telling Jed about Murillo and how he had researched the scene they were to shoot tomorrow. Father Ricardo, returned from Barcelona, turned out to be something of an expert himself where the painter was concerned, and between the two of them, they kept up a flow of conversation that carried us through the meal. We were just finishing our coffee, and I was intently following the scriptwriter's account of Murillo's last days – so intently, in fact, that I feared he might question my extreme fascination with what he had to say – when I felt a hand on my shoulder. I looked up into the face I'd last seen framed in the doorway to Quiepo's room.

'The clue to Murillo,' said Carlos, eyes trained on the scriptwriter, 'is that he lost his children. Nine children – yes? – and by the end only one of them is left. Six die, his daughter enters a convent, Gabriel goes to America. This is why he paints the beggar boys. But because these paintings are secular, they are not enough for him. So he starts the final altarpiece. And he dies as he has to die, with a brush in his hand, falling from the scaffold in the Capuchin church. Artist to the last.' Without taking his eyes off the scriptwriter, he clapped me forcefully, almost painfully, on the shoulder and continued imperturbably: 'A man dying in the service of God. Of God and his art. That's what we have to convey. Fuck what Al wants.'

'Indeed,' assented the scriptwriter nervously.

Carlos turned his attention to Jed. 'You were very good today. I'm only sorry I have to keep you from your studies. But then I'm sure your tutors know how to make up for

lost time.' At last his eyes came to rest on me. 'Isn't that the
job of a teacher? To make up lost time?'

Intending to plead a headache and thus escape the room,
I pushed back my chair – but as I did so, I became aware of
Quiepo watching like a hawk from the top table.

'Right,' I said briskly. 'Jed! What about an ice-cream in
the square?'

'Now?' He could hardly believe his ears or his luck.

'No time like the present.' I looked directly into Carlos's
gaze. 'Isn't that what you're saying?'

Carlos laughed. 'What people say and what people
do . . . Very different things, I always find.'

'You can say that again.'

There was a dangerous pause, into which stepped Father
Ricardo.

'Right!' he intoned, getting to his feet. 'Ice-cream time!'

I held out a hand to our expectant charge.

'Vanilla for me. What about you?'

Once in the square, though, I changed my mind and settled on a brandy instead; two brandies, in fact, since Jed had
ordered himself the most expensive confection on the
menu, a confection that would take him an age to con-
sume.

Jacqui's joke about being hung over – frightened, lonely
and depressed – rose to the surface of my mind, bringing
with it a heightened awareness of just how messily I'd
betrayed her trust. For the second time that day, I heard
myself apologising.

'I'm so sorry.'

Surprised, Jed looked up from his ice-cream.

'What Peter means,' said Father Ricardo smoothly, 'is
that this won't happen every day.'

'Indeed,' I said. 'Not if I have anything to do with it.
That I promise.'

'But Peter!' Jed's voice was plaintive. 'It's only an ice-cream.'

'And this,' I said, holding up my glass, 'is only a cognac.'

Frightened, lonely and depressed. Words that covered a multitude of sins.

Thirteen

*T*he next day I kept pretty much to my room. I tried to read, and because I hadn't slept the night before, dozed a good deal. At lunchtime I ventured into the square for a sandwich and a beer. The hotel foyer was deserted, as was the square – siesta time – making me feel the entire country had, out of exquisite tact, retired to another room.

At four o'clock there was a single, rather strangulated ring from the phone by my bed. It was the manager.

'Señor Smallwood?'

'Yes?'

'I have a call from England.'

There was a pause, followed by a whooshing sound, followed by a faint and unfamiliar voice: 'Peter?'

'Yes?'

'It's P.J.'

'P.J.?'

'Your agent, darling. Remember?'

'Oh, P.J.! I'm so sorry, I—'

He didn't let me finish. 'Who's been a naughty boy, then?'

'I beg your pardon?'

But already he was rushing on, voice expanding and

contracting in concert with the static on the line. 'Look, darling, I'm not in this business to judge people. I'm simply here to pick up the pieces.'

'Wait a minute . . .'

'Darling, this line is awful. Don't interrupt, or we'll only . . .' His tone changed, and I heard him shout: 'Not now, Paul!'

I could imagine his office, how he was leaning back in his chair, feet on the desk, with Paul in the doorway. He continued: 'Basically, dear, what happened is neither here nor there, though when you get to London, if you want to tell me about it, we can of course—'

'What do you mean, when I get to London?'

Again his tone changed. 'Fuck it! I might have known.'

'Known what? What's going on?'

'No one's told you?'

'No one's said a thing. I . . .'

'Peter, sweetie, just listen. Carlos wants you off the movie. He didn't go into details – well, actually, it wasn't him I spoke to, Al called from the States – but whatever you've done, my advice is to clear out as soon as possible. Carlos isn't someone you argue with. I've got them to agree they'll make you a severance payment, and if there's anything else that needs settling, we can do it from here. All right?'

I didn't answer immediately, and after a moment he said: 'Are you still there?'

'Yes, ' I said woodenly. 'Still here.'

'Did you hear all that?'

I said nothing.

'Listen,' he continued, 'I realise I'm not on the spot and I might not be in possession of all the facts. If there's anything you'd like to tell me, do, and I'll take it up with Al. I mean, if there's been a misunderstanding . . .'

'No,' I said then. 'There's no misunderstanding. The only thing is Jed. Jacqui's in Los Angeles. I—'

'Surely the priest can cope?' he said briskly. 'I mean, he is being paid. Now, what about a flight?'

The initial shock had passed. My mind was beginning to function again. 'That's okay. You don't have to do a thing. I've still got the return half of my ticket. I can make my own booking from here And Jed . . .'

Jed, I was thinking wryly, *is better able to look after himself than his chaperone.*

'You sure?'

'I'm sure.'

'Well, ring me if you need anything.'

'I'll ring. Don't worry. I'll be fine. It was very good of you to call. I—'

I was interrupted by a crackle on the line, after which the phone went abruptly dead. I dropped the receiver into its cradle and stared blankly at a crack in the wall, trying to take comfort from the fact that Quiepo did at least know Carlos, that perhaps this had happened before, that he must know how to protect himself. Otherwise he wouldn't have lasted as long as he had. My pity I could reserve for myself – though the speed with which Carlos had acted left me unable to feel anything very much except a sort of grudging admiration. He had learnt well from his political idol.

I expected the next interruption to come from Jed, but by eight o'clock there hadn't been any knock on my door, and I could, if I'd chosen to, simply have stayed in my room. Mindful, however, not only of Quiepo's plea, but more crucially of the need to protect Jed from unpleasantness, I knew that tonight I absolutely had to put in an appearance.

The success of each day's work was always echoed in the evening meal. Some nights there was hilarity; on others, an undercurrent of unease. That night, as I stood in the doorway surveying the tables, I could tell the day had been exceptional. The hilarity was edged with hysteria, especially at the high table, barometer to the rest of the room.

I made for my empty place, and, as I did so, caught Quiepo's eye. He was in mid-guffaw, and though his expression didn't change, he managed to flash me a message of silent support.

'Guess what?' I was barely seated before Jed was demanding my attention.

'What?'

'Mummy gets back tomorrow.'

'Tomorrow? I thought she wasn't coming until the end of the week?'

Father Ricardo chimed in with a mild explanation. 'Apparently they've had a change of plan.'

He gave no clue as to whether or not he was party to what had happened. All I could cling to was the fact that at least my actions had resulted in Jacqui coming back to claim her rightful place; and indeed, it was the radiance of Jed's features that gave me the courage to say, as I reached with seeming nonchalance for the wine: 'Well, I have news too. I have to go back to London.'

'When?' It wasn't a frown exactly, that crossed his face, but almost.

'Tomorrow or the day after. I've had a call from my father. He's not well.'

'Nothing serious, I hope?' said Father Ricardo.

'No, no!' I shook my head quickly. 'I just feel I ought to be there.'

'When will you come back?' demanded Jed.

I shrugged. 'That's the problem. I can't say. It all depends.' I looked at Father Ricardo. 'You'll have to take over, I'm afraid.' And to Jed: 'Besides, Jacqui will be here. I don't suppose you'll notice I'm gone.'

He didn't like admitting weakness, and now he shrugged with elaborate unconcern. 'I'll be fine,' he said. 'You don't have to worry about me.'

I could see, though, that my announcement had taken the edge off his earlier excitement.

'Forgive me,' I whispered, leaning over to ruffle his hair. 'That's the way it goes.'

'You'll miss Sean Connery,' said Father Ricardo.

I made a face. 'Just my luck. I come all this way, and who do I miss? James Bond.'

When we'd finished eating, and because I wanted to clear my final hurdle as soon as possible, I got up and crossed to the high table. The Italian starlet was in the midst of some anecdote, but she tailed off at my approach, and the whole table fell silent.

'Yes?' asked Carlos quietly, fingers tapping lightly on his glass.

I swallowed. 'I'm sorry to interrupt, but I thought you ought to know. I've had a call from London . . .'

'Yes?' repeated Carlos.

'My father's been taken ill. I have to go back.'

'No!' It was Mercedes, looking genuinely horrified. Obviously she didn't know the full story. Maybe no one did. Maybe they never would. I had no idea how Carlos liked to play this sort of thing.

'It's nothing serious,' I continued hastily. 'I'd just feel better if I was there.'

'Of course.' Carlos gave up tapping his glass. 'When do you leave?'

'The day after tomorrow? I thought I'd wait until Jacqui got back.'

'Is that wise?' To an outsider, the question would have sounded quite innocuous. Only he and I knew its true import.

'I'm only thinking of Jed,' I said steadily.

'There's Father Ricardo,' replied Carlos. 'He can cope, surely?'

Quiepo came to my rescue. 'I understand,' he said. 'Jacqui gets back tomorrow, no? There might be time for an evening flight.'

'Poor you,' said Mercedes. 'That's horrible.'

I shrugged. 'These things happen.'

Carlos stood up. 'So, Don Pedro!' His tone was splendidly neutral. 'We might not see you again?'

'Probably not.'

In the depths of his steely eyes, there was a glint of ironic amusement. 'Just as long as we made you feel at home.'

I don't know how I managed to get through the rest of the evening. I started by treating Jed to another illicit ice-cream, and tried, without making too much of my impending departure, to let him know he would stay in my thoughts. I'm not sure I succeeded. As Father Ricardo had indicated, Jed lived in the present. Talking about tomorrow made him uneasy, as indeed did any overt display of emotion. In the end I opted for an entirely coded way of getting across my message: I read him three chapters of *The Lion, the Witch and the Wardrobe.*

He was already asleep by the time I put down the book, mouth slightly open, hand dangling from the side of the bed. I lifted it and laid it across his chest.

'You'll be all right,' I told his sleeping form. 'I know you'll be all right.'

His face went out of focus, the result of unwanted tears. I leant forward and kissed him on the forehead. 'Look after Jacqui.'

Back in my room, there was a surreptitious knock at the door. Opening it, I found Quiepo in the corridor. He slipped inside.

'I can't stay,' he whispered. 'Only Carlos . . .' He was having more than his usual difficulty in finding the right words. 'I'm sorry for Carlos. Sometimes he is very . . .'

'Jealous?'

He frowned. 'You are angry. Is it me?'

I shook my head. 'If I'm angry, it's with myself. I don't like to think I've made things difficult for you. Or for Jed.'

He shrugged carelessly. 'Carlos and I, we go back a long way. I can care for myself.'

'Can you?'

He appeared not to hear me. 'But you . . .'

'I don't regret a thing,' I said. 'I needed to do what we did. For me it was . . .' I had to fumble for the words. '*Muy importante. Guapo?*'

I put out a hand and felt for his face.

'You must go.'

For a moment he didn't move. Then, taking my hand in his, he bent over it, and in a gesture of quite ludicrous courtliness, kissed my fingers. 'If I teach you to touch,' he said, 'Quiepo is happy.'

Then he was gone.

One final surprise lay in store for me. The next morning – having waited until I was sure the crew had left for the day's filming – I opened my door to discover that an envelope had been propped against it. Inside was a card which Jed had drawn my father. A crooked camera, the clapper boy and a group of stick figures cavorting in the dam. 'Get well soon,' it said. 'Love from Jed.'

I took a coffee in the square. Afterwards I found a travel agent and ascertained there were frequent buses from Castres to the coast, where I would be able to catch a train to Barcelona. I enquired about flights, but did not book one. That I would do in Barcelona.

Errand completed, I returned to the square. A black car

was parked outside the hotel. I thought nothing of it until I'd mounted the hotel steps and heard, emanating from the foyer, an unmistakable American drawl. I was about to flee when Jacqui made an operatic appearance in the doorway.

She and Al had obviously come straight from the airport, and before that a Hollywood do. She was dressed in a black cocktail frock, her shoes had bows on them, and tucked under her arm was a small silver bag. Her make-up, too, was thicker and more elaborate than warranted by a transatlantic flight.

In any other circumstances, I might have burst out laughing, so incongruous did she look, dressed for a party on the mid-morning steps of the Reina Cristina, the Spanish sun cruelly highlighting the ravages of jet-lag. The expression in her eyes, however, put paid to laughter.

'So there you are! We wondered where you'd be skulking!'

She came clicking down the steps, high heels drumming on the concrete.

'Jacqui . . .' I began.

'What the fuck have you been doing?'

Close to, I could smell the cigarette smoke on her breath, and the cognac.

'Do we have to have this conversation here?'

'I just want to know,' she continued relentlessly, 'what the fuck you think you were doing?'

'It sounds to me,' I replied levelly, 'that you know all about it. In more detail, perhaps, than me.'

'How did you think you would get away with it? What did you think would happen? Did you think he wouldn't mind? Did you think he was going to say, you want my boyfriend, have him, he's yours?'

'It wasn't a question of wanting him. Not like that.'

'Oh, really? What was it then? Scientific curiosity?'

'He wanted it too. It wasn't only me.'

She tossed her head angrily. 'Did you stop to think of the consequences?'

'Actually,' I said, taking a deep breath, 'I rather took a leaf out of your book and said to hell with the consequences.'

I thought for a moment she might hit me. She didn't, though, just tautened with fury.

'And Jed?' she demanded. 'What about him?'

'Leave Jed out of this!'

'You were supposed to be looking after him.'

It was then that my temper snapped. 'So that you could fly to Hollywood and have it off with Al? Pardon me!' I came a step closer. 'Sorry to be biblical – it's rather catching here – but let him without sin.'

Without finishing the quote, I spun round and walked away. Almost immediately, I heard the click-clack of her pursuit. I ducked into a side street, and would have broken into a run, except that something silver whistled past my head. It was her bag. It fell in front of me, bursting open and spilling its contents – lipstick, lighter, packet of cigarettes, mascara – onto the cobbles.

The sight of her belongings splashed like that across the street brought me up short. I was reminded of how, in Kilburn, her saucer had sailed across the street and into Mrs Sargeson's trolley. That had been the start of our adventure. This signalled the end. I turned to face her.

I was expecting at least one further verbal assault, but in fact we had said everything there was to say, except, perhaps, sorry. She knelt and gathered up her possessions. I stood and watched. She straightened up, her breath coming in short, uneven bursts. I wondered if it would help to say the word that had been left unsaid, but she pre-empted me with a quiet: 'If I were you, I'd get out of town as quickly as possible.'

'Is that a threat?'

She regarded me evenly. 'All right,' she said eventually. 'Stay and find out.'

Seconds later she had click-clacked from sight, and I was left alone in the street – unless, that is, you count an indifferent cat draped like a shabby fur across a neighbouring wall.

I let an hour elapse before returning to the square. The car had vanished – up to the village, no doubt – and when I put my head through the hotel door, the foyer was mercifully deserted. I went straight to my room, packed my bag, then returned downstairs.

The foyer was still empty, and I was able to complete my final task without explanation or hindrance. I located a pen and paper behind the reception desk. The picture I drew was of the door in the back of the cupboard in the Professor's house.

'Sorry I couldn't say goodbye,' I wrote underneath it, 'but if I don't go now, I'll miss my bus. Keep socking it to 'em, and don't give Father Ricardo a hard time. Lots of love, Peter.'

I placed the note in Jed's pigeon-hole.

The travel agent had explained where the buses left for the coast – not from the square, where my wait might have been observed, but from an open space on the edge of town. Approaching it through the sun-drenched, somnambulant streets – siesta time again – I came to the square with the church.

The sight of its door, set like a challenge in the blank façade of the building, induced in me a wave of sudden, inexplicable anger. Too many doors were closed to me.

Indeed, I had only to see a door for it to be slammed in my face. Unlike Jed, who at least had Father Ricardo to guide him forward.

Taking a deep breath, I marched up to the church and put my hand on the door. Cumbersome though it looked, it acquiesced to my touch, and all at once I was on the threshold of this other, foreign world.

The church vaulted skywards, cool, daunting and indifferent. Far ahead of me, a sort of journey's end, was the curlicued canopy of the altar, gleaming dully in the gloom: as massive and as complicated as it was unobtainable. Immediately in front of it, head bowed, sat an old woman in regulation black.

Not wishing to disturb her, I slipped into the nearest chair and waited patiently for the church to initiate me into its mystery, to make me feel welcome. The longer I sat, though, the more aware I became that I did not possess the key with which to unlock the building's stillness. The whitewashed walls, interrupted at regular intervals by the stations of the cross, the rows of miniature chairs, the stone pulpit, the cloying smell of incense: all conspired to emphasise the fact that this particular path to salvation was one for which you needed a very particular map. No help for the uninitiated.

Crossing herself meticulously, the old woman got slowly to her feet and began to approach down the aisle. I saw with a shock that it was none other than Maria, my father's one-time lover. As if in prayer, I buried my head in my hands. Her footsteps stopped as she drew level with me. I kept my head lowered. There was silence, and then − just when I thought I wouldn't be able to endure the silence a minute longer − her footsteps started up again. I waited until I heard the door close behind her. Only then did I lift my head. The altar was as distant as ever.

I turned towards the door. In the corner, before a side chapel, I saw a bank of candles, and, on impulse, went across, dropped some money into the box, and lit a pair of them. One for Jed, one for my father. Then — angry, even as I made the gesture, with its manifest uselessness — I snatched up my bag and ran outside.

Fourteen

*A*ttaining the coast was every bit as easy as the travel
agent had indicated. Admittedly, I had to wait an
hour for the bus, but once it came, we rattled speedily
onto the coastal plain, mountains dwindling to a shadowy
serration set low in a sheet of sky. We crossed the motorway, and shortly afterwards pulled into an open space on
the outskirts of Alaroig.

I stepped from the bus into another, more hectic world.
Little sign of siesta here. A collection of tourist buses lined
the perimeter of the open space, and about them milled an
assembly of portly Germans interlaced with backpacking
youngsters of every nationality and an equal number of
unencumbered locals. I fought a path through the seething
mass and found a bar. The train station, I was told, was also
on the outskirts of town, about a mile away. I reached it just
minutes before a train to Barcelona.

The line ran more or less parallel to the sea. I sat with my
face to the window, catching glimpses of beach and rocky
coves, holiday resorts, dry river beds, the occasional town
and the even more occasional ship far out to sea where the
sparkling turquoise of the water darkened into a band of
blue that underlined a paler sky. We stopped at a number of

stations, soporific with sun, their platforms empty of all but a handful of passengers. We passed through a city, emerging into a continuation of the journey's Mediterranean refrain: pine forests and olive groves, more beach and cove, other, drier river beds. We came to another town and slid into another somnambulant station. Sitges.

It had been a week of impulses, and, without really thinking, I grabbed my bag and descended from the train. Since leaving Alaroig, the sense had grown in me that I wasn't ready for London, and I remembered the starlet pointing to that sign on the motorway: '*Bellissima!*' A spot, I thought, that might be conducive to contemplation.

The station opened onto a square full of taxis, beyond which ran a busy road, its pavement lined by shops. Crossing the road, I found the streets on the other side to be narrower and more interesting, the buildings older. In one of them a child was practising scales, and the hesitant, repetitive run of notes hung sweetly in the air, like blossom. I came to an equally narrow but much busier street along which a stream of people were taking their evening stroll. To my left, down a side street, I caught a hint of blue.

The sea front was fringed by two parallel promenades, one of earth, one paved, separated by a strip of grass planted with palms and oleander. I crossed them to the beach, which had been dissected, by means of breakwaters, into clearly defined bathing stations, each clotted with deckchairs. To the left, at the very end of the promenade, towered a church, and bracketing the bay at its other extremity was the outline of a vast hotel. Before me, the soothing stillness of the Mediterranean. *Bellissima*.

I began to hunt for a hotel, finding one in what had once been a house in one of the narrow streets that ascended the hill from the promenade. The reception area was a tiled courtyard from which, in a steep swirl, a wrought-iron staircase twisted to the top of the building. And yes, said the man behind the desk, they had a room, no bath, but it was at the back, very quiet.

The room was simple in the extreme: a single bed, a cupboard, a table and chair under the window. The window overlooked a second courtyard, where chairs had been placed under the vines and a suntanned couple were sitting out, drinking beer. Essentials only – the essentials of relaxation in the courtyard, the essentials of comfort in the room. Nothing extraneous.

I woke the next morning to a sky of translucent blue. I dressed in a T-shirt and shorts, packed my swimming things, and, after a leisurely breakfast in the courtyard, wandered down to the front.

The various segments of beach were bristling with people, either lounging on the deckchairs, playing quoits, or splashing in the water. I strolled along the promenade, and quickly came to a concession that was, or so it seemed, entirely and blatantly male.

Had I secretly known about Sitges? Or was I leaping to conclusions? Whatever the case, it seemed – in the fittingly clear light of day – that my decision to stop over had been more cunningly dictated than I'd realised. Essentials only. Some essentials! I walked down the steps and found myself an empty deckchair.

The scene before me comprised a sort of global seduction: seduction by sun and by flesh. Immaculately muscled bodies would twist this way or that to accommodate the rays of the sun, and when they got to their feet, would saunter sensuously to the water's edge. A man with a box slung over his shoulder passed like a town crier between the deckchairs, selling his wares. '*Agua*! CocaCola!' He fired the words at his supine customers. 'CocaCola! CocaCola!'

After a while, unable to contain the mixture of simple

relief and more complicated excitement my surroundings engendered, I got to my feet and entered the water. It was very flat and very warm and I was able to swim a long way out before turning onto my back and allowing the sea to cradle my pent-up body. An hour must have passed before I returned to the beach and flopped onto my deckchair.

'Good, huh?' It was the man next to me, dark-haired, moustached, body compact.

'Indeed.'

He nodded towards my book. 'I saw you were English.' He levered himself partially upright and lowered his voice. 'Quite a relief, too, if you don't mind me saying so. One gets so tired of incessant Germans.'

'One does?'

He grinned. 'Not that I'm against bratwurst – certain brands anyway – but everything in moderation.' He extended a trim hand. 'John. From Manchester.'

'Peter,' I replied. 'From London.'

We angled our bodies for conversation.

'I haven't seen you around,' he began. 'Just arrived?'

I nodded.

'First time?'

Again I nodded. As I did so, John's eyes flickered quickly but comprehensively over a passing form in the merest hint of tangerine.

'Not bad,' he chuckled. 'Even if it is from Dusseldorf.'

Thus invited, I allowed my eyes to follow his.

'Where are you staying?'

I explained.

He nodded. 'I know. Next to Angelo's.'

'Angelo's?'

'The restaurant? Heavenly food, heavenly waiters.'

'I'll remember that.'

'There's one, hung like the proverbial ox, who really

should be in the movies. And I don't mean *Mary Poppins*.'
He rolled onto his back. 'Found the bars yet?'

I shook my head.

He rattled off a list of where I ought to go.

'You certainly know your way around.'

'I ought to. This is my sixth visit.'

'What else should a newcomer know?'

'Apart from the bars? Well, if you're feeling energetic . . .'
Again he levered himself upright, this time to gesture over
my head. 'At the end there, past the hotel and along the
coast a bit, there's a nude beach. Not as nice as this – it's
awfully pebbly – but still' – he grinned suggestively – 'it's
always pretty busy. But I'm for a beer. Want to join me?'

The invitation was offered so easily, so naturally, without
a hint of come-on, that I found myself accepting without
demur.

Over our beer, and the two that followed, which we
drank sitting on the terrace of a bar overlooking the beach,
I learnt that my new-found companion had recently broken up with his boyfriend of ten years' standing.

'It was just too much for him,' said John wryly.

'What?'

'The fact that I'm HIV positive.'

He said it with extreme casualness, much as one might
admit to an allergy, then saw my confusion and came
swiftly to the rescue.

'It's okay. You don't have to say anything. And I can't say
I blame him. Alex, that is. I might have done the same in
his position.'

'He wasn't?' I asked. 'Positive, I mean?'

Which caused John to chuckle richly. 'You can say that
again.' He took a sip of his beer. 'I've been through all the
emotions. Anger, self-pity, hatred. Now . . .' He shrugged.
'Now I just live. At least I won't ever have to see this place

spoiled, which – if the rest of Spain is anything to go by – they'll do eventually.'

I followed his eyes along the promenade and down to the beach, where the muscle-proud men came and went. There was another element to the dance now, a hint of shadow fringing the light.

John, though, was smiling dreamily.

'"The Lobster Quadrille,"' he said.

'I beg your pardon?'

'"Will you walk a little faster?" said a whiting to a
snail,
"There's a porpoise close behind us and he's standing
on my tail."'

I completed the refrain. '"Will you, won't you, will you, won't you, will you join the dance?"'

'Lobsters,' he said. 'Lobster-red from the sun, and endlessly, endlessly dancing.' He finished his beer. 'Another dip?'

In between further dips and a sandwich for lunch, John told me the salient facts of his life. How he'd come out, how he'd dealt with his parents' reaction, how he'd met his lover, how he'd discovered he was HIV positive, some of what it meant to live with the disease. I listened intently, absorbing his story as greedily as my body was absorbing the sun, only joining in when, with his wandering glances, he invited me to share his sometimes amused, sometimes lecherous appraisal of the lobster quadrille.

At five o' clock, he announced his need of a shower and a nap.

'Doctor's orders,' he explained. 'Lots of rest. But what about a drink later?'

I said I'd like nothing better, so he made me accompany

him as far as the steps leading up to the church, where he pointed out a pavement café.

'Eight all right?' he queried.

'Eight would be perfect.'

Back at the hotel, I too took a shower; then, pole-axed by sun, even more by the fact that a gay beach could yield such a pleasant companion, I threw myself onto the bed and fell instantly asleep. I came to at seven, had another shower to wake me up, then wandered onto the front where, although I was early, I settled at the bar indicated by John.

The road at this end of the promenade had been widened so that cars could turn, and on the beach there was a cluster of sailing boats pulled up on the sand, bare masts pointing skywards. It wasn't details like this, however, that exercised my attention. It was the men – some single, some in couples – who traversed the promenade, eyes peeled for others like themselves who, under cover of their evening stroll, were continuing the day's assessment of what the town had on offer. I felt excitement, fear, resentment, disgust, relief. For better or for worse, for richer or for poorer, I had – it seemed – found my church.

'Peter!'

The voice was unfamiliar. Swinging round, I saw a vulture-like figure loping across the road. Of all people, the Canadian scriptwriter.

'Goodness!' I hoped my smile would mask how unwelcome I found his sudden appearance. 'What brings you here?'

He threw himself into a chair and waved an imperious hand at the waiter. 'I could ask you the same. Shouldn't you be on location?'

'I was called away to London.'

He smiled crookedly. 'And you came to Sitges!'

'I couldn't get a flight.'

The waiter came up, and he ordered a beer.

'Nice butt!' He nodded his head in the direction of the departing waiter, then patted his pockets to locate his cigarettes. 'So! Il Duce thrown anyone off the set yet?'

I took a sip of my drink and replied with what I thought was laudable evenness. 'Why? Is he likely to?'

The writer lit his cigarette. 'You saw how he treated me. The moment anyone stands up to him, questions his authority, he gets rid of them. Mind you, I'm sure he's happy with the Yorkshireman. I mean, what's *he* ever done? *Coronation Street*!' He enunciated the title with massive disdain. 'He'll do exactly what Carlos tells him.' He leant forward conspiratorially. 'Besides, he's so repulsive physically, there won't be any of the other trouble.'

'Other trouble?' Sensing revelation, I was suddenly alert.

The writer lowered his voice still further. 'I used to live with this producer, schmuck called Harold. Harold has a big mouth. There was very little Carlos hadn't heard about me, and I don't mean in the writing department.' The waiter had brought his beer, and now he took a deep draught of it, wiping the foam from his lips when he'd finished. 'We work on the script, Carlos works on me, and when I suggest it might be – well, friendly – to include Quiepo, he goes apeshit. He actually asks me if I think he's gay? Catholics!' He gave the word the same intonation he'd given *Coronation Street*. 'I mean, what do you say to self-deception like that? I'm supposed to let him play with my dick because he's heard about it from Harold, but when I suggest that Quiepo's his piece, he goes overboard.'

I'd hardly had time to take this in – or to consider the light it shed on my own brush with Carlos – when John appeared.

'Sorry I'm late,' he began.

I got smartly to my feet. 'John! Let me introduce you.' I turned to the writer. 'I've forgotten your name?'

'Brett.' Without rising, the writer extended a lazy hand.

'We met on this film,' I continued, stumbling over the words in my rush to explain to John that this wasn't a pick-up. 'Brett was doing the script. And now here he is in Sitges.'

'I've seen you around.' Although he had taken the writer's hand easily enough, I sensed that John wasn't sure whether or not to believe my explanation. 'On the beach.'

'That's what I love about Sitges,' said the writer. 'It throws up all sorts. I mean . . .' He fixed me with a leery grin. 'When we met at Carlos's, I thought you were with that chick. You know, the gold-digger.'

The waiter came to take John's order, and the writer – blithely unaware of the effect his presence was having – ordered another beer ('Make it a large one this time') and capped his insult with: 'Mind you, they're two a penny in Hollywood. Chicks like that. Spread their legs for anyone.'

A silence fell on the table, broken eventually by John, who said: 'So you're a writer? Anything I might have seen?'

The writer shrugged. 'I've just been working with Tarifa. That's where I met Peter. Before that Spielberg.' I noticed he didn't mention any films by name.

If John found the writer as crass as I did, he gave no sign of it; but then he couldn't know what I now suspected, that the writer was only in work because of the press Harold had given a certain part of his anatomy.

'Well?' prompted John. 'Have you met Mel Gibson?'

The writer lit a cigarette. 'Who hasn't?'

'And?'

'And what?'

'Is he as gorgeous in real life?'

The writer snorted. 'Guy's a midget. Comes up to my

waist. If you passed him on the street, you wouldn't look twice. It's only the eyes. That's what the camera loves.'

'Not just the camera,' said John.

The writer ignored the interruption. 'Sure I know Mel. Mel and Bruce and Richard. If you live in Hollywood, these people are your neighbours.'

'Tell me,' I said. 'How much do you know about Carlos?'

'Like?'

'Well, how exactly did he get where he is? What I mean is, for an orphan from Tarifa . . .'

'I know what you mean. You've only got to look at that villa. Those ceramics, for example, in the top living room?'

I nodded.

'Some duke or other – what do they call them? Grandees? One of Franco's main supporters, helped fund the old generalisimo when he launched his attack on the mainland, you know, at the start of the Civil War. Duke of Tarifa, I guess. I don't know. Anyway, he had the hots for Carlos. Met him at some function or other. Carlos moved in, and when Duke Baby died, out moved a whole lot of stuff. It was quite a scandal. The family tried to sue. But by then Carlos had used his connections to get in with the establishment, he was working at the Opera House . . .' The writer flicked the stub of his cigarette into the street. 'The rest is history. God, what a country! Where are you guys eating?'

John shot me a questioning look – to which I replied with an imperceptible shrug.

'We hadn't decided.'

'Well, actually,' said John, 'I thought, since you hadn't been, we could try Angelo's.'

'Angelo's!' said the writer. 'I know Angelo's. Angelo's is great.' He got to his feet. 'First, though, I need a pee. You guys settle the bill. I'll pay you later.'

'I'm sorry,' I said as the writer threaded his way through the tables. 'He just descended.'

John grinned resignedly. 'I thought he was a pick-up.'

'God, no!'

'Well, we're obviously stuck with him, so we might as well make the most of it. I want to know if it's true about the gerbils.'

'Gerbils?'

'You mean you haven't heard?' John laughed. 'My dear, you *are* on a learning curve.'

In fact, I'd had enough revelation for one evening, but over our meal the gossip continued unabated. Brett was a conversational litterer, dropping comments, opinions, statements of fact and of fantasy with a total disregard for his surroundings.

During dessert, in an attempt to let John know I wasn't unaware of the reason why he'd chosen Angelo's, and thereby reminding him of the confidences we'd shared on the beach, I said: 'Well, you were right. This place is certainly something.'

He shot me a pleased look, and – making it clear that this was a secret joke – answered quietly: 'And the waiter?'

Not secret enough, however. The waiter was obviously famed for his appendage, and the writer just as obviously resented sharing his billing.

'You think that's impressive? Feel this.'

Taking John's hand, he guided it under the table. There was a frozen pause, at the end of which John disengaged his hand and said evenly: 'Sorry. Not a size queen.'

'That's what they all say.' If he was put out by the tone of John's voice, the writer didn't show it. 'It's like those creeps in Hollywood who pretend they're not there for the money, only because they love film. Size is everything. In bank accounts, in real estate. Why should sex be different?'

'Because sex,' said John, 'isn't just about genitals.' He pushed back his chair. 'Now, if you'll excuse me, it's late and I'm for bed.'

I should have had the courage to stand up with him, but we didn't know each other well enough for that. All I managed was: 'See you tomorrow?'

John shook his head. 'Tomorrow I'm going to Barcelona.'

At first I thought this was a way of saying we wouldn't be seeing each other again, but immediately he added: 'Day after, though?'

'Perfect.'

'God!' said the writer the moment John had left the table. 'You English! Uptight isn't the word.'

'And you?' I could have answered. 'Heard of subtlety?' What I said, though, and as pleasantly as I could, was: 'John's fine. Just tired, that's all. Me too. So if you'll forgive me.'

Only when I reached the street did I realise – with immense delight – that we'd left him to pick up the bill.

The next morning I woke feeling at a loss. In the space of a single day, John had become both map and guide. Without him, I didn't know where to start, or even if I wished to. My Father Ricardo. Over breakfast, though, I became more bullish. That John had travelled further than me, and could therefore point me in the right direction, I didn't doubt. But at the end of the day, I had to hack my own way through the undergrowth. This was what the summer had been about. So, after finishing my coffee, I set off to find what I'd known I would want to explore ever since John had mentioned it.

As I progressed along the promenade, the hotels on the right gave way to a line of splendid villas, and the vast hotel which dominated the end of the bay came into sharper focus. After the hotel, grandeur became a stretch of pebbles littered with sea-scoured plastic, rusty cans and blackened wood. There was a golf course, a discotheque, some sort of sewage plant, then the dusty, terracotta path, which now ran parallel to a railway line, mounted a rocky headland.

Although it was only mid-morning, the heat was intense, and I was bathed in sweat by the time I reached the summit. Insistent cicadas called from the pine forest across the line. Then the line itself began to sing, and seconds later a train swept past, taking the singing with it. In the silence that followed, I heard a whistle. A man dressed only in underpants, body thrown into erotic relief by the whiteness of his briefs, stood in a grove of pine trees on the opposite side of the track. When he saw that I had noticed him, he slipped a suggestive hand between his heavily muscled legs. I was overtaken by a wisp of a man in lycra who, when he reached the base of the headland, crossed the line and mounted the hillside opposite. The man in underpants withdrew into the trees. The man in lycra ducked after him. Minutes later Lycra reappeared and continued his progress to the beach. Underpants took up his original position and began to caress his nipples. Another man came up, and the process was repeated. Communicants, I thought, partaking of the body and blood. Though what Father Ricardo would have made of this particular church, this particular body, I shuddered to imagine.

There was a second headland past which, in the cove between it and a third, even bigger headland, was a crescent of pebbles on which I saw maybe half a dozen bodies, all nude, all male. I came off the path and began to slither down the incline that led to the cove. The earth here was an even fiercer red, and had been ravaged by erosion. There were cigarette stubs and strips of tattered tissue festooning the shrubs that clung with vegetative obstinacy to the hillside. On the beach itself there was even more litter, only a hint of sand, and a grubby plastic structure which, although closed, I took to be a bar. If the beach in town was a sexual supermarket, this was a bargain basement: no packaging, just the goods themselves. What you might call naked consumerism.

I spread my towel at an appropriate distance from two men whose dramatic tans and golden hair led me to assume they were German, though, as it happened, they turned out to be Dutch. One was reading the paper, the other was lying on his back. Both contrived to study me as I slipped out of my shorts.

Part of me wondered where the hell I thought this would lead? Another part experienced the same relief and excitement that the beach of yesterday had triggered. Though on the beach of today this sensation was both heightened and less unsettling. No pretence about this cove, and pretence was what, in stepping from the train, I had come to Sitges to escape.

There was a glint of silver in the sky. A plane was making its descent into Barcelona Airport. Behind me, the impatient rattle of a train. Another plane, and ten minutes later, another train. Men trickled down the incline onto the beach. The bar was opened. The man with the paper put it aside, slipped into revealing shorts, and mounted the incline. His friend went into the water. More planes, more trains. The man in shorts returned in company with a dark-haired boy dressed like a game ranger in immaculate khaki. His friend, fresh from his swim, shook his head delightedly, sprinkling them both with water. The traffic was constant, the beach that point where, for a moment, various modes of travel – stellar and terrestrial – intersected.

The Dutch couple giggled with their catch over the fact that when you went for a walk in the pine forests, you seldom returned alone. A balding man with a paunch had settled on the other side of me, and every time I turned in his direction, I found he was staring at me. Overhead, the sun did service as a masseur, unknotting muscle, allowing my limbs to slacken and stretch. Another plane, another train, and on the beach the slow, remorseless unfolding of a ritual that was as flagrant as it was covert, as sordid as it was innocent, as perverse as it was natural. Utterly human.

I consulted my watch. It was two o clock. I was as hot as the beach was now full, so, negotiating pebbles and bodies with equal care, I entered the water and swam beyond the breakers to a point where, ironically, I was granted a Harry Lime-like perspective on my chosen stretch of coast. The men who toiled up and down the incline to the pine forest were no bigger than ants. On the beach, their supine counterparts blended with the pebbles in a causal arrangement of flesh and stone. And in the water there was a third commerce of bodies, this time between the beach and an adjoining cove. Either singly or in pairs, heads bobbed above the water to disappear behind the rocks which formed the limit of the beach.

I decided to investigate. The cove was tiny in the extreme; less cove, in fact, than an opening in the rocks that extended from the foot of the cliffs into the sea. I swam closer, and saw that through the opening there was a cave. A group of perhaps a dozen men emerged from the opening. I waited until they'd cleared the rocks, then coasted in on the swell. The sea floor banked steeply. I found my footing, and, wading clear of the water, stepped into the cave.

At first I thought it was deserted. Then, through the gloom, I made out the figure of a man leaning against the rocks at the back of the cave. He was in his late thirties, tall, blond; someone who clearly looked after himself. He had well-defined pectorals, a sculpted stomach, traceries of golden hair. He wasn't erect, though the size, angle and shape of what hung between his legs suggested that either he had been, or soon would be. I came a step closer.

His chiselled perfection was on the one hand banal; the stuff of pornography. He was too obviously a man of whom dreams are made. But in conjunction with the rocks behind him, and even if this does sound panegyric, his body took on an aura that approached the sublime. I don't wish to exaggerate, but so at one was he with the rock behind him that it seemed as though this wasn't a person I was approaching, but some god of the cave, placed there by the mountain itself. A living extension of the landscape. I put out a hand and reached for his cock.

What followed took all of two minutes. He came alive in my hand, body arching away from the rock. He pulled me closer. Our bodies merged. Fingers teased, explored, became urgent. Tongues too, lips and hands. Self was released into the strangeness of another, strangeness become something infinite, familiar and welcoming, then we were both returned − by each other and, it seemed, the cave itself − into our separate identities. Mortal again, he squeezed my neck and, with the briefest of nods (thanks? goodbye?), strode to the water's edge and plunged into the sea.

Have I exaggerated? Yes and no. What exists is what one sees, and if in those moments I saw more than was actually there, if I fashioned a god for myself where none existed, it is nevertheless true to say that after his departure I wanted to shout with joy. I could hardly believe that so brief and so physical a transaction could cause me to feel so healed. Because that is how I felt. As if what Quiepo had started, but left unfinished, was finally complete. And when, moments later, I swum out between the opening in the rocks and turned to look back at the cave, I was reminded of Carlos in the village, disappearing through the door of the church. Here, by contrast, was a door that stood forever open, a door that would admit anyone, even the likes of me. All one needed was honesty, determination, foolhardiness, luck.

The beach was a *petit mort*: grubby and distasteful. Scooping up my towel, I dried myself briskly, and avoiding the stare of the man with the paunch, slipped into my shorts, gathered up my things, and mounted the path. I didn't want epiphany to be compromised by reality.

I was halfway along the promenade when I heard my name. John beckoned from the terrace of the café where we'd sat the day before, the trimness of his moustache accentuating the brilliance of his smile. For the second time in as many hours, I felt as if in coming to Sitges I had somehow come home; completed a journey. What had yesterday been strange and threatening was now oddly normal.

'So!' he laughed as I settled opposite him. 'Three guesses where *you've* been.'

'You need three?'

He leant across the table. 'Find what you were looking for?'

I deflected his question with one of my own. 'How was Barcelona?'

He shrugged. 'Too hot and too crowded. I came back early.'

A waiter approached and I ordered a beer.

'Was our friend the writer in evidence?'

I grinned. 'If he was, I didn't see him. Or the tool of his trade.'

'I'm sorry about last night,' said John. 'I couldn't stomach any more.'

'You weren't the only one.'

The waiter deposited my beer on a little mat. The taste of it was sharp and clear.

'Maybe,' I ventured, 'we could try again? Tonight, I mean. Somewhere off the beaten track.'

John chuckled. 'Not Planet Hollywood.'

So as to minimise the risk of bumping into the writer, John called for me at my hotel, and we headed straight for a restaurant he knew in one of the back streets, where we were given a table in the garden, under a fig tree. He made me tell him more about my day, and when I mentioned the man in underpants, burst out laughing.

'She's there every day,' he smiled. 'Same spot, same time, for as long as I can remember. She has a plastic cock ring to help her keep it up.'

'And the forest behind the beach? More of the same?'

He speared a prawn. 'Always reminds me,' he said, 'of when I was a boy. Playing hide and seek. The excitement of the chase. Wanting to hide where no one will find you. Wanting to be found.' He bit into the prawn. 'It's our nature to hunt. Male nature, that is. How can we avoid it?'

'And the dangers?'

He shot me an enquiring look. I attempted a list.

'Being mugged. Rejection. Loneliness.'

'AIDS?'

He supplied the danger that had been uppermost in my mind. I nodded.

He speared another prawn. 'Because we're not total animals . . .' Here he grinned. 'Oh, for a total animal!' Then he was serious again. 'We can, if we wish, hunt politely. Safe sex. Also kindness.'

The garden of the restaurant was lit by candles, one on each table, and in their flickering light he looked impossibly boyish. On impulse, I reached across and took his hand in mine.

'I'd like to thank you,' I said, 'for making what could have been horribly lonely exactly the opposite.'

He smiled deprecatingly. 'At the risk of bumping into your writer friend, what say you to a walk along the beach?'

I released his hand. 'Sounds good to me.'

As we stepped onto the promenade, we heard music, half jolly, half wistful. A brass band was playing in the centre of the promenade, on a platform draped by the Catalan flag. At the base of the platform, in three circles, were some local dancers. Each circle had a leader who, as the band played and then replayed its tune, would shout instructions to his group. *Uno, dos, cambio!* The feet of the dancers skimmed the earth as they skipped first to the right, then to the left, knees bending, feet kicking, arms always linked. *Uno, dos, cambio!* The words became a refrain, the trumpets and tubas circled the notes as fleetly as the dancers circled each other, the spectators were smiling.

'Sweet,' whispered John. 'And, under Franco, treason. Weird what people find threatening.'

We crossed to the balustrade that separated beach from promenade. The deckchairs had been stacked away, and the only movement was of waves turning from white into black as they made their rippling assault on the sand; another version of the dance. To our left was the floodlit façade of the church, to our right the distant outline of the hotel, and in the sky the occasional star that on closer inspection turned out to be the lights of a plane making its descent into Barcelona Airport.

'I had a Dutch friend once,' said John, 'we were a sort of item. Well, for a while. He used to say: life is what happens just when you've made plans for something else.'

I didn't reply.

'What do *you* think?' he continued. 'Is there life after death?'

'The way I feel,' I said hesitantly, 'is that there's death in life, and life in death. I don't see that you can tell them apart.'

The moon had appeared from behind a cloud, turning the ripples into the train of a global wedding dress, opulent and camp. John rested a hand lightly on mine.

'Pumpkin time,' he announced; and then, in a huskier tone: 'Would you like to come back? To my hotel?'

It was a question I'd been expecting – hoping for, even – and one that I had no difficulty answering.

His hotel was by the station. The boy behind the desk didn't bat an eyelid when John collected his key and ushered me towards the lift. Nocturnal assignations were obviously the norm in this particular marbled hall.

In his room, he switched on the light above the bed – 'At my age, overhead lighting is to be avoided' – and showed me the bathroom. When I emerged, he had turned back the coverlet and stripped to his underpants. His body was in pleasant contrast to that of the underpanted man in his grove of pine trees. The one had been a human billboard, advertising availability. John's was too thin, too thin and too vulnerable, for pornographic perfection.

'Here!' he commanded softly, and, when I obeyed, began, very slowly and with a sort of wry self-absorption, to undress me. When he reached my underpants, I took his hand in mine and squeezed it. He lifted both our hands to his mouth, kissed the back of mine, then rubbed my cheek.

'Bed?' he queried.

I nodded.

'Right side or left?'

'Whichever.'

He pushed me into a sitting position on the bed and enfolded me in his arms. Through the hair on his chest I could feel the pulse of his heart. He brushed his lips against my hair, then vanished into the bathroom. When he returned, he turned out the light and slipped beneath the sheets, gesturing me to do the same. He gathered me into his warmth.

'I don't know about you,' he whispered, 'but I'm bushed.'

He made the announcement with the same firmness he had displayed in undressing me, the same gentleness with which he was currently tickling my back.

'That's nice,' I murmured. 'What you're doing.'

He snuggled closer and kissed me on the neck.

'You smell of the sea.'

'You too.'

'Sweet dreams.'

Without the slightest difficulty, I surrendered myself to the movement of his fingers and the comfort of his arms: to sleep.

When I woke, it was morning already and John, fully dressed, was drawing the curtains.

'Sleep well?' He came to sit on the edge of the bed.

I reached for his hand and kissed it. 'Like a baby.'

'Your face goes all soft when you sleep. No lines.'

'It's the feel of your arms.'

'That powerful?' He flexed them in parody of a muscle man.

'Magic certainly.'

He leant forward and kissed me lightly on the forehead.

'That's because you're so good to hold.'

'You can hold me some more if you like.'

He stood up.

'I have a plane to catch.'

'This morning?'

'This morning.'

'You didn't say.'

He crossed to the table between the windows and held up a piece of paper.

'My number in Manchester. I have a car, and we're very close to the Peak District, also the lakes. Perhaps you'll come up some time? The flat's pretty small, but the bed's accommodating.'

Whereas he had been the one to do the commanding the night before, now I felt the initiative lay with me.

'Come here!' I whispered, and when he had, slipped a hand beneath his shirt. 'Closer!' My other hand I placed on the curve of his neck, forcing his lips onto mine.

Did I run a risk by kissing him? I couldn't imagine so.

'Look after yourself.'

He giggled. 'My dear! As you can see, these days I do nothing but.'

Back at my hotel, I took breakfast in the courtyard — then, despite the fact that the day promised to be every bit as glorious as yesterday, I went to the desk and enquired about trains to the airport. This section of my journey felt complete, but the journey itself was not yet over. There was still my father.

Fifteen

The flight to Heathrow was entirely atypical. A storm was brewing, and, after banking over the Mediterranean, we were tossed by turbulence into France. Then, hemmed in by trays of food and the ministrations of the cabin crew, we flew more calmly until we reached the channel.

I remembered the first time. Jacqui and I drinking cognac, Jed playing his electronic game. Still on Level One. Which level now, I wondered, and what of Jacqui? Would she realise, without anyone to tell her, how much her son had missed her?

I had a window seat, and as the engines throttled back, I was able to chart our descent: an estuary dotted with islands, a pattern of fields, roads, town, city, the winding thread of the Thames, Greenwich Observatory, Lloyd's, St Paul's, the Houses of Parliament, Battersea Power Station, each headliner in this urban vaudeville more suggestive of home than the last, right down to the chorus line of suburbs.

The distance from the railway station to my father's house was a fifteen-minute walk: too close to take a bus, too far to be agreeable on foot, especially with a suitcase.

To distract attention from my aching arm, I concentrated on the houses, the subtle gradations of class and style that distinguished one road from another. From the air, these houses looked identical, muted accompaniment to an urban symphony. Close up, they were themes in themselves. This street boasted basements, that bow windows. This house was pebble-dashed, that had a porch. These gardens were profuse, those paved.

Turning into Winterbourne Road, I was confronted by a sight I'd never have thought possible: my father on the pavement, conducting a divertissement in which Barbara and Jim were cutting back the hedge. Despite the heat, my father was dressed, as always, in cords and a cardigan. Barbara wore overalls. Jim – who, when he wasn't writing his pamphlets, favoured the gym – was stripped to the waist and in shorts.

Barbara saw me first. Dropping an armful of clippings onto the mountain that was building on the pavement, she dug her conductor deftly in the ribs: 'The prodigal returns.'

If I hadn't known him better, I would have sworn the look that transformed my father's face was almost one of delight. But I did know him better; apart from which, by the time I had entered his orbit, his expression was every bit as guarded as usual.

'I thought you were in Spain?'

'I was. I got back this morning.'

He looked at his watch, not to check the hours, but the date. 'Three weeks. They can't have finished the film? Or did he have a smaller part than you were led to believe?'

'No, no,' I said. 'His part was central. Still is. It was mine that was peripheral.'

Again, if I hadn't known him better, I could have read his answering look as one of concern. Except that the hand he waved in front of his face was to ward off a wasp, and his frown was for the insect, not me.

Barbara pushed a strand of sweat-dampened hair from her forehead and said: 'Well, if we'd known, we wouldn't have started this. Would we, Jim?'

'I rather like it,' said Jim, muscles flexed. 'Good exercise.'

'Narcissist!' spat Barbara.

'I think,' said my father quietly, 'I'll put the kettle on.'

I followed him round the side of the house. The back garden was as wild and jungle-like as ever.

'Saving this for me?' I asked as we passed into the kitchen.

'Actually,' said my father, 'I wasn't expecting you back for at least another month. September at the earliest. What happened?'

I deposited my case by the door.

'A disagreement with Carlos.'

'Over Jed?'

I shook my head.

'Well?'

'It's a long story.'

Kettle in hand, my father hovered by the sink, waiting on elaboration. When none was forthcoming, he abandoned the kettle and gestured towards the fridge.

'Why don't we have a glass of wine instead?'

'If you want.'

He busied himself with extracting a bottle from the chaos on the lower shelf.

'There are glasses behind you,' he said; and as I twisted round to reach for them: 'So how is Jed?'

'Jed,' I said, handing him the glasses, 'is a star. An absolute star.'

'But now you're not there?'

'There's Father Ricardo.'

My father snorted. 'I might have known there would be a priest.'

'A very good priest, actually.'

'Aren't they all?' He thrust a glass at me. 'Is Jed becoming a Catholic?'

'Actually,' I said quietly, 'I think he might be.' I took a sip of my wine. 'Would that be so awful?'

'For Jed?'

'I wasn't thinking of myself. And you haven't answered my question.'

He went to stand at the window, where, cardiganed back towards me, he surveyed the viridescent spawn of summer.

'Perhaps you haven't been reading the papers,' he said eventually. 'But every time the Pope makes another pronouncement, my blood runs cold.'

'Forget about the Pope,' I said. 'Forget about the Church. Just to have faith. To have belief. A guiding principal. Is that so awful?'

He turned to face me.

'Well?'

The expression on his face was utterly inscrutable.

'They always say of Thatcher that at least she believed in what she was doing. At least she had commitment.'

'As with Stalin, you mean?'

My riposte was unthinking, part and parcel of our historic sparring, and it had the effect of causing my father to look sideways again, in the direction of his less truculent garden.

'I was thinking nearer home.'

'Talking of home . . .' My tone was conciliatory. 'Is it all right if I stay? Here, I mean.'

'Your disagreement extended to Jacqui?'

It was my father's turn to twist the knife.

'Jacqui and I are fine.' The words came automatically.

'Just fine. I don't feel like being at the flat. That's all.'

My father placed his glass on the window sill. 'There's that camp bed in the box room. If you don't mind the junk.'

'Of course I don't.'

'That's settled, then. Now, what about supper? The hordes will be ravenous.'

He moved towards the pantry. I extended an instinctive hand.

'Can't they fend for themselves? It isn't every day I come back from Spain. I thought we could eat out, just this once. Just you and me.'

'You have something to tell me?'

The directness of the question was as uncharacteristic as it was unnerving. I swallowed.

'Yes,' I said. 'As it happens, I have.'

A sort of skittish disbelief flared in his eyes, half wary, half flattered. Then, with a nervous giggle, he patted the pockets of his cardigan. 'Goodness! Well then, where shall we go?'

We settled on the Indian in the High Road, and whilst he went to inform the workers they'd have to cook for themselves, I went to claim the box room. Returning downstairs, I heard Barbara's strident tones emanating from the kitchen, Jim's purring bass providing the accompaniment. I took myself outside to wait on the front steps. The hedge had been shorn to within an inch of its life, and as a result the house looked sadly vulnerable. Deprived of cover, its Gothic extravagances seemed overly architectural, too starkly revealed, not strictly necessary. The hedge was vital to the fairy tale. Without it, the Prince was redundant. Jed would have been horrified.

My father appeared. Like me, he had changed his shirt. He was also wearing a tie.

'Acceptable?'

'The Khyber Pass,' I said, 'is hardly the Ritz.'

'Still . . .' He fingered his tie. 'It isn't every day your son asks you out.'

I got to my feet. 'I'm paying, am I?'

He feigned surprise. 'Aren't you?'

I laughed. 'Of course. Let this meal be on Carlos.'

Which details are crucial? As with Quiepo's hotel bedroom, if I think back to the evening in the Khyber Pass, it defines itself by means of fragments, some visual, some tactile, some aural. The waiter's wrist, oddly feminine and yet coated with hair, as he fits our beers to the mats at the side of our place settings. The metal warming trays, the dishes of curry, the hillocks of nan, the steaming napkins in their plastic skins. Velvet wallpaper, sepia photographs of an imperial past, the woman opposite, vermilion nails as vivid as her lips, her featureless partner. My father's fingers as he snaps a papadum, the waiter again, wanting to know if everything is to our satisfaction, my own face in the glass of the picture beside my father's head, features superimposed on a line of Indian soldiers with rifles at the ready, a ghostly, younger echo of the older, warier eyes, nose, forehead, chin and mouth which, as my father's fingers pluck at his tie, is saying: 'But I thought it was you we'd come to discuss.'

'In essence,' I reply, 'it's a photograph.'

'A photograph?'

I think of the plastic lilies. The pictures on the wall, of Christ and of Franco. The photograph of Edward, the one of Maria. A small museum of self-deception.

'Of a woman,' I say, 'who lives in Castres. A very old woman, though not in the photograph.'

'Maria!' Mantra-like, my father combines the name with an exhalation of breath, and I am reminded, ridiculously, of the song from *West Side Story*.

'Maria,' I repeat, giving the name a more prosaic emphasis. 'For Maria. With love always. Edward.'

I turn the inscription into a challenge. There is a long silence, in the course of which, though he doesn't take his eyes from my face, I know he is looking through me, past me, at some other point of focus. Then, feeling for his teaspoon and starting to tap it against his saucer, he begins to speak.

'We travelled through France by train. There were half a dozen of us. A Scotsman, I remember, and a Welshman; the rest of us from London. We were smuggled into Spain by lorry. We went to Tarragona. Training, they called it, though all it amounted to was a bit of square-bashing, rifle practice, a lot of soccer. We were there for three months. Then we moved to Castres. It was towards the end of the war. Teruel was under siege. They needed reinforcements. There was some argument, though, between the divisions. We never got to Teruel. We stayed in Castres. Kicking our heels. Doing pointless manoeuvres in the mountains. Charging pine forests. Laying siege to olive trees. Beniplacar. Valliguera. It was awful, pointless, mid-winter, none of us had sufficient clothes.' The tap-tap of his teaspoon increases in tempo. 'Though what really happened was the realisation I'd come to Spain under false pretences. That actually I was a coward.' His lips form a self-deprecating smile. 'I didn't want to die. I didn't want to suffer. Even when we were play-acting – bang-bang you're dead, count to a hundred, like little boys – even then I was scared.'

'Maria,' I prompt, transfixed by what he is telling me, but not wanting him to get side-tracked.

There is a further silence. Then: 'We'd taken over the church in Castres. Stripped the altar, made that a table. Thrown out the pictures, the statues, the candles. We slept in the side chapels.' He stops the tapping, and, denied accompaniment, his voice becomes oddly hesitant. 'One day we came back from some manoeuvre in the mountains – charging a pine forest, arresting an olive tree – and there was this girl in the church, kneeling in front of the altar, praying to our plates. The others set on her. They chased her round the church, cornered her in one of the side chapels, started to rip off her clothes. I managed to get between them.' He's taken up his teaspoon again, is turning it between his fingers. 'I actually stood up to them. Got her out of there. I took her home. We. . . .'

He doesn't finish the sentence, nor is there any need. I know what happens next, at least in essence.

'And then?'

He replaces the teaspoon in its saucer. 'Two weeks later we were pulled back to Tarragona. A month later I was back in London.'

'You never saw her again?'

He smiles, only this time the smile has a certain radiance. 'I saw her all the time. It wasn't a face you forget.'

'Apparently not.'

He shoots me a puzzled look.

'I saw the similarity.'

'Similarity?'

'You know what I mean.'

I don't know what effect I'd imagined my saying this would have on him, but I certainly wasn't prepared for the way in which my words caused his face to crumple, nor for the tears. I reached across the table and clutched his arm.

'I'm sorry if this is painful. I need to understand.'

He fumbled for his napkin and wiped away his tears, then folded it neatly and placed it on his side plate. 'After Spain,' he said eventually, 'I left the Communist Party. It

wasn't just Maria. It was everything I'd seen. The politick-
ing. The cruelty. My cowardice. It was all so hopeless.'

'Why have you never told me this?'

He began to fiddle with his napkin. 'What was there to
tell? That people are irredeemable? That politics is a sham?
What kind of a message is that?'

'All the same . . .'

'I wanted to protect you.'

'Back in London, then,' I said, steering the conversation
onto its original track. 'What happened?'

'Lots of things. I lived, I worked, I met your mother. She
hadn't lost her faith, either in people or in politics. She was
active. Committed. Full of idealism. And as you say: the
similarity.' He forestalled the question he knew I would
ask with a frown. 'Don't forget, I was in my late forties.
Your mother seemed like a second chance.'

'I thought . . .'

He appeared not to hear me. 'And then she died. Just
when it looked like maybe she was right – politically, I
mean – that things could change. Nineteen-seventy . . .' He
was still frowning. 'After her death, and having you, I don't
know – I felt I owed it to her memory, especially in the
eighties, when things began to go wrong, when people
were crowing over the death of communism, I felt I owed
it to her not to lose faith. I'd been a coward once.' His
frown deepened. 'People's greed, their stupidity, their cruelty, their self-satisfaction. Why should it triumph?'

I was reminded of Father Ricardo and the holograms:
the whole contained in every part. Except that the whole
was only in focus when all the parts were present. Cut off
a bit, and you got a blur.

'Do you remember,' I whispered, 'when I was seven,
maybe eight, I found a box in the attic?'

'Your mother's clothes.'

'And something of Maria's.'

He looked at me blankly.

'A lace mantilla.'

He gave vent to a sudden laugh. 'No, no! You misunderstand. How I met your mother, she was in a production of *The House of Bernarda Alba*, one of the sisters, amateur dramatics. I was helping with front of house. The mantilla was hers.'

My mouth fell open, and as at the start of our conversation, my face mirrored his, except that whereas his mouth was open in laughter, mine gaped in disbelief. Certain things had been clarified; others complicated. Each piece of the mosaic had a corollary. Two sides to every coin. Heads you win, tails you lose.

'I suppose I owe you an apology?' My father's eyes had finally come to focus purely on me.

I shrugged. 'I certainly wish I'd known. Earlier, I mean.'

He shook his head. 'No, no! The clothes. When you found that box. I was unnecessarily harsh.'

Which led, of course, to that part of the mosaic which was mine to complete. Exactly how, all those years ago, my mother's clothes had made me feel. The effect of my father's anger. What I had discovered in Quiepo, and in Sitges.

A plan was forming in my head, though because I felt we had done enough talking for one evening, all I did was call for the bill.

'What's done,' I said, 'is done. Where we must look is the future.'

Back in the box room, I put my suitcase atop a teetering pile of *Socialist Workers* and rooted through it for my toilet bag. My hand found an envelope: the card which Jed had drawn my father. The crooked camera, the stick-like clapper boy, the figures in the dam. Get well soon. Tears sprang to my eyes. Then, in an effort to shake off the past, I shoved the card between the yellowing newspapers. All right, so I had, in Jed, lost a surrogate son, just as he had lost a surrogate father. But in another part of the picture, another son was, piece by piece, putting together an image of another father.

Sixteen

Neglectful of the fact that the hot-water system for the whole of my father's house passed through the box room, I had forgotten to open the window, with the result that the next morning I woke feeling as if I'd been subjected to a nocturnal drubbing. It hurt to swallow, it hurt to move my head, and, thanks to the contours of the camp bed, it hurt to move my arms and legs. I staggered to the window, where a fresh morning breeze went some way towards cooling my body. Then, mindful of what I had to achieve if I expected to put my plan into action, I took a hurried shower, dressed and went downstairs.

There was a note from my father on the kitchen table: 'Back this evening. Barbara's cooking.' Next to the note was the cooking rota, which confirmed that indeed it was Barbara's turn to cook, and next to that a shopping list headed, in red, by the name of another functionary: Roger. Everything in apple-pie order, at least within the People's Republic of Winterbourne Road.

I made myself coffee and began a list of my own. Top of it was to phone P.J.

'Darling!' he cried when Paul had put me through. 'Where are you? Why aren't you back?'

'I am. It's just the line.'

'Where are you phoning from?'

I told him.

'Norwood?' The tone of his voice made it plain that on his map, South London was on a par with Outer Siberia.

'I just wanted to check about the severance payment. You said you'd spoken to Al.'

'A minute, darling.' I heard him call Paul, then he must have put his hand over the receiver, because all I heard was a muffled exchange, followed by: 'Why don't we have a drink? What about Friday?'

The last thing I wanted was a drink with P.J. I didn't see the need to supply him with gossip which, I was sure, he would only use against me.

'I'm afraid I can't. As of tomorrow, I won't be around. I just need to know if the money's on its way.'

'The money is indeed on its way.' He mentioned a figure I couldn't quite believe.

'Are you sure?'

'Darling, if they want to break a contract, they have to pay for it. There was nothing in the small print about where to put your dick.'

'Well, well!' If P.J.'s laconic manner had ever made me question his negotiating abilities, the amount of money he'd extracted from Al put paid to that. 'Thank you. I never thought . . .'

'It'll take a day or two for the cheque to clear, but it should be in your account by the end of the month. All right, Paul, you can put her through! Listen, darling, I have to go, but if you ever make it as far as the West End, you know where to find us.'

The phone went dead.

Delighted at having dealt so quickly and profitably with item number one, I lit a cigarette and called my bank.

Already my account, into which P.J. had been paying my salary, showed a healthy balance. Reassured, I started on the car rental firms, settling finally for a Ford from Hertz. Then I walked to the High Street and the local travel agent, Boots and the bank. Lunch I had in the Queen's Head, surrounded by cautious pensioners nursing their daily quota of bitter.

Back at the house, I found myself alone with Barbara, who had returned early to prepare a stew.

'So!' She looked up keenly from the chopping board. 'We're dying to know.'

'Know what?'

'Why you're back so soon.'

I repeated my evasion of the day before: 'I had a disagreement with the director.'

'Film people! You can never trust them!' She butchered a carrot. 'I hope they paid you?'

'Barbara . . .' I leant against the counter. 'I have a favour to ask. I think Edward could do with a break. I want to give him a holiday. I was thinking Spain. The problem is, I know he'll worry about the house, about you and Roger and Jim. I'd really be grateful if you could back me up. Give him permission. You know.'

I'd never asked anything of her before, and her reaction left me wondering if perhaps that was her problem – that, politics apart, no one did. Vegetables forgotten, she was the picture of solicitude.

'But of course. You're absolutely right. The last few years . . .'

She tailed off.

'What about the last few years?'

She looked at me defiantly. 'I don't expect you to understand. Or to sympathise. But when you've given your life to something and people shit on it, it's very hurtful.'

The concern in her voice quite surprised me, and once again I felt that perhaps I'd underestimated her.

'Indeed,' I assented, reaching for a slice of carrot. 'But isn't he stronger than that?'

She snorted. 'If everyone claimed *your* ideology was nothing but a cheat, if they wanted you to think that everything you'd fought for was an utter waste of time, how would you feel?'

I shrugged. 'Not good.'

She removed the rest of the carrots from my reach and threw them into the pot. 'I'm with you all the way. A holiday would do him the power of good. You leave it to me. I know how to handle your father.'

And indeed she did. On the pretext of needing to wash her hair, and with strict instructions for Edward to keep an eye on the stew, her first step, on my father's return, was to cede us the kitchen.

'Some tea?' queried my father. 'I'm parched.'

'Thank you,' I said, and when he handed me my mug: 'I've been thinking. About last night. I want to take you back.'

'I beg your pardon?'

'To Castres.'

Hands cupping his mug, he allowed the implication of what I was suggesting to sink in, then shook his head; just the once, and very firmly. 'You don't understand. I ran away. How can I go back? What would I do? What would I say?'

'It isn't only you and her. It's also me.'

He shot me a startled look.

'All three of us.' I put down my mug. 'I never told you this last night, but when I met Maria, I got the impression that knowing you . . .' I paused in order to find the correct wording for what Quiepo had told me. 'That maybe you made it impossible for her to go on living like before. That having been with you – a foreigner, someone on the other side – she became an outcast. Life hasn't been easy for her.' I touched his arm. 'Besides, we've never spent much time together. A trip to Spain . . .'

'Who's to pay?'

'Me.' At last I was on surer ground. 'This morning I phoned my agent. I did rather well out of this film. Better than expected. We're going to rent a car and drive to Spain. Just you and me. End of conversation. Okay?'

He didn't exactly agree, but neither did he demur; and, true to her word, that evening at supper Barbara kicked off with: 'Exciting, huh? About Spain.'

'What about Spain?' Cornered, my father fielded the question as if it were a missile.

'Peter's been telling me,' continued Barbara smoothly, 'and I have to say, speaking selfishly, your timing is perfect. I told you, remember, that Jesse and Arnold wanted to come down for that seminar? They could use your room. Well, if you don't mind. They're very neat, and they'll hardly be here. When do you leave?'

Although the question hadn't been directed at me, I was the one to answer it. 'The day after tomorrow. There's an early-morning ferry from Newhaven.'

'Dieppe,' said Jim. 'I love Dieppe.'

My father was staring into his stew.

'All booked.' I didn't give him a chance to raise any further objections. 'All you need is your passport and some clothes.'

'And not too many of those,' supplied Barbara. 'I looked in the paper. Barcelona's in the eighties.'

'There's a bar by the port,' said Jim. 'Fantastic seafood.'

Barbara frowned. 'What the hell are you talking about?'

'Dieppe, of course.'

I raised my wine glass. 'To holidays!'

'Holidays!' chorused Barbara and Jim.

There was one further chore that needed doing. To visit the flat and remove the last of my things. Tell Mrs Sargeson that it would be a while before Jacqui returned, and would she mind continuing with the post?

'Mr Smallwood! Come in, come in! This drought. Terrible, isn't it? No rain for a week. Now mind the step!' She shuffled ahead of me down the corridor, hand on the wall to steady herself. 'How is Jed? You've no idea how quiet it's been without him. I was just about to put the kettle on.'

She gestured me into her antimacassared sitting room. Every chair, every sideboard, every table profusely protected by lace.

'You'll have a scone? I made them yesterday.'

I'd made the mistake once before of accepting tea from Mrs Sargeson, and wasn't about to repeat the error. Owing to the slowness with which she moved, even something as simple as tea could take half an hour to prepare.

'That's very sweet of you,' I said, 'but actually, I've just had some. And I'm in a bit of a rush.'

'Just a scone, then,' she pleaded. 'You must have a scone. I made them yesterday.'

To this I felt I had to acquiesce, so I took my place in the crowded sitting room and waited patiently whilst she buttered a scone and brought it through on a plate which, in keeping with the furniture, she'd covered with a doily.

'Mmm!' I said, biting into the floury offering. 'Delicious.'

'My scones,' said Mrs Sargeson, sinking into an armchair, 'have always been admired. Oh, dear! This heat. I find it very trying.' She dabbed her forehead with what looked like an off-cut from one of the antimacassars. 'Back, are we?'

'Well,' I said, 'only me. Jacqui and Jed are still in Spain.'

'Hot,' she said. 'Spain. Much worse than here.'

'I need the key,' I said. 'To the flat. To collect a few things. I'll take the post up.'

'My niece,' she said, 'is in Greece, and next week Mrs Hadland and I are going to Clacton. Just for the day. Her son-in-law's taking us. You know, the one who works for British Gas. That's something to look forward to.'

I'd finished my scone, and before she could continue her itinerary, stood up and said clearly: 'That was delicious. Now, if you'll excuse me, I'll get the key. I'm not staying, I'm off myself tomorrow, so I won't be long.'

'The post is in the hall. You can leave the door on the latch. It's quite safe.'

'And the key?'

'In a saucer.'

There were maybe a dozen letters, all bills, and the key in a saucer that looked naggingly familiar. Last seen, it had been spinning through the air like a frisbee.

The flat upstairs smelled delicately of dust. I took the post into the kitchen and left it on the table, then went to my room. Winter clothes, my books from school, a collection of paperbacks, my personal papers: there was more than I remembered, and I was going to need a taxi in order to get it back to Winterbourne Road. I took down my suitcase and set about filling it with clothes. The books I decided to junk, and for my papers, I found a box in the kitchen, which, once packed, I took downstairs to put by the door.

Back in the flat, I lugged the suitcase into the hall and closed the door on my room. It wasn't only the dust, I decided, or the silence, that gave the flat such an air of being in limbo. It was the absence of people. A memory of Jacqui suggested itself. A black velvet dress, a flower behind

her ear, two bottles of champagne. *My God! Teachers! So he
misses some school? You think it won't be a learning experience,
two months in Spain? Working on a film?*

The door to Jed's room was ajar. I pushed it open and
stepped inside. He'd been under strict instructions, before
we left, to tidy up, but even so, clothes spilled from his
cupboard, and though the majority of his toys had been
piled in the corner, a few still lay in the centre of the
floor: a Lego jet, a fire engine and a tank, remnants of a
forgotten war in which Jed, because he'd imagined the
conflict, would always be victorious. I thought of how my
father had played at another war (*bang-bang you're dead,
count to a hundred, like little boys*), and how, in Sitges, men
stalked each other through the pine forests behind the
beach. All of us, in our different ways, doing battle with
reality, but only Jed, and only for a while, able to exercise
control.

On the chair by the bed, underneath a sock, stood the
cardboard casing for his set of *The Chronicles of Narnia*. It
was empty – Jed had taken the books to Spain – and it
brought to mind the cupboard into which Peter, Susan,
Edmund and Lucy had stepped. And yes, I thought, as one
door shuts, so another opens, until the unfolding of what
Lewis called the real story, which goes on forever and in
which every chapter is better than the one before.

Downstairs, I replaced the key in its saucer and put my
head round the living-room door. Mrs Sargeson had turned
on the television and was lost in *Neighbours*.

'I've put the key back,' I said, 'and if you don't mind
continuing to take in the post, that would be wonderful.
I'm sure Jacqui will ring to let you know when she's getting
back.'

I was sure of no such thing, but I didn't want Mrs
Sargeson to feel put upon.

'Take care of yourself,' I finished. 'And thanks for everything.'

Outside on the pavement, as I waited for a taxi, a young
man strolled past, cropped hair, white T-shirt, jeans
moulded to his lower body. At the corner he paused, osten-
sibly to get his bearings, and in the seemingly innocent
process of checking the street names, subjected me to a
knowing scrutiny.

S e v e n t e e n

*B*y seven the next evening we were sampling Stella
Artois outside a small *auberge* on the outskirts of a
town to the south of Limoges that was, in every aspect,
postcard perfect.

The day had unfolded in a series of such images: a shaft
of early-morning sun on the lighthouse at Beachy Head;
the concrete cob and cluttered harbour of Dieppe; roads
regimental with plane or poplar trees; the cathedral of
Chartres asserting its ascendancy, like some spiritual grain
silo, over the wheatfields of Normandy; obedient sunflowers, blackened heads bowed in prayer; walled cemeteries;
shops selling *brocante*; towns like the one where we had
stopped, with central squares of honey-coloured stone, gift
shops, *charcuteries*, *boulangeries*, vine-clad *auberges* and bab-
bling brooks.

'It's a bloody advertisement,' exclaimed my father.

'For what?'

'For France.'

I had to smile. 'It *is* France.'

'It's different.'

'Of course it's different. It's France.'

He held up his hands in mock surrender. 'I'd forgotten, that's all.'

I still needed reminding that the last time he'd been out of the country was when he'd gone to Spain.

'Also different,' I suggested, 'from the last time. No? I mean, that was almost sixty years ago.'

He nodded ruefully at the garish figure of a passing pedestrian. 'Shellsuits,' he said. 'Is that what you call them? I certainly don't remember those.' He finished his beer. 'Shall we eat?'

'Do you remember,' I asked as we waited for our soup, 'when you taught me how to shave?'

He looked at me blankly.

'A-levels. I was doing my A-levels.' We were sharing the dining room with a party of some thirty couples, all French, all in late middle age, all under the aegis of a Falstaffian thirty-year-old who lumbered between their tables in concert with the waitress, serving jokes as a condiment, and I had to raise my voice against their laughter in order to make myself heard. 'You came into the bathroom one morning, I was shaving, and you took the razor out of my hand and you said: "Not like that. Like this." I used to run the razor all the same way. You taught me to scrape upwards under the chin. You said that was how your father taught you.' The waitress arrived with our soup. 'I remember it, that's all.'

'What *I* remember,' he said quietly, 'is that you never much liked being told how to do things. Certainly not by me.'

'Did it ever occur to you I might have been jealous?'

'Jealous?'

'Of the others.'

'What others?'

'You know. The lodgers. And the endless meetings.

Your life. It seemed more important than mine. I resented that.'

He didn't flinch from my troubled gaze. 'Are you saying I neglected you?'

I looked down at my soup. 'I think what I'm saying is that I let you neglect me. Perhaps I felt more deeply about not having a mother than I wanted to let on. Perhaps I felt different. Perhaps I was different.'

I was remembering the box of my mother's clothes, the thrill of finding them, the force with which my father had snatched them away. Both needing to say what was on our minds, both failing.

'It's very simple,' I heard myself saying. 'I'm gay. I love other men. I'm not what you think. I'm different.'

I could no longer see my soup. Sudden tears had reduced my vision to a blur, making everything sparkle, like jewellery.

'When I was a child – I don't know, I never felt wholly at ease with my body. It was even worse as an adolescent. I was too tall, too thin, I hated my legs. I used to look at those men in the adverts. God, how I envied them! They had it all. They were how I was meant to be. I don't know. I wanted them.' I laughed harshly. 'Does it matter?' I looked up and into his eyes.

The expression on his face was unlike any I'd seen before. Unyielding. Inscrutable. I looked quickly away, at the faces of the couple on our right, blasted by sun. English, I guessed, on their way home from a fortnight in Spain. The cigarette the woman was lighting was identical to those smoked by Zeynep. Long and thin. Anaemic. Like me.

'Say something,' I begged, still not looking at him.

'What?' He sounded startled. 'What do you want me to say?'

What *did* I want him to say? That he understood? That he loved me? That I had his blessing?

'I don't know. You're my father. I'm your son.'

'If you want my blessing . . .'

There was a scraping of chairs on the other side of the room. The party of French were being shepherded to bed by their jovial leader. There was a great deal of kissing, and of shared instructions, and the French equivalent of sleep well. The waitress arrived with our second course, and the English couple leant inwards across their table and lowered their voices so they wouldn't be overheard in the sudden silence that had descended on the room. My father was concentrating on his steak, cutting it into manageable strips.

'Looks tasty.' He ferried a strip of meat from plate to mouth. 'Superb, in fact.'

'Goodnight. Sleep well.'

It was the English couple, who'd finished their coffee and were getting to their feet.

'Sleep well,' I echoed.

'I know I shall,' said my father. 'All that driving, and now this meal. I shall sleep like a log.'

'I'm not sure I shall.'

'Of course you will.' His tone was brisk; parental, almost. 'All that driving. You'll be out like a light.'

'All I'm telling you,' I persisted quietly, 'is who I am. That I need to be myself.'

'Eat!' he commanded. 'Or your steak will get cold.'

By lunchtime the next day we'd paused in our progress along the Autoroute des Deux Mers and pulled into a lay-by from which we had a view across the plain to the walled fastness of Carcassonne.

'I'm familiar with the arguments, of course,' said my

father suddenly, 'but even so: is it sufficient, even as a gay person, simply to be yourself?' It was the first reference he'd made to my confession of the night before. 'You remember George?'

I had to think a moment. 'Blond hair? Well built? Had the room next to yours.'

'He was gay. Used to say it was his right, his political right, I mean, to explore his sexuality. After all those years of repression. Now, I don't subscribe to the idea of a plague, or God's wrath and all that, but even so: AIDS didn't come from nowhere.' He frowned. 'A great deal of nonsense is talked about liberation. It's an understandable impulse, of course, especially when, as a group, you have been repressed, but freedom is really a myth. There's a price on everything. All we can do is try to ensure that the price is borne equally. Take Carcassonne.' He gestured at its distant walls and turrets. 'The inhabitants of Carcassonne, they knew that in order to protect themselves they had to build a wall. I know this sounds old-fashioned, but people need standards. What worries me, when I look at the modern world, is nowadays morality is left to the individual. It's a contradiction in terms: individual morality. Morality has to do with the common good. It can't exist in isolation.'

I don't think I'd ever heard him speak at such length, though what struck me was the fact – the hope – that perhaps, albeit obliquely, he was actually expressing concern for my safety.

I chose to laugh. 'You ought to meet Father Ricardo. The two of you would get on like a house on fire.'

He snorted. 'Not all moralities are equal. Or desirable.'

To the left and right of us the Autoroute des Deux Mers ran in a silvery ribbon from sea to sea. An hour earlier, when we'd joined the motorway at Toulouse, we'd seen the first signs for Barcelona. The Mediterranean was within striking distance, and, at our backs, across the scrubby plains of the Midi, was the long, low hump of the Pyrenees.

'Aren't you hot?'

Despite the supremacy of sun and sky, my father was still in corduroys.

He ran a hand across his brow. 'A little.'

'Shall we have lunch at the coast? It'll be cooler.'

'Why not?' He detached his gaze from the walls of the distant town, and, raking the fields of vines and sunflowers with his eyes, turned to stare thoughtfully at the mountains.

'Not long now,' I said softly.

'They smuggled us in, you know. In a lorry. From Perpignan. Over those mountains.'

'I know. You told me.'

We were embraced by mountain: Haut Languedoc to our left, the foothills of the Pyrenees to our right. The geographical smörgåsbord that was France – the wheat-fields of Normandy, the lushness of the Lot, the flatlands of the Midi – was almost over. The Pyrenees marked the start of simpler, harsher fare.

At Narbonne the motorway divided. We turned south and were granted our first sight of the Mediterranean: a vast inlet of sun-drenched water, pale and baleful as the sky.

'The grand object of travelling,' declaimed my father.

'I beg your pardon?'

'Doctor Johnson.' He waved an explanatory arm out of the window. '"The grand object of travelling is to see the shores of the Mediterranean." Didn't he say that?'

'Search me.'

I took an exit marked Leucate. We drove along another inlet. Close up, the water gave off an unpleasant stench. Holiday apartments stood in tiers against a hillside whose rocks were so white they could have been salt deposits left there by the sea. The glare from the sun hurt my eyes, and it was with some relief that I parked the car opposite a stretch of beach and led my father onto the shaded terrace of a blue and white hotel. Across the bay, in the glittering distance, I could still see the Pyrenees: constant reminder of our destination.

'Just a sandwich,' said my father. 'This heat has robbed me of appetite.'

I placed our orders at the bar, then went to join him on the terrace. A group of sun-darkened Germans were drinking beer at the table next to ours. I looked at my watch.

'If it's okay with you, I think we should spend tonight in Perpignan. Then, if we leave early, we can make Castres by nightfall. I wonder if you'll recognise it?'

He was staring across the bay at the distant mountains.

'I recognise them,' he said. 'They haven't changed.' The waitress brought our food: stringy ham in a roll that had been moistened with tomatoes. 'But everything else . . .' He left the sentence unfinished, and together we tackled our rolls.

'I'm boiling,' I announced. 'I need a swim.'

On the sand I stripped to my underpants and dived into the soupy water. Dead Sea-like, it kept me to its surface, cradling my limbs in its sticky embrace. On the terrace of the blue and white hotel I saw my father ask the waitress for another beer. He looked very vulnerable, sitting stiffly upright in his wicker chair, neck and face as lined and white as his badly ironed shirt. Out of place – certainly when compared to the lounging Germans – and almost out of time.

'Come,' I said, dressed again and running my fingers through salt-slicked hair. 'Perpignan.'

Swallowing the last of his beer, my father got dutifully to his feet.

Now we were headed straight for the looming mountains. To our left was the sea, to our right another inlet over which, butterfly-like, skimmed a solitary windsurfer.

'Does this mean,' asked my father, 'no more Jacqui? Was that what happened on the film?'

'In a way. But Jacqui and I, we were never . . .'

'Never what?'

'Exactly a feature.'

'And Jed?'

I was lanced by a sudden sense of loss. Jed on the upper deck of a London bus, small hand in mine, as we rattle through the Sunday suburbs. *You're lucky to have a father.*

'Perhaps,' said my father, fingers tapping the dashboard, 'perhaps this Catholicism is no bad thing. At least it gives him a centre. I wouldn't like to think of things being difficult for him. Would you?'

'No,' I said dully. 'Indeed I wouldn't.'

We were on the outskirts of Perpignan, in the grip of a merciless traffic jam, and it took us the best part of an hour to infiltrate the city centre and find a space to park.

'That hotel there,' I said, pointing across the road. 'Look okay?'

He shrugged. 'You're the boss.'

We had supper in a nondescript restaurant across the street from the hotel.

As the waiter filled our wine glasses, my father lifted his in a toast and said quietly: 'I suppose I should thank you.'

'For what?'

'Bringing me. All this way. It's been . . . very educative.'

Was it the journey he meant, or what we were discovering about each other?

'To sons!' I said.

He smiled. 'To fathers!'

We clinked glasses.

Perhaps it was my imagination, but in that moment his face seemed particularly in focus. As if I were seeing all of it. All the constituent parts. The hologram complete. Well, almost.

I only hoped he saw me with equal clarity.

Eighteen

*T*he motorway had changed its name. Now La Catalane, it pointed directly at a break in the mountains, the only hint of geographical hesitancy in the barrier thrown up between Spain and the rest of Europe. My father said very little. The passing landscape engrossed him utterly. I, for my part, was mulling over the irony of our double act. My father had spent most of his life in search of an ideal. He wanted to distance himself from what the capitalists would have him believe was the essence of human nature, shunning greed and the desire for ownership, turning his back on market forces, working for the common good. I, by contrast, was travelling not away from what I was, but wholeheartedly towards it. My father wanted to be other than purely, meanly human. My salvation lay in the stark, unalterable facts of myself.

Or was that historical? Maybe, I thought, the purpose of this journey is to take us each in the opposite direction? Him towards himself, me away.

We negotiated the final *péage*, watching as a pair of gendarmes officiously waved a lorry to one side. Then, in a moment akin to take-off, the road had lifted to become encased in mountain. There was a French customs post, through which we drove without stopping, and a bureau de change. To our right, perched on a crag, was what looked like a monastery. To our left, a latter-day Aztec pyramid, monument presumably to Spain's imperial past, and token, therefore, of its probable future. There was a second customs post, and, running parallel to the motorway, sections of the old road, the road along which a lorry had once smuggled my father; unless, of course, that road was even older, and no longer in evidence. There were a couple of tiny towns, then the motorway had rejoined the earth, our flight was over, and we were speeding past the ugly outline of modern-day Jonquera.

The motorway surged southwards. Already the mountains were a thing of the past. The land was flat, planted with either bamboo or the remains of billboards, many of them little more than an array of metal struts, all without lettering. One was in the shape of a bottle: sometime advert for brandy, or sherry, or wine.

We stopped for coffee at a filling station just north of Barcelona, then continued southwards, bypassing the city and curving round to join the coast. This section of motorway I knew: the glimpses of sea and of holiday apartments, the exit to Sitges, a profusion of oleander in the central reservation, the mountains to our right. We crossed the Ebro, and still my father remained silent, unable or unwilling to give voice to his emotions. We left the motorway and turned towards the mountains. We passed a man on a mobylette, head encased in a brown plastic helmet. We drove through a village that was nothing more than a line of houses edging the road, a bar whose door was obscured by a metal fly-screen, a woman in a floral dress, washing strung between trees. The orange groves gave way to terraces of olives, deep green transmuting to silvery grey. The mountains became starker.

We entered Castres. I looked at my watch. It was half-past three.

'Continue up this street,' said my father, 'turn left, straight on for a bit, and you're in the square.'

'You remember!'

'Stop here!' He was gripping my arm.

'Here? But—'

'Here!'

Here turned out to be a bar set slightly back from the road. I pulled over and turned off the engine. My father emerged from the car as if from a chrysalis, standing stock-still on the pavement to look slowly about him. Then, without so much as a glance in my direction, he vanished inside. I followed suit.

The bar was as drab and featureless as the building which housed it. The tiled floor was awash with paper and cigarette stubs. The tables were of yellow formica, the chairs also. A trio of men stood against the counter, drinking cognac. A woman wrestled with the espresso machine. There was a fruit machine too, against the one wall, and on a shelf above the bar, a television tuned to a music channel.

My father stood in the centre of the room, a look of wonder on his face. I approached him gingerly.

'Are you all right?'

He didn't reply, just continued to drink in the details of the room.

'Why don't we sit?'

Still he didn't reply, so, taking him by the elbow, I guided him towards the nearest table.

'A cognac?'

Suddenly he was grinning. 'Veterano?'

'If you'd like.'

His grin did not evaporate. 'Fitting, wouldn't you say? Veterano.'

I caught the eye of the woman behind the bar and raised two fingers. '*Dos Veteranos, por favor.*'

She nodded curtly and indicated she would bring the drinks to our table.

As if it were braille and he could read it for secrets, my father was stroking the formica with his fingertips.

'You knew this bar?'

He nodded.

'You used to drink here?'

Again he nodded.

'Well then!' I raised my glass. 'To the journey's end!'

His only response was to lift his glass as I had lifted mine.

'Shall we find a room?' It was a moment I'd been dreading. What if Carlos and the crew were still in residence? How would I face them? What would I say?

My father provided temporary respite from the problem.

'I think,' he said slowly, 'I'd like to drive into the mountains. Can we do that?'

'Of course. Nothing simpler.' I tried not to let relief show in my voice. 'Whatever you want. There's plenty of time to find a room. It isn't dark till seven.'

'What you mustn't forget,' he said once we'd left Castres and were winding upwards – no sensation of take-off on this road, just a slow, tortuous ascent – 'is that in the thirties, living in the shadow of Hitler, it wasn't unusual to support the Republicans. We all felt the need to combat fascism. What I did – what the others did – it wasn't that remarkable.'

'Going to war?' We had reached the bridge beyond which lay the dam. 'It sounds remarkable to me. This bridge, for example. According to Jed, it was blown up. Do you remember that?'

He appeared not to hear me. 'And there was Father, of course.'

The change of tack was as unexpected as it was sudden.

'Father? You mean your father?'

'You know he was a Baptist minister?' My father chuckled. 'Well, lay preacher, actually. In his spare time. At weekends.'

'You've never told me that.'

'We didn't get on.' He was staring out of the window, but what he saw was in the past, not in the present.

'I thought he was a clerk.'

Again my father chuckled. 'He was. Monday to Friday. But at the weekend he became someone else. Hellfire and damnation.' He was drumming with his fingers on the dashboard. 'I suppose I felt the need to find a gospel of my own. Adolescent rebellion. As predictable as that. Silly, really, though of course it was real enough at the time.'

We passed the monastery and turned into the valley.

'Valliguera!' Decanted from past into present by the huddle of whitewashed houses on their hill, my father uttered the name in a tone of awestruck recognition.

'Unchanged?'

Gripping my arm as fiercely as when we'd entered Castres, he once again ordered me to stop the car. We were opposite the path along which I'd walked to Castres.

He got out and ventured a yard or two off the road. I stayed in my seat. Mirror images. He on his path, me on mine. He in rebellion against his father, me in rebellion against him. The means by which we define ourselves. I'd never known my grandfather. Only, and briefly, my grandmother, who I remembered as a creature so gnarled, so bent and unimaginably old, that I'd thought of her as a witch. A character out of a fairy tale. Like the tales I told Jed. Except that the tale which, section by section, my father was telling me wasn't fictional. It was the tale of himself, and by extension, me. Told not as a prelude to sleep, but in order to come awake.

I opened the car door and stepped into the singing silence. The only sound, apart from the hum of insects, was that of a distant dog. I remembered how, when I'd walked the path, the mountains had felt so empty; inimical to humankind. Scant sign of human passage.

My father was sitting on a rock, staring at Valliguera.

'Mountains!' he said. 'They seem so unassailable. Impossible to conquer or cross. Dividing this valley from that, this country from that, these people. But climb a mountain, and there's always something on the other side.'

I saw them in a different light. As an extension of the Pyrenees, the Pyrenees a continuation of the mountains which dissected France, and so on, and so on, right back to the cliffs which guarded England and the lighthouse at Beachy Head. The postman, I thought, used to walk this path every day, bringing news from the coast. These mountains carry news of their own from south to north, and vice versa. News, too, from past to present. Part of the hologram.

'It isn't easy,' said my father, 'for fathers and sons when they're different. Much easier if we're all the same. No disagreements. No differences. But that isn't life. Besides . . .' He was staring skywards at a speck of bird riding the thermals. 'Perhaps we're not that different. We're both pretty good at self-deception.' He allowed himself the glimmer of a smile. 'Other than we'd like to be. Cowards.' He made a clicking noise in his throat, reminiscent of Carlos. 'What's important is to be honest. As honest as we can. With ourselves and with each other.'

'Goodness!' I was smiling through my tears. 'A new manifesto.'

'Your mother,' he concluded quietly. 'I did love her. And you. Just didn't know how to say it, that's all.'

'Come!' I slipped my hand beneath his arm. 'Let's find
that room.'

I was greatly encouraged, on reaching the Reina
Cristina, to see no sign of a van, and my luck continued to
hold inside. The boy on reception was new and it was the
work of moments to sign in and be handed our keys. In the
corridor outside our rooms my father paused.

'I think, if you don't mind, I'll take a walk.' He looked at
his watch. 'Rendezvous at eight?'

'Okay. I'll see you in the square.' I was unwilling to push
my luck; safer to meet away from the hotel, safer to eat out.

I had a shower, changed, and then – because I felt too
restless to stay in my room – returned downstairs. There
was a rack of postcards on the desk, and I thought of finding one for John. 'Guess where?' I would say. 'Back in
Spain. Not Sitges, though. I'll tell you why when we see
each other. Maybe I can visit you in Manchester? Or would
London be more fun? You decide.'

I was prevented by the familiar face of the manager, who
had taken over from the newcomer.

'Señor!' A smile of startled surprise was spreading across
his features. 'You come back!'

In careful English, I told him I was on holiday with my
father, had wanted to show him Castres, it was such a pretty
town, and of course there were the mountains.

'And the film?' I asked cautiously. 'Where is everyone?'

He shrugged. 'Film finish. Finish yesterday. They go
Sevilla. Only English señora.'

At first I thought I must have misheard him.

'She stay. Others go.'

'The English señora?' I repeated the phrase dumbly.

He pointed. 'In the bar.'

She was all alone, slouched at the counter with a glass of
whisky in her hand. Cigarette smoke spiralled from an

ashtray at her elbow. She was staring into the mirror above
the bar, and that was where our eyes met, in the mirror.
There was a moment in which neither of us moved. Then,
levering herself upright, she swung round and demanded
boozily: 'What the fuck are you doing here?'

I advanced into the room. 'I could ask you the same.'

She lifted her glass and smiled crookedly. 'Isn't it obvi-
ous?'

Close up, I saw that her eyes were bloodshot and that she
was having difficulty focusing.

'Tomorrow,' she said, 'tomorrow I shall be frightened,
lonely and depressed. But what the fuck! I'm here to have
a good time, not a long time. What are you having?'

I shrugged. 'Cognac?'

She banged on the bar. 'Ramón!'

The barman appeared through a door in the far wall. If
he remembered me, he didn't show it.

'*Un coñac, por favor*,' said Jacqui. She drained the liquid in
her glass. 'And another of these.' She reached for her cigarette. 'What have you been doing lately?'

Because, in her question, I heard an echo of my cue, and
because it was simpler to take this coward's way out, I
replied: 'I went round the world, you know, after . . .'

Despite her drunkenness, she segued into the scene
faultlessly: 'Yes, yes, I know. How was it?'

'The world?'

'Yes.'

'Oh, highly enjoyable.'

'China must be very interesting.'

'Very big, China.'

'And Japan?'

'Very small.'

She threw me a curved ball. 'Did you eat lots of dicks,
and take your clothes off, and use condoms and everything?'

For a moment I was at a loss as to how to proceed. Then, meeting her gaze full on, I let Coward's original line do the work for me: 'Practically everything.'

She put down her glass, and to my horror, I saw she was crying. I laid a tentative hand on her sleeve.

'What is it?'

'The fucker was married. I was just somewhere to park his dick. Then wifey got suspicious. Came over with some awful brat in tow. Hair curlers and polyester.' She shuddered. 'It's what he deserves.'

'He dropped you?'

She drew erect. 'Actually,' she said, enunciating the words with care, 'I dropped him. I told him to go fuck himself. Which, since the only person he really cares about is himself, will probably give him a bigger thrill than he deserves.'

'And Jed?' I ventured. 'How's Jed?'

'With the unit.' She had slumped onto the bar again. 'I'm joining them tomorrow. I just needed a little time. And anyway . . .' She grimaced. 'There's saintly Father Ricardo. Our Jed' – she stabbed her cigarette into the overflowing ashtray – 'our Jed has made a few discoveries of his own. He wants to take instruction. Is that the phrase? Father Ricardo and I have been talking. I may let him go to school in Tarifa. You know.' She let out a hollow laugh. 'The one for orphans. Though it's going to cost, of course, flying him to LA for the holidays. But what the fuck. I'll earn that.'

'LA?' She was going too fast for me. 'You're moving to LA?'

'Al might be a dickhead, but at least he introduced me to some useful people. There's a lot going down in LA. Not like London. You'll have to come and visit. All those surfers. You'd have a ball.' She ran a quick hand through her hair. 'Do you hate me?'

'Of course I don't hate you. Why should I hate you?'

It was as if she hadn't heard me, or hadn't asked the question. 'I mean, it is more stable. For Jed, I mean. Being in a school like that. I'm all over the place. And his Spanish, you should hear his Spanish.' She fumbled in her bag. 'Well, I hate you.'

'You do?'

'You walked out on me. People never . . .' She frowned. 'Not since Durban.' She produced a crumpled envelope, which she thrust into my hand. 'It's for you. He wanted to tell you himself. About his instruction. Ramón!' She hit the bar with the flat of her hand. 'Anyway, America – I don't want to bring him up there. No place for kids.'

I made a show of consulting my watch.

'Listen, I have to go. I'm here with my father. He's expecting me.'

'Your father?' She looked behind her, as if expecting to find him propped against the wall. Then, and not without difficulty, she refocused on me. 'Where is he?'

'Outside.'

'He wouldn't like LA.' She attempted to light a cigarette. 'Not his scene at all. We'd have to leave him behind. But he could always come across with Jed. They like each other. Don't they?'

I pushed back my stool. Her fingers, as they reached for my wrist, dug so sharply into my flesh that I winced.

'Have another one. Go on!'

I shook my head. 'I'll come back later. You keep a place for me.' I patted my stool. 'After I've fed my father.'

He was at a table in the square, cup of coffee at his elbow.

'Are you all right?'

He could see from the expression on my face that something untoward had happened.

'Of course I'm all right.' I waved the crumpled envelope in the air. 'And look what I found! A letter from Jed!'

'What does it say?'

'I haven't read it yet.' I sank into a chair. 'But what about you? Have a good walk?'

He nodded.

'Tomorrow,' I said, keeping up my flow of words, 'we can find Maria. She isn't far from here.'

'I've been thinking . . .' He began to toy with his tea-spoon. 'I know the purpose of the trip was to see Maria, and I'm sorry if you feel I've wasted your time, but in actual fact . . .' He paused. 'She's an old woman. I'm an old man. It was a long time ago. Another life.'

I reached across the table and took his hand in mine. I could feel, in the fragility of his bones, precisely how old he was, and how feeble.

'It's all right,' I said. 'It was just an idea. Probably not very wise. At least it got us here.'

He returned the pressure of my fingers. 'I found the church. Where we used to sleep. You know. Different now.' A dreamy smile illuminated his face. 'Like it always was. Like it ought to be. There was an old woman, she was praying, she lit a candle and put some money in the box. I lit one too. Three, in fact. One for Maria. One for your mother. One for you. Silly.' Tears had sprung to his eyes, but he made no attempt to remove his hand and wipe them away. 'I'm glad,' he said. 'I'm glad you brought me. But now I want to go home.'

I could, I suppose, have told him who I guessed the woman in the church to be, but perhaps he already knew.

'We can leave tomorrow. We can take a different road. Via San Sebastian, maybe, and Bordeaux. Whatever we feel like. And now . . .' Without releasing his hand, I got to my feet. 'Now we should find ourselves something to eat.

I don't know about you, but I'm starving. I'll read us Jed's letter.'

He allowed himself to be pulled upright.

'Indeed,' he said. 'Ravenous.'

'Right!' I didn't let go of his arm. '*Vamanos!*'

☐ A Summer Tide	Tony Peake	£5.99
☐ The Smell of Apples	Mark Behr	£5.99
☐ The Virgin Suicides	Jeffrey Eugenides	£6.99
☐ Charms for the Easy Life	Kaye Gibbons	£5.99
☐ The Seduction of Morality	Tom Murphy	£6.99
☐ Eden Close	Anita Shreve	£6.99

Abacus now offers an exciting range of quality titles by both established and new authors which can be ordered from the following address:

> Little, Brown & Company (UK),
> P.O. Box 11,
> Falmouth,
> Cornwall TR10 9EN.

Alternatively you may fax your order to the above address.
Fax No. 01326 317444.

Payments can be made as follows: cheque, postal order (payable to Little, Brown and Company) or by credit cards, Visa/Access. Do not send cash or currency. UK customers and B.F.P.O. please allow £1.00 for postage and packing for the first book, plus 50p for the second book, plus 30p for each additional book up to a maximum charge of £3.00 (7 books plus). Overseas customers including Ireland, please allow £2.00 for the first book plus £1.00 for the second book, plus 50p for each additional book.

NAME (Block Letters) _____

ADDRESS _____

_____

_____

☐ I enclose my remittance for £ _____
☐ I wish to pay by Access/Visa Card

Number ☐☐☐☐☐☐☐☐☐☐☐☐☐☐☐☐
Card Expiry Date _____